DAUGHTERS
OF
JUPITER

A NOVEL BY:

E. M. LEANDER

For all those who reach for the stars

CHAPTER 1

NORA, THE RAPSCALLION

They were doomed.

Nora felt it in the pit of her stomach — a freezing, wrenching, nauseated feeling. Her hands were clammy, and she realized after a few moments that her lungs were aching. Somehow, in the midst of what she was witnessing, even the primitive parts of her brain had forgotten how to function and to keep her breathing.

She took a breath and brushed a dark curl back from her eyes. How had it come to this? One moment they were flying through the Current, that supraluminal highway that connected their solar system to that of the J'nai, on an emotional high after making history. Instead of using the Star Ports like a train station for jumping off the Current, they'd leapt off in the middle using their new — and untested — P2 device. The next moment ...

"What is *that?*" Donovan asked. He was their communications officer, a supremely talented linguist with unruly brown hair and thick-rimmed glasses. He was a true polyglot, fluent in several Earth languages as well as J'nai and Qaig dialects. He was also one of the top ten most anxious people Nora had ever met, which did make her wonder why he'd been assigned here in the first place. His voice cracked on the last word.

To be fair though, the sight before them *was* catastrophic.

"It's a hundred Qaig ships, what does it look like?" Soren snapped.

Nora turned to look at her — the J'nai woman's pale-yellow hands were flying over the controls at the captain's chair, though Nora couldn't for the life of her figure out what she was doing. Despite minor anatomical differences, like four-fingered hands, the underlying similarities between J'nai and humans had allowed them to build a ship both could operate interchangeably. Captain Soren was tight-lipped and sweating as she swiped icons on her screen aside, typing out something rapidly as the rest of them sat in stunned silence. Soren's tapping fingers kept beat with Nora's fluttering pulse — what were they going to do? As a student, Nora shouldn't even have been here! And she wouldn't have, if Bastian and Soren hadn't insisted on her help piloting the ship! This was supposed to be a simple mission, a test for the P2. Getting this close to the Qaig hadn't been part of the plan at all! And where was Terra Prime? Where in all the universe had they ended up?!

Their ship was damaged. The P2 was also completely fried. It had allowed them to jump off the Pangalactic Current without exploding, but they were a little off-course from the J'nai home world —a few million miles, give or take. Then the P2 had fizzled out, like the jerry-rigged piece of junk that it was. The technology of the Star Ports them-selves was ancient and exceptionally difficult to replicate. Like stops on a subway station, the two-kilometer-wide rings had tech that allowed travelers to disembark the Current. Unlike a subway, one could 'jump on' to the Current at any time with the right hyperdrive — like their own PuddleJumper-class ship, or PJ as they were affection-ately known.

The materials and man-hours involved in making and maintaining a Star Port were staggering. With the revolutionary portable star port, the P2, that Thalia and her team had engineered and mounted onto the underside of the *Rapscallion*, they could jump on and off the Current at will — and, theoretically, be undetected while doing so. It was a discovery that was going to change the course of the Qaig-J'nai War. It was easy to guard a single Star Port and bottleneck any oncoming enemy ships. If the Qaig, the slimy long-time enemy of the J'nai, knew that Ganymede Station had P2 technology, the results would be …

well, Nora guessed that they knew now, so the implications were likely to be discovered soon.

One glance at Bastian's console, every engine now capped with a glaring red symbol to indicate it was no longer functioning, told her that their luck had just run out.

Bastian. He looked up at her, his blue-gray eyes unfocused as he computed thousands of scenarios per second, his hands flying over the keyboard. Their pilot. Her mentor. For this mission, he'd also been the captain, only taking back the controls of the ship from Nora when the P2 had been engaged. No one else in the universe was skilled enough to maneuver that transition off the current — they could have been blown into a trail of metallic dust a thousand light-years long. Despite everything, her heart warmed just looking at him.

He bent back down to his work, swiping aside warning symbol after warning symbol. The only thing that seemed to be working was the subluminal xenon engine. At best, it would accelerate them at a few hundred meters per second until it got them up to true near-light speed — which would take days.

And the hundred blocky, green Qaig ships, their cannons locked onto the *Rapscallion*, didn't seem likely to give them that much of a head start. Each one, she thought with a shudder, looked large enough to carry a hundred — no, a thousand — of the ruthless, reptilian Qaig.

"Captain?" Donovan wheezed and took a pull at his asthma inhaler. The bobble-head toys on his console were preternaturally still, even the one that kind of looked like Soren. Donovan's obscure band T-shirt was dark with sweat. He was perpetually pushing his glasses back up his long nose, especially when he was nervous. Like now.

"They're... it looks like they're hailing us. Trying to send a sound file."

"Don't open it," Soren snapped, her hands never ceasing their motions. "It's probably a trick of some kind, a way to take over the electronics on our ship."

"Aye aye," Donovan said, leaning back in his chair. His hands hung at his sides.

"So... now what?" Asher asked. Usually the most dramatic and loudly pessimistic of the crew, now he was eerily quiet.

"Now we—" Soren said.

The ship lurched suddenly, pulled forward, like a fish caught on a hook. They all stumbled and leaned, grabbing onto whatever console or armrest was closest. Nora was thrown against the straps of her chair hard enough to sting — she wouldn't be surprised if her shoulders were bruised later. She looked up, and saw that the *Rapscallion* was moving, and not of its own accord. It was being dragged towards the Qaig ships, which loomed larger and larger in the view panel. The console in front of Bastian began blinking more angry red lights in response to the action.

"Thalia, take your team below and get that P2 back online," Bastian shouted. The tug lurched them forward again — now the motion was unmistakable. Something was pulling them towards the Qaig fleet, some invisible force. Nora swallowed hard, bile making a sickly taste in the back of her throat.

"I can't," Thalia said, slamming her fist against the wall of the ship. Her dark curls were a thunderhead around her, struck through with bolts of blue and teal, like lightning. Her sage-green flight suit was only half-zipped, the arms knotted around her waist, revealing her assorted tattoos. Once, Nora had admired the daring look. Now, there was little about Thalia that she admired, though there was no questioning her brilliance behind the P2 drive. She knew every line of code, every micrometer of wiring in the device. If Thalia thought the drive was beyond repair, then it was, and that thought made Nora want to vomit or pass out. Maybe both.

Overhead a panel dropped open, and a twisted bundle of wires fell out, showering them all with sparks. Several more panels rattled as the *Rap* shook, straining against the force moving them inexorably toward the Qaig.

"Try," Bastian said through gritted teeth — for a moment he and Thalia stared each other down. It was like the whole thing was happening in slow motion — Nora could track each spark that fell down between the two of them, taking as much time as a gently drifting leaf to reach the floor. The tension from Thalia was a palpable force, her innate instinct for self-preservation battling her desire to cause drama.

While they might have been cloned from the same, brilliant ancient philosopher — Hypatia of Alexandria — Nora and Thalia were like night and day, or oil and water. Thalia clenched her hands at her sides, her lips pursed.

After what was probably only a few seconds, Thalia frowned, grabbed Sun by the arm, and motioned to her other teammates to follow. Her scientific team was made of all clones, besides Daven — after all, that's what the clones, or Faxes as they were known, were brought to Ganymede to do. They did the science and left the running of the station to the Originals. There were an Edwin Hubble and Sun, a Chieng-Shung Wu clone, on Thalia's team — and then there was Daven, the gray, wraith-like J'nai who was a renowned scientist on Terra Prime. The P2 team stormed from the Bridge after Thalia, their booted feet echoing as they ran down the hall.

"Donovan, can we get any sort of message back to Ganymede?" Soren asked. Her own long, white hair was askew, falling loose from its braided hold, streaked dark with sweat.

"Negative, Cap... I mean, Commander Soren," he replied, looking over his console, which glowed red like the others. "Since the P2 is down, and we're nowhere near a star port, there's no way for me to get the signal back onto the Current — if I send it to the relay station at the Terra Prime port, maybe it would be sent on through one of those automatic programs, if it hasn't been compromised by the Qaig invasion there."

"Do it," Soren said. Nora frowned. At best, that signal would take weeks to reach Ganymede. At worst ... Nora twisted her sweating fingers together in her lap. Was there nothing she could do? She couldn't fix the P2 — that she'd have to leave up to Thalia and her crew. Bastian was working the flight console, which was the only thing she had any sort of business operating on this ship anyway. She felt stuck, trapped, and helpless. She watched Bastian run a hand through his hair, pushing the sweaty bronze strands back from his eyes.

"If you have any more brilliant ideas, now would be a good time," he said, glancing at her. She shook her head, looking down at the floor, feeling his steely gaze like a physical touch. Moments later she heard his fingers return to their staccato dance over the console, while she continued to wring her hands. She'd never felt so useless in all her life.

"It's some sort of projected gravitational field," Asher said. Nora glanced up at him — his usual pastel-green skin gone gray. The J'nai were proof of the theory of Convergent Evolution — the idea that two species, given similar environments, would evolve similarly. In this case, other than the number of fingers (and hearts — the J'nai had two), the two species were more alike than different — except the J'nai had skin that was colored every shade of the rainbow from the various environments they'd lived in, from pale, pink pearlescent to darkest green scales. They were an amazingly adaptable species, quickly shaping themselves to fit any planet, any environment once they'd started colonizing the galaxy centuries ago. The *Rap* had three on board now — Soren, the captain/engineer; Asher, the green-skinned J'nai who managed the more complex computations and navigations required for the Current; and Daven.

"They're using it to pull us in — I think to that one," Asher said, pointing. The crew all followed his gaze — the *Rap* had turned slightly and now moved at a sedate but steady pace towards a massive rectangular structure. It was a harsh-looking thing, with each of the panels — like windows on a skyscraper laid on its side — opening and closing at intervals, letting out smaller shuttles or allowing them to land.

"We can't let that happen," Soren said. Bastian swiveled in his chair to look at the J'nai woman — the woman who had been his captain, his leader, and his teacher. Though Bastian had been appointed Captain for this particular assignment, it was clear, now, that he still needed her leadership, her experience.

Bastian and Soren locked eyes. Another shower of sparks fell from overhead and Nora covered her head, but Bastian seemed not to notice them at all. There was a conflict going on here, silently, one that she couldn't follow. Something so terrible that they didn't even want to speak it out loud.

"You know we can't let this ship — not its crew, not its communication equipment, not the P2, none of it — we can't let it fall into their hands," Soren said, her voice weirdly soft amongst the clanging metal and creaking of the ship. Still, every word was as clear and deadly as a laser beam. No one on the Bridge moved — not Donovan, or Asher, or Nora or Bastian. Their fates — and those of Thalia's crew — hung by the slenderest thread.

"We should wait until we're a little closer," Bastian said at last, and Soren nodded. He turned back to his console, his spine as rigid as a pole. His lips were set in a hard line, and he moved automatically, like a robot, unfeeling, unthinking. As if the mere thought of what he was doing might disrupt his self-control.

"Wait for what?" Nora asked. The words barely made it past her lips, and she had to repeat herself to make sure Bastian had heard her. He swallowed hard but didn't answer. She put a hand on his arm, gripping the thick material of his flight suit, and he finally turned to face her.

"Wait to blow up the ship," he said. His voice was tight, his face composed, like he'd had to force the words past his vocal cords. "There's a ten-second timer on the self-destruct sequence. If Thalia can't get the P2 working by the time we reach the Qaig ship, we'll …"

"Blow up the *Rap*. And take part of their ship with us," Nora said. She knew what it meant — that they would all die here, today — but it didn't really seem to register in her brain. That she was going to die. That Bastian was going to die. That her life was over, when it had barely gotten started. That she'd never get to tell her friends goodbye —she'd never told them the truth about this mission in the first place. The thoughts fluttered through, but barely, like they were skittering across the surface of her brain but not making any kind of impression. It was a thought too large and too terrible for her to comprehend. She'd known this mission was dangerous, but the naïve part of her had believed it was still going to be all right.

"Nora," Bastian said, breaking her stream of thoughts. She released his sleeve — she'd been holding it so tightly her hand was starting to cramp — and looked up at him. He reached up and brushed the back of his fingers against her cheek, before cupping her face gently in his palm.

"I am sorry," he said. His blue-grey eyes locked onto her, like he had more to say. Nora swallowed, her gaze flickering to his lips, now so close to her own. His fingers were cool, steady against her flushed face.

God, she was about to get herself blown to bits and all she could think about was kissing him. It wouldn't be the worst way to go.

"Uh, Captain? Command... damn it, Soren? That thing — we're picking up speed," Donovan said, his words coming fast and high-pitched. His hands were flying over his console, knocking over the few bobble-heads that hadn't toppled already, swiping at messages and sequences on the screen.

Bastian turned to look — the spell was broken. She took a wobbly breath.

"Thalia — Thalia, are you there? How's the P2? Can we jump?" Soren demanded over the intercom.

For a moment there was no response. The Bridge crew was fixated on the Qaig ship, looming impossibly larger and larger in the view screen, until it filled the entire panel, blocking out the stars with its mammoth bulk. This close, they could see the irregularities in the metal it was constructed from, the dents and scorches along its flanks, like it had been assembled hastily, and from parts of other ships, with no regard for aesthetics or aerodynamics.

Then, Thalia's voice crackled over the speakers, shrill and fast.

"I told you there's nothing I can do down here. I'd need a week, at least, to —"

"You've got about fifteen seconds before I blow this ship up. Let me know if your situation changes."

There was what sounded like a scuffle on the other end of the comm, and then a pounding of feet up the hall to the Bridge.

"WHAT?" Thalia demanded, her chest heaving. Her face was sweaty and red with anger, her hands gripping the sides of the door to the Bridge like she would tear them off and heave them at Soren if she could.

"You're wasting time," Soren said calmly. "You knew this was a risk. We cannot let your tech fall into their hands."

"They've already *got* this technology," Thalia barked. "Didn't you see how they just popped out of nowhere? Do you *see* a star port anywhere?"

"The decision has been made, Thalia," Soren said, her green eyes level. Nora felt Bastian's hand grip hers, and she squeezed it tightly, not daring to take her eyes off the scene before them. Everything seemed to be moving in slow motion. Except her heartbeat — that was beating so fast, it felt like a thousand hummingbirds fluttering in her chest. Like a thousand hummingbirds with razor-sharp beaks and claws, tearing at her sternum.

"You don't know what they want — you wouldn't even listen to their audio file. They could have blasted us into pieces long before now, but they didn't!" Thalia shrieked.

"I will not subject my crew to their tortures — we J'nai are long acquainted with the way the Qaig treat their prisoners, Thalia," Soren said, her voice rising. The J'nai woman stood, somehow looking taller than she really was, an impenetrable wall. "And neither will we be hostages to be bartered with."

"Soren…" Asher said, breaking the tension — everyone turned to look. The Qaig ship had opened a larger side panel, like a massive garage door, and the gravitational beam seemed to be pulling them directly into it. It looked to be a large holding area, like a hangar bay, empty and vast.

"I'm sorry, Thalia," Soren said, and turned. Her hand paused for a microsecond, before hitting a glowing red button on her console screen.

"*NO!*" Thalia screeched, falling to her knees. Overhead, the rattling remnants of the comm system started the grim countdown.

"Ten," the voice filled every corner of the ship. It was a pleasant voice, Nora thought, a calm female voice, without any evidence of panic or fear in it. It echoed down the hall behind them. She heard it as if from a great distance, as if she were somehow already detached from her body.

"What have you *done*?" Thalia screamed. She screamed so loud, her lips pulled back over her teeth, that she almost looked like an animal. She clutched her head, pulling at her hair in despair. She screamed again, incoherent, and ran from the Bridge.

"Nine," the voice continued, breaking whatever reverie about her clone-twin Nora had been momentarily lost in.

"Eight."

She thought about Sophie, and Cat and Zoe and Raina, and about Lara and Mike and all those friends she'd known and lost. She thought about Aditi, her mentor and friend, and regretted never knowing what the Ganymede underground was truly about. She thought about Louisiana, and the humid air, and live oak trees, and her parents. A tear fell down her cheek, quickly followed by another, and she found herself sniffling.

"Seven."

"It will be okay, Eleanora," Bastian said. His accented voice sounded thick, choked. It might have been the sparks and smoke and dust floating around them. Her own throat, too, felt raw from the mixture in the air. He unlocked her chair wheels, pulled it close to his, and wrapped his arms around her, resting her head against his chest. She clung to his flight suit, gripping it tightly in her clammy fingers, listening to the slow, steady pulse of his heart against his chest. Memorizing the sound.

"Six."

She felt his lips brush the top of her head. She squeezed her eyes tight, willing the tears to stop. There was no more room for thoughts in her head. She thought she'd have a flashback — didn't people with near-death experiences always claim to have those? Some rapid movie-style montage, a highlight reel? Instead, her mind was blank, overloaded with terror and regret. She was a deer in the headlights, waiting for the oncoming truck.

She breathed deeply, savoring the feel of Bastian's arms around her, warm and strong, grateful to have a friend here, at the end.

"Five."

"Four."

"Three."

"Two."

"One."

CHAPTER 2
SOPHIE, GANYMEDE STATION

"Earth to Cat," Sophie called, waving a manicured hand in front of her roommate's face. "Come in, Cat."

Cat winced, and blinked rapidly, her eyes unfocused behind thick glasses as she tried to look up. Sophie sighed and turned away from Cat's bunk to plop herself at the table in the middle of their room.

"They're not giving out prizes for sleep deprivation, you know," she said. "Or are you thinking about that hunky Xerxes you're tutoring again?"

Cat turned pink and redoubled her efforts at studying her tablet. Sophie rubbed her own eyes — and a smear of eyeliner came off on her hands, damn it. She'd forgotten that she was wearing it, which was a testament to how tired she was, since she *always* wore makeup. She probably looked like a raccoon now, and that just wouldn't do. Sophie pushed herself up with a huff and headed to the bathroom at the back of Room 10013. The room was an elongated rectangle, with the bunks stacked in pairs along one wall, and a massive window overlooking Ganymede Station and the moon itself on the other. Tonight, Jupiter was half-full in the sky, casting shadows on Ganymede's cratered, brown surface. The red storm on the surface peered down at them, like an all-seeing eye. She hated that red spot. She stalked down the room, feeling its gaze on her like a sunburn.

Raina and Zoe were curled up on Raina's bunk, reading something together on her tablet. Sophie's eyes flickered to the neatly made bunk atop her own, where Nora was conspicuously absent.

"Asteroid mining, my ass," she muttered, and went into the bathroom. She peered into the mirror, wishing the harsh white light in here was a little more flattering.

Yep, she was right. Raccoon eyes. She grabbed a towel and cleaned off the black smudges as best she could. She turned and looked down the room. Six girls had started here. Now there were just the four of them left. Lara was dead. Nora was gone who-knew-where, most definitely *not* mining asteroids or whatever. No one was saying anything, and the silence was going to drive her crazy. No one would ever suspect they were clones of the most brilliant, bad-ass women in history, not with the way they looked now, demoralized and exhausted and silent.

"How can you all just SIT THERE!" Sophie yelled, throwing the eyeliner-streaked towel the length of the room. It landed on the table, scattering tablets and cups and spare parts for their various projects. She heard a loud *thump*, which turned out to be Zoe's head hitting the top of Raina's bunk as she sat up in surprise. A string of muttered curses was followed by Zoe's angry face peeking out at her, glaring down her aquiline nose.

"Hey, drama queen, keep it down, will you?" she said. Sophie stuck out her tongue. She'd already completed that day's task as part of the plan to save Ganymede Station. Each day, a new task was sent out to their tablets, depending on their particular skills. Cat, as a Marie Curie clone and the smartest in their year, was working on the Star Port repairs, or so Sophie thought. Raina and Zoe were helping repair the shuttles since they weren't as scientifically minded, which generally left them covered in sweat and grease and stinking to high heaven. Sophie doubted their illustrious warrior-queen DNA had prepared them for grunt-work, but they threw themselves into it with an unrivaled passion. Since they'd lost their roommate, Lara, an Eleanor Roosevelt, in the Qaig attack, they'd all wanted to chip in and do their part. Sophie had been tasked with scanning known frequencies (and some unknown) for any potential J'nai communications. Spoiler alert:

there had been none. They'd had no news at all from Terra Prime. The futility was draining. Sophie crossed her arms.

"We miss Nora too, you know," Cat said quietly. Sophie turned, but couldn't see Cat, buried as she was into her bunk. She sagged into a full-body sigh and went over to see her.

Cat had scooted over, patting her hand on the blanket for Sophie to sit. She did, and Cat looked up from her tablet momentarily to smile at her, eyes magnified by her lenses. It made her appear somehow younger than she was. She was barely seventeen anyway, as some sketchy circumstances had brought her to Ganymede a year early. She was pretty, Sophie always thought, with her mass of light brown curls, though she'd never bothered to do anything with it. Sophie's fingers itched to tame it, to apply a little blush to Cat's pale cheeks. The thought distracted her for a moment.

"She'll be okay, Sophie," Cat said. Sophie shook her head.

"Not even you can know that for sure," she said, and she bit her lip to keep tears from falling. She could cry on command — and frequently did, as the damsel-in-distress act was the best in her arsenal — but this time, the tears were real.

"She's good, you know," Cat said, powering down her tablet. Sophie was surprised at that — she'd thought the thing was glued to Cat's palms, the way she'd been working lately. Cat was giving Sophie her undivided attention.

"Who?" Sophie asked, sniffling.

"Nora," Cat said. She cradled the tablet to her chest, pulling her knees up.

"I know we don't know where she's at, but she's a great pilot. And she has Sebastian with her. Nothing will happen to her."

"Thalia's there, too," Sophie muttered. If there's one thing she could count on Thalia for, it was her survival instinct. Nothing would happen to the *Rapscallion* while Thalia had anything to say about it.

Cat nodded, and blinked a few times, before closing her eyes and rubbing at the spot between her brows. She rolled her head from shoulder to shoulder, working out muscles that had tightened up as she'd worked. When her eyes opened again, they were rimmed with red. Sophie frowned.

"Migraine?"

"It's not so bad," Cat said, but her voice shook, and the words were faint. Sophie grabbed the bottle of acetaminophen from the shelf in Cat's bunk and shook out a few pills, handing them over.

"Here," she said.

"Thanks," Cat whispered, and took the pills. She took a sip of cold coffee that sat in a cup on the shelf in the side of her bunk.

"You know caffeine and sleep deprivation can trigger migraines," Sophie said, and Cat winced.

"Yeah."

"And gray hairs. Want me to pull this one out for you?" Sophie said, smoothing Cat's hair back from her forehead. The gesture was gentle, but the frown on Sophie's face was not. She would not tolerate an errant hair, especially one that was such a contrast to Cat's ash-brown mane.

"Don't bother. I'm getting more and more of them," Cat grumbled. She curled up, closing her eyes. Sophie noticed the sharply circumscribed violet shadows under her eyes, usually hidden by the glasses. Cat was working too hard. They all were. She let out a long breath, hoping that wherever Nora was, that she was safe.

"Hey, sleep deprivation causes wrinkles too!" came a shout from the next bunk. Sophie rolled her eyes.

"That's why there's Botox!" she shouted back. Cat winced at the volume of Sophie's voice — not a good sign.

"Get some rest, Cat. You'll feel better in the morning," Sophie said, and dimmed the light in the bunk. Cat was already asleep, nestled with her tablet in her arms. Sophie removed Cat's glasses and pulled the cover up. She pulled the curtain on the bunk closed to block out the light from the room. Cat's migraines made her extra sensitive to things like light, and noise. And smells. Basically, any kind of stimulus.

"As for you two," Sophie said, strolling past Zoe and Raina to her own bunk, "take a shower, will you? It smells like the hangar bay in here."

"Yes, mom!" Zoe called, cackling. The two of them had been thick as thieves lately. Zoe — a clone of Zenobia, a fearsome Syrian warrior queen — had fought to keep her own exercise routine up, to keep herself in fighting form. They'd had lessons in hand-to-hand combat, in "Fight Club," before the Qaig attack. Before the curfew that Admiral Savaryn had enforced, for 'their own benefit,' 'time to rest and recharge.'

Not many could stand against Zoe in the ring. Sophie'd like to see her box Savaryn for keeping them locked up like prisoners sometime. Sophie used to watch, from the safety of her stationary bike, while the students in the officer-training group trained. Zoe moved like a massive jungle cat, nearly six feet of muscle and grace. She exercised in their room now, even after spending a day hauling ship parts in the hangar bay. As a result, she *did* tend to smell rather ... foul.

Raina, a clone of Rani Lakshmibai — an Indian queen who hadn't known the definition of surrender — was more into yoga. It kept her simmering temper generally under tolerable control. Raina had gone to "Fight Club," too, but reluctantly. Instead of giving her an outlet for her temper, it tended to stoke it. Still, when she and Zoe were together, they made heads turn when they strode through the hangar bay, with all the swagger that their heritage instilled in them. Two queens, no matter what the circumstances. Sophie envied their closeness — it made her miss Nora even more.

Sophie climbed into her own bed. It was late, well past curfew, but she wasn't tired. Maybe she'd read a book — the colossal digital library at Ganymede went much further than just boring old science books. There was plenty of fiction too, and the classics, and occasionally new updates from Earth were sent over. She'd delved into the romance novels — some even written by her own fellow Ganymedeans — and enjoyed winding down with one on nights when she couldn't sleep. Like this one. Tonight, she felt electrified, every muscle aching. She hadn't been allowed to the gym lately, which was probably part of the problem. Zoe might have been able to move a few dumbbells around, but there was no way Sophie could move an entire stationary bike in here.

She was restless. She wanted to know what was going on, *really* going on. Her last attempts to hack into the mainframe had left her cross-eyed and disappointed. She sighed dramatically, dropping back onto her pillow. She wondered what Hedy would do in this situation.

Sophie had known she was a clone long before most of the other Faxes — Hedy Lamarr had been too famous, too recent. As a result, she identified with the movie star quite closely. It had been a rare misstep in the Board's stringent cloning process, when usually clones weren't told their lineage until they were nearly adults. Too much risk of the clones being 'duds,' or having medical problems from the cloning process. But Hedy wouldn't have given up! She *would* find out what was going on here, and —

Ping.

Her tablet chirped at her. It was probably Tylajah, she thought with a grin, and picked it up. He wasn't very chatty, and they hadn't had much time together, anyway. Best she could do was flirt with him over the messaging app and flirt she did. She liked to imagine him blushing at the other end of her texts.

But when she pulled up the app, the message wasn't from Ty.

It was a blocked name; a feature she didn't even know the app had. She opened the message, intrigued.

Sophie Bauer? It read.

Who's asking? She replied. A pause.

Someone who wants the same things you want.

Impossible, she thought, grinning. That was a long, long list. The message continued.

Someone who wants answers.

That got her attention.

What kind of answers? She typed. While she waited for a response, she ran a check on the app, to see if she could back-trace where the message was coming from, who was sending it. Nothing happened. It was like the message was coming from nowhere. She frowned. Not many people on this station had that level of security encryption on their tablets, and none should be able to send anonymous messages.

I want to know the truth about Ganymede Station. Don't you? Don't you want to know where Nora really went?

Sophie went cold.

Who the hell are you? And where is Nora? She wrote. Her fingers typed out the message in a furious staccato, her painted nails clacking against the tablet's surface.

I'd like to meet you. Tomorrow, after curfew lifts. The cafeteria. We can help each other.

Sophie rolled her eyes. There would be a hundred people in the cafeteria then. How would she know who to meet?

Why me? She asked.

Because we need someone with your particular talents, they wrote. Another pause, before they sent another message —

And because Lara trusted you.

Lara. Her loud, hilarious, Australian roommate. A clone, like the rest of her roommates, Lara was the only Eleanor Roosevelt to have been made, and Sophie never had figured out why. Lara had been Cat's bunkmate. She was a rising star in the officer training track, until the attack on Terra Prime — when she'd been killed, along with half of Ganymede's fleet.

Sophie sat back, stunned, and smacked her head against the wall of her bunk.

Ow, she thought. Not for the first time, she questioned the bunk's design. But her interest was piqued, to say the least. And whomever she was meeting in the cafeteria couldn't have picked a more public place on the whole station. She'd be safe there, meeting them. What did she have to lose? Sophie was nothing if not curious, which had been known to get her into trouble on occasion. She wanted to know who was capable of this kind of encryption, and she really wanted to know what they knew about Nora.

Tomorrow, she wrote, and closed the app.

———

B y the time curfew was lifted, Sophie had been up for hours. She couldn't help it — she was too worked up. She'd sent Ty a few messages, but he hadn't responded (he was probably still asleep, like any sane person). She'd showered, curled her hair, and reapplied her signature cherry-red nail polish. She'd polished the already-gleaming buttons on her navy uniform. And still she'd sat, waiting, drumming her fingers on the table. When the curfew lifted, the door lock unbolted automatically, and she dashed out the door. True, she'd hacked the lock before, but there was no point getting caught by the Night Guard for something like this. The mysterious person awaiting her wouldn't be at the cafeteria yet anyway. Better save the sneaking out and risking detention for when it really mattered — like when she needed ice cream.

She walked swiftly through the halls, her shoes clicking softly. Hardly anyone else was up yet; she could make out alarms going off in the dorm rooms as she passed, waking the occupants. She pressed on and entered the cafeteria. The large dome had clear panels overhead, showing Jupiter's watchful eye. Inside, though, it looked like any food court back on Earth, just cleaner, and everything was made out of white and blue plastics. A few tired-looking people and J'nai made their way through the lines, grabbing coffees and breakfast. It was a quiet bunch, fatigued and subdued. Sophie joined them, craning her neck to see if anyone seemed out of place, anyone looking for her, but no one was. She got her coffee — large, with lots of cream and sugar — and took a seat at an empty table. She pulled up her tablet, attempting to look busy, as she watched the early morning crowd. She didn't have to wait long.

"Good morning, is this seat taken?" a cool, vaguely British-sounding voice asked.

She turned, and was greeted by a tall, teal-skinned J'nai man taking a seat across from her. Sophie arched an eyebrow, looking him up and down. She thought she had seen him before. He was usually with a bunch of the officers and definitely was not a student. He wore the uniform of Ganymede Station, but the J'nai here were mostly of the Delta class, a somewhat-outcast standing. She'd been told that the other J'nai classes looked down on those who deigned to come to Ganymede to work, though mostly the J'nai students viewed their time here as a kind of exotic exchange-program, a chance to see 'alien' humans up close and learn about their culture.

This man, though, was no outcast. He had delicate white and gold tattoos scrawled across the back of his hands, up his neck, and over his face. This marked him as a member of the highest caste — the Alpha class. J'nai royalty. She hadn't noted *that* on any J'nai before. It was like meeting a prince — enough to make any girl's head spin, even Sophie's.

"Good morning," she muttered, and took a sip of her coffee. The cup was warm in her hands, and she wrapped both palms around it. It steadied her. She was nearly trembling in anticipation. This person was not what she'd expected — but really, what had she been expecting? Maybe one of the Einstein clones? She'd considered that the person meeting her would have been MacGregor, the XO, who was a Charlemagne clone. He'd been known to be a friend to fellow clones before, including Nora, and didn't stand for any of the Fax-Original feuds. She wouldn't put it past him to go against Admiral Savaryn's orders.

"Thank you for meeting me, Sophie," he said, sipping his own coffee. He glanced casually around the room, but everyone else was either too busy or too tired to notice them.

"Mmm," she muttered, taking him in. He wore his straight white hair long, like most J'nai. It was pulled back a bit on the sides, revealing ears that were slightly too pointed to be human. In fact, other than the tattoos, there was nothing all that distinguishable about him. Royalty? He didn't really look it. His uniform was impeccable, true, but he moved slowly, as if he was exhausted. He sat casually, as if they were just two friends having coffee together — or perhaps he was too tired to put up any sort of pretense. This man before her was handsome, for a J'nai, but Prince Charming he was not.

Sophie tossed her hair. So. Royalty, was it? She'd played this role before — or at least, Hedy had. Sophie was, after all, a clone of Hedy Lamarr. The Austrian American star of the silver screen, Hedy was the co-inventor of technology that had led to the development of Bluetooth and GPS. And so, Sophie prepared to channel her inner Princess Veronica, in *Her Highness and the Bellboy*. She would not be intimidated, J'nai royalty or not.

"Is there... anything you'd like to ask me?" he said. Sophie huffed, a very un-princessy sound. A thousand questions rattled in her head, clamoring to be asked—

"Where's Nora?" she said. First and foremost, she had to know that.

"No idea," he said simply. Sophie rolled her eyes and went to get up. The J'nai held up a hand to stop her.

"Please, sit down." He gestured towards her seat. This wasn't a question. It wasn't really a command, either — Sophie would have chafed at that — but almost a plea. Almost.

She glared at him a moment, considering, then sat, crossing her arms.

"What I meant was, no one knows where she and the *Rapscallion* are. But they are definitely not mining asteroids," he said, leaning back and crossing his ankle over his knee, completely at ease. Sophie drummed her nails against the sleeve of her uniform.

"I knew that already. I mean, sort of. Anything else? I'm going to be late for my assignment."

He sighed. "Sophie, I need your help. Ganymede needs your help."

"Then get in line, Prince whoever-you-are. In case you haven't noticed, there's a crisis going on here about every other minute. I'm already working eighty hours a week on Savaryn's orders, so forgive me for not volunteering for whatever extra projects you've got going on."

"Jaxon."

"Excuse me?" she blinked.

"My name. It's Jaxon. Lara always spoke highly of you. Are you really going to dismiss me so soon?" He smiled and took another sip of his coffee. How dare he look so relaxed, so calm when he said her name. Losing Lara had been like losing a limb. The ache had receded, eventually. The sensation of not being whole though, not being complete, remained, and at times caught her off-guard. Like now.

"How the hell do... did you know Lara?" she asked with a glare. A few students at the next table over glanced their way. Sophie continued to stare him down.

"We met after one of her classes, I was tutoring. We ... became friends," he said. Sophie arched an eyebrow. He pursed his lips, and when it became obvious she was waiting for more, he added— "Good friends."

"I see," Sophie said. Her brain was whirling. Was *this* the 'mystery boyfriend' Lara had been keeping from them last year? A J'nai, and royal to boot? No wonder she'd been so secretive. Sophie hadn't seen that one coming, and she generally prided herself on her snooping. As Lara would have said, good on ya.

So, Lara had liked this guy, trusted him, had wanted to be close to him. Why hadn't she told Sophie about this? True, J'nai-human romances were a rarity — though Sophie knew enough about J'nai anatomy to be fairly certain that it *could* work — but it was no different to Sophie than if Lara had been dating an Original (which, to be fair, was also pretty rare since most Originals — besides Ty — were pompous jerks). Memories of her boisterous Australian roommate hit her like a tidal wave, from her obnoxious photographic memory to her infectious laughter. Sophie raised her eyes — she just knew that her emerald green gaze was now ringed in red, not an attractive look — and met Jaxon's.

"*I* got Lara access to the shuttle that took her to Terra Prime. I had wanted her to see my home world. She wanted to see it, I think, to understand my affection for it. I," Jaxon said, stopping a moment, lost in thought. Sophie's chest clenched, the wound that Lara's death had left feeling raw all over again.

"I am the reason Lara is dead."

"Wow, I really want to help you with your secret project now," Sophie said, standing abruptly. She hadn't been prepared for the rush of sadness that had struck her when he'd mentioned Lara. Now, it was like she could think of nothing else. She grabbed her tablet. "Thanks for that, Prince, but I have work to do. Real work. Trying to save this station. And for the record," she said, raising a finger. "I don't like you."

And she walked out.

CHAPTER 3
CAT, GANYMEDE STATION

BEEEEEEEEEEEEEEEEEEEEP!
Her alarm blared like a foghorn in her ear. Cat pushed the button on her tablet — which she'd forgotten to charge again, as she'd fallen asleep with it in her hands — and shut it off. The noise was unbearable. It felt like needles driving into her brain, stabbing and stabbing and stabbing. She fumbled for the power cord to her tablet, and it took three tries to get the darn thing plugged in. She reached for her ragged stuffed bunny, the one she mostly kept hidden under her pillow. It reminded her of Muffin, her old pet back home ... well, back on Earth, anyway. The migraines hadn't been so bad then, but the stuffed rabbit always seemed to calm her, even if his glossy, black eyes were now opaque with scratches, and his once-white whiskers were frayed and drooping. There was a bald patch near his tail, where she used to rub as she'd hold him tight and wait for the pain to pass.

Migraines. *Always* with the migraines. She lay back and squeezed her eyes tight, so tight that bursts of color appeared in her vision, like fuzzy fireworks. The pain at her temples was so bad, it was hard to focus on anything, even breathing. *Hydrogen, Helium, Lithium, Beryllium...*

"Here," a voice — Zoe — said, and Cat pried open her eyes to see the tall girl handing her some pills and a glass. She clenched her eyes tight again against the light.

"Thanks," she croaked. She held out her hand, and Zoe dropped the pills into it. Cat took each pill and swallowed them, one by one, with a sip of water. *Boron, Carbon, Nitrogen…*

"Bad today?" Zoe asked quietly, walking toward her locker. Zoe tried to be quiet, she really did, but today even her soft tread felt like elephants stomping to Cat's overly sensitive neurons. Cat focused on the periodic table. On naming the elements, in order. Usually by the time she reached Iridium, the pain would start subsiding.

"Yeah," Cat said, cautiously opening her eyes again, but the needles in her brain were already withdrawing, the glare of the overhead lights already becoming less intrusive. "Didn't sleep well. Common migraine trigger. Aura's not so bad though." Sometimes the aura, or associated symptoms, of her migraine included holographic visual changes, sound sensitivity, vomiting … the list went on, interminably.

"Uh huh," Zoe said, grabbing her uniform. "Hey, you see Sophie this morning?"

"I think I heard her leave just as the alarms went off," Cat mumbled. *Bromine, Krypton, Rubidium.* The door shutting behind Sophie might as well have been a gong for the way it had rattled her skull.

She pushed back the blankets, pushing Muffin back under her pillow, and got up out of bed, momentarily nauseated. She was almost always nauseated lately. It felt like she was walking on a ship at sea. She straightened, closed her eyes for a second, and the feeling passed. *Ruthenium and Cadmium …* no, that wasn't right. *Rhodium.* That was next. Then … *Indium?*

"Come on, Cat," Raina said, getting up from her bunk and stretching. She looked tiny and petite next to Zoe — but not fragile like a flower. Fragile like a bomb. "Let's get you something to eat."

"I'll grab a bar. I've got to get to…"

"It can wait five minutes for you to get a proper meal. I heard there's peach pancakes today," Zoe said, crossing her arms. "I mean, there's *always* peach pancakes. And peach smoothies. Peach protein bars. Peach tea. Anyway, the carbs will be good for you. Gives you energy."

Cat sighed. They were right. And besides, it wasn't worth the effort it would take to fight them. Her head was already spinning, going over her computations from last night. She was working — she thought — on the code and structure for a new Star Port. It was a fusion of human and J'nai tech that they hoped to deploy at Terra Prime to rescue the J'nai from what was assumed to be — at best — a Qaig invasion. That it might have been a complete genocide, a planet-wide obliteration, no one wanted to even contemplate.

Cat got herself dressed, pulling on her white shirt from yesterday and her uniform pants and jacket, which pulled a little across her stomach. She ran a comb through her hair, agitating the frizz, then pulled it up in a bun. No one cared about what she looked like. Well, she wasn't going to see anyone she was interested in impressing, anyway. She fiddled with her earrings, the cluster of stars she'd designed and had 3D-printed for her roommates. She wondered if Nora was wearing hers. It calmed her a little to think of that link between them, wherever she was.

Tin, Antimony, Tellurium.

It took Raina and Zoe a few more minutes, but soon the three of them were headed out of the room and towards the cafeteria. Cat thought she glimpsed Sophie rushing out of the dome just as they entered. Zoe nudged her.

"Hey, Earth to Cat. Breakfast, remember?"

"Oh. Yeah," she said, and drifted after Zoe and Raina. Food presently acquired, they sat to eat. Cat absently picked at her pancakes and pulled up her latest task report on her tablet.

"That's strange," she mumbled. Zoe and Raina had been talking and stopped.

"What is?" Raina prompted after a moment.

"Huh? Oh," Cat said, looking back at the tablet in her hand. It was like an extension of her arm these days. "There's some issue with the Observatory. Telescope is malfunctioning. Should be an easy fix," she said. In a way, she was grateful. She missed her time there for Astronomy class. The moons of Jupiter were her favorite thing to look at, and she was sure she'd discover a new one, a small one of course, if she just had the time. She'd love to name one after Marie Curie. Taking a break from looking at the Star Port calculations — loathe as she was to do so — might actually be a good thing. Her brain felt numb from the computations. Besides, it shouldn't take too long, the message on her tablet had said. She'd be back in the computer lab in a few hours.

I t took more than a few hours. And, as luck would have it, she *did* run into someone worth impressing. Well, sort of. She almost *literally* ran into him. She was rounding a corner on her way to the telescope when she saw Raphael, the Xerxes clone she'd been tutoring. She'd abruptly stopped and retreated, flattening her back to the wall. She clutched her tablet to her chest and took a deep breath. He was on the other side of this corner, just a few feet away. His back was towards her, but she could tell it was him. She could always tell him apart from the other Xerxes. He stood differently, somehow, looked more regal. His dark hair swept back in waves, longer than the others. His words to her were kinder. And when he'd asked for her help with his Chemistry homework, and turned those unfathomable eyes on her, she hadn't been able to resist.

Her heart pounded in her chest. Relax, Cat. She told herself to take a deep breath, to consider her options rationally. What would Sophie do? She considered. Sophie would walk past him, flipping her long hair over one shoulder, and give him the brightest smile she could muster. Cat could try that — but wait, her hair was in a bun, and really it was too curly to flip properly anyway, so scratch that idea. Besides, had she even remembered to brush her teeth today? It would be just her luck to have food stuck between them. She'd have to come up with another plan.

As Cat pondered her approach, she heard Raphael's gravelly voice. He was talking to someone — an Original, she wasn't sure which one. She could recognize the voices of most of the Faxes by now.

"Oh, I'll have plenty of time later," he was saying.

"I thought they'd assigned you extra projects in the Chemistry lab," a voice — female — said.

"Only because I'm suddenly so good at it," he said, and laughed. "It's the price I pay for having Cat do my work for me."

Cat flushed. She didn't do it for him, exactly. She just helped him. And if he didn't have the time to sit and listen to her explanations — which would take hours, and there was a curfew to consider — that wasn't her fault. And honestly, he was hopeless at Chemistry. She had no idea why he'd actually been assigned there, except maybe to help wash the glassware.

"In fact," he said, chuckling, "I'm suddenly such a prodigy that they're going to be giving me my own project soon. Of course, I'll let Cat do that for me, too."

Cat's migraine pulsed, suddenly so intense her vision blurred. *Promethium, Samarium, Europium.* She squinted her eyes shut, as if blocking out the light would also block out his words. It wasn't the first time she'd been in this position, wasn't the first time that someone had pretended to be friendly to her just so she'd do their homework for them. But he'd been nicer than the rest. She'd thought they *were* friends. And when he gave her a smile or a wink, she'd just melted.

Overhead, the lights flickered once, twice, and the talking stopped.

Then, she heard some low giggling, and the voices faded, moving away down the hall as Raphael and the girl walked away. Cat swallowed, but there was a lump lodged in her throat that wouldn't budge. It was like she'd gotten a big glob of peanut butter stuck there. There had been no room to misinterpret his words — no excuse she could make for him now. Between the migraine and her crush stomping on her heart, she thought, it was shaping up to be a pretty terrible day.

Focus, Cat. He's no different from all the rest. So what if he'd made you feel … seen. Her vision blurred again, and not from pain — there were tears forming in her eyes. She blinked hard, looking up at the lights. She'd read that doing that would keep the tears from falling, and it kind of helped. Then she took a deep breath, rounded the corner, and continued on, focusing on the task at hand. The telescope. She had to fix it. People were counting on her. And Raphael had been right about one thing — she was good at her work.

C at blew a stray bit of hair away from her eyes, and readjusted her glasses, which were foggy from sweat. Her head still pounded. It had been pounding all day. She was grateful to not be staring at computer screens, grateful to be left alone to repair the telescope, for the lack of audio stimuli other than her own tinkering, but she wished she'd brought some meds with her. Her migraines had never been this bad back on Earth. She remembered her handlers — like foster parents, hired by the Board to raise the clone children — bringing her to neurologists, who prescribed her a few different medications. They all made her feel fuzzy. She couldn't think clearly while taking them, so she'd stopped. She'd suffer through a few migraines each month if it meant that the rest of the time she was clear-headed.

Today though, the pain was so bad that she was thinking about as clearly as a mud puddle.

The telescope was a brilliant piece of engineering, and getting to work on this 3D-printed masterpiece was a privilege. Each delicate piece had been crafted and put together with precision that bordered on the nanometer. Ganymede had an atmosphere, but just barely, so the gamma rays, the infrared spectrum, as well as the long-wavelength radio waves blocked by Earth's atmosphere, could all be accessible from the moon-based station. Not even the Hubble telescope and its progeny orbiting Earth could compare to this hydra-headed behemoth. She'd heard one of the da Vincis calls it the "Ferrari of Telescopes," and he'd laid a hand on it fondly, like it was an old friend, an animate thing with a soul.

And here she was, taking it apart like a jigsaw puzzle.

She was on a small ladder, in the underbelly of the beast. She'd really just needed to recalibrate most of the sensors, and it was working fine. She'd taken a peek through each of them — purely for confirmation that they were working correctly, and definitely not so that she could scope out Jupiter's moons. She could see the thin glittering rings around Jupiter with a clarity that took her breath away. But the darn radiation sensors ... she strained her arm, ignoring the crescendo pounding in her head, trying to reach the thin connection wire so she could remove the last...

Clang.

The whole piece dropped, the connection severed, and Cat fell with it, in a scrabble of bolts and screws. She shrieked, a high-pitched yelp that echoed in the otherwise-empty dome, the sound cut off sharply when she struck the ground, and the air left her lungs in a great *whoosh*.

For a moment, she didn't move. Then, she took a deep breath and opened her eyes, assessing. She had not hit her head. She had not lost consciousness. Her knee throbbed, and the back of her shoulder, too, where it had struck the ground. She moved both gingerly and was pleased to note they seemed to be functioning appropriately. When she was sure nothing was broken, either on herself or the piece of the computer she held, she sat up.

"Ow," she said, rubbing her knee. That would definitely be a bruise. She was lucky she'd just been a few feet up the ladder. Fortunately, the fall hadn't seemed to damage the microprocessor in its casing. She hoped.

"God, Cat, are you okay?" Sophie came out of nowhere, like a guardian angel. Cat had startled at the sound of her voice, nearly dropping the case again. She let Sophie help her to her feet, then pushed her glasses back up on her face.

"I'm fine," she mumbled, stooping to collect the pieces and bolts that had fallen. She gazed up over her glasses as she worked and saw Ty standing by the door to the Observatory, leaning on the doorframe, waiting. She glanced back to Sophie.

"Sophie," she whispered, still looking at Ty. "What is he doing here?" She liked Ty more than most of the boys on Ganymede — he was quiet and never pestered her for help on his homework. Plus, Sophie liked him. But that didn't mean Cat wasn't awkward and shy around him.

Sophie stood, brushing her hands on her skirt, and tossed her head, waving to Ty to come over.

"I just wanted to check on you. Tylajah offered to walk me over," she said with a wide smile. Ty gallantly offered Sophie his arm, which she took, beaming. Cat wasn't sure how the jacket seams kept from bursting over his biceps when he flexed them like that. A blush came over his dark face as Sophie looked up adoringly at him.

"Oh," Cat said, feeling like a very obvious third wheel. "I mean, I'm fine. Almost done."

"Migraine gone?" Sophie asked, her bright green eyes still fixated on Ty.

Cat frowned.

It *was* gone. The migraine was gone. In fact, it had been gone since she fell. She rubbed another bruise forming on her arm. Not that she wanted to try falling down every time she got a headache, but it had triggered something to release the pressure on her brain. There wasn't even a trace of pain left, no nausea. Nothing.

"Yeah," Cat said, brightening, and straightened up a little at the realization. "Yeah. I'm good."

"Marvelous," Sophie said. "And now what's going on with this telescope? Will you be done by curfew?"

"I think so," Cat said, sighing. She looked back dejectedly at the parts she'd strewn across the floor, mostly the housing of the telescope and bolts and screws. It would take her a while to put it all back together. She bent and started gathering them, placing them neatly in a cart.

Sophie's tablet buzzed — and she silenced it, without looking at it.

"So, what's with that piece?" Sophie asked, nodding to the chunk of metal in Cat's hand.

"There's something off with the radiation sensors. I've got the rest of them back online, but this one —" Cat said tapping the processor in her hand, "isn't working. I'm just going to take it back with me," she said.

"Not much that's radioactive out here," Ty said. His voice was low and grumbly, and echoed in the large dome like rolling thunder.

"This should be able to detect even the cosmic microwave background," Cat said, tapping the device again. "But I can't even get a reading from Callisto. All that registers is noise."

"Callisto the moon or like, Callisto Station?" Sophie asked. Ty turned to look at her.

"Callisto Station? I thought the moon was just a dump for old fusion products," Ty said. Cat shook her head.

"No. There was some kind of station there, before Ganymede. It'd be a good place for it, I mean, there's water, some oxygen, and…"

"…and then their fusion reactor had an epic meltdown, and they all had to evacuate. So, we're now on Ganymede," Sophie finished. Cat and Ty looked at her, silent. "What? I read about it one of those times I was trying to find out where Nora went. A whole big file, too. I didn't get into the details." She fluttered a hand in front of her, as if to wave off the remark.

"Well, Hubble Junior should be able to detect the gamma and beta particles from Callisto Station easily, and he's not," Cat said, patting the telescope affectionately.

A chime sounded overhead. Ten minutes until curfew.

"Can I walk you to your room?" Ty asked — he was looking at Sophie, which confused Cat, since she'd clearly be walking the same direction. Sophie glowed and squeezed his arm.

"Hey Cat," Ty called back to her. She grabbed her tablet and the processor and was following them out. She could plug the microprocessor up to her tablet back in her room; she had most of the necessary equipment there to work on it. Just because it was curfew, and she had to be in her room didn't mean she couldn't keep working.

"You remember Wesley, my roommate? Medical guy?" he asked. Cat nodded, still thinking about radiation signatures.

"He was asking about you. I think Nora told him you were having headaches, and he wanted me to pass on to have you stop by and see him."

Thoughts of gamma particles — and of Raphael — were suddenly shoved to the back of her brain. Something felt squirmy in her stomach. Thinking about science was easy. Thinking about herself was harder. As she worked, she could forget that her migraines were getting worse, could ignore the niggling feeling in her gut that told her there might be a bigger problem, a darker problem. Did she have a brain tumor maybe? A glioblastoma would certainly account for her symptoms. She shook her head, clearing out the dark thoughts. Better to focus on the telescope. She could drive herself crazy otherwise.

But did she want to go see Wesley? She considered as they walked back to Room 10013. Cat knew both Nora and Wesley had been concerned that there was something more sinister going on, something that went all the way back to the cloning process itself. Or, Cat thought, something that went back to the DNA of Marie Curie. After all, it had been pretty heavily radiated. Sometimes, she was surprised she didn't glow herself.

"Yeah," Cat said, surprising herself. "Tomorrow. I'll come by tomorrow."

CHAPTER 4
SOPHIE, GANYMEDE STATION

Her tablet buzzed at her all day, the same stupid message each time. *Username: Blocked.* She huffed, for the millionth time, and stuffed the device back into her jacket pocket.

"Task stuff?" Ty asked, eyeing the device. Sophie rolled her eyes. It had been another long day monitoring for J'nai distress calls — none had been found. Her eyes felt dry and her back ached and she was overall very grumpy.

It was futile. No J'nai ships would — or could — get a signal out. Still, Nora could be out there for all she knew, stranded maybe, the *Rapscallion* could be sending distress calls through the Star Port, so she kept looking, kept listening. Kept finding nothing. And sometimes she played 'Qaig Attack,' a new tablet game, with a first-person shooter perspective that was 49% something to occupy the cadets and 51% propaganda. It kept her busy while her search programs ran sweeps across every possible communications frequency. She had one of the top ten high scores in the entire station, under the username "🤍*Hedy* 🤍.""

"No," Sophie said after a moment, brushing a long piece of hair back from her face. She considered telling him what was going on. It's not like he was officially her boyfriend or anything. He hadn't even kissed her yet. Still, he was a good listener, and when he didn't say anything else, just watched for her reply with his infernal patience, she blurted out the whole story — about the texts from Jaxon, his connection to Lara, and his request for her help. Ty shifted his bag to his other shoulder, rubbing at a spot on his collarbone.

"The guy sounds pretty desperate," he said. Sophie bristled at that.

"You think he's coming to me as a last resort?"

Ty flushed, which amused her. Getting a rise out of him always amused her.

"No," he said, slowly, thinking. "But you said he's an Alpha. Royalty. Why come to a student for help with something about the J'nai when he has his own people here, and the Admiral?"

"I guess he doesn't trust them," she mused. She'd considered the possibility. More likely he just wanted her help hacking the mainframe to get into the Admiral's files, so he could do his own snooping. He wouldn't be the first person to ask. Being notorious for her computer hacking skills — and curiosity — came at a price. Though he had dangled a carrot in front of her — Nora's mission — and not everyone who requested her services did. There wasn't much she wouldn't do to make sure that Nora was safe. It was a good carrot, indeed. Jaxon had considered his request carefully, had done his research.

"So, he's a J'nai royal, stranded from his home, from his people, with no resources," Ty listed, frowning. Sophie could hear the sympathy in his voice, and it irritated her.

"He's the one that got Lara killed."

Ty stopped — they'd been walking to the Observatory to pick up Cat. People in the narrow hall flowed around his massive shape like water around a boulder.

"The Qaig killed Lara," he said, tilting his head. Sophie clenched her fist.

"She was only on that ship because of him. She shouldn't have been there at all — she is, or was, a Fax, and we aren't supposed to be on those trips. He told me himself; she was only there because she wanted to see his homeworld."

Ty started walking again, and so she did, too. The crowds thinned as they got close to the Observatory. With classes cancelled indefinitely, no one came out here much. He was quiet for a while, quieter than he usually was. Sophie punched his arm, and he winced, mocking her.

"What are you thinking?" she asked him.

"Well," he said, slowly. "She wanted to see his planet. Learn more about him. It sounds like they had a real connection. And maybe," he said, looking sideways at her as they walked. "Maybe he's hurting from her loss, too."

Sophie considered this. She was opening her mouth to say something when she caught sight of Cat. The girl was perched precariously on a step ladder, reaching for a piece on the telescope, her back to the door.

And then, Cat fell.

Later that night, after Ty had walked them back to their room, Sophie got ready for bed. Cat's fall had rattled her, but the girl seemed all right. With her migraine gone, Cat had been chattier this evening, even though she was working on her tablet with the pieces from the telescope spread out on the table. Cat had been mooning over a boy named Raphael — a notorious flirt, Sophie knew. Sophie'd recognized it in his attitude the moment she'd first laid eyes on him — and then Cat had told them about the abrupt end of her crush, without fading into the least bit of melodrama. She'd even laughed when Zoe broke Raina's concentration as the feisty girl went through her evening meditation sequences, and Raina had stuck out her tongue. It was good to see Cat laugh.

Sophie spent more time than usual brushing out her long hair, lost in thought. Was Ty right? She thought about Jaxon's perspective. She didn't know much about him. He was an Alpha, but one with no family, no pack. It sounded awfully lonely. She looked back over her shoulder from the bathroom into her room, catching sight of Cat at the table with her tablet and the pieces from the telescope, and Raina and Zoe loading up the laundry, smiling at each other. Something tightened in her chest. They were *her* pack. Lara and Nora were her pack. This room, though sometimes it felt like a cage, was her home. And she would defend it.

She put her hair up into a bun — wispy pieces artfully arranged —

and got into her bunk, pulling up the messaging app on her tablet. Jaxon had sent her one message. The repetitive buzzes all day were from him checking to see if she'd read it yet. She pulled her blanket up, cuddled against her pillow, and replied.

Okay.

Okay, came the rapid reply. Sophie chewed on her bottom lip. It wasn't like messaging Ty, or her roommates. Jaxon outranked her, in several different ways. He was older — though by how much, it was hard to say, since J'nai aged differently. He was an officer, not a cadet. And he was royalty. The whole situation was weird to the extreme. Still, he'd come to her for help. And maybe he could answer some of her own burning questions.

What do you need? she typed.

We're meeting in the last lab in the chemistry wing. Do you know it? She winced. Yes, she knew it. She'd hosted a very public Halloween party there last year. And then had the worst hangover of her life. It was not an experience that she was eager to repeat. Still, the lab was isolated, which is why it had worked so well for her party.

I know it. Who's 'we'?

The Mutineers.

Now *that* got Sophie's attention. Intriguing. The code names, the covert messages. It was like a moth to a flame, calling to her — maybe burning her too though, who knew. She sat upright, a fierce determination growing in her chest.

When? she typed.

Now.

Sophie pulled on her sneakers.

"Um, curfew, hello," Raina called, toothbrush in her mouth. She'd given up on her yoga that evening, a fact which Zoe was still cackling about and claimed full credit for.

"Yeah, yeah," Sophie muttered, brain spinning. She pulled on a sweatshirt, lifting the hood up and over her head, tucking her hair inside.

"Clandestine meeting?" Zoe said, grinning from her seat at the table, watching some video on her tablet.

"Don't wait up," Sophie said, blowing a kiss to her roommates. She waved a little wave and hotwired the door to break the lock that the Admiral's curfew automatically engaged at night, to prevent little expeditions just like this one.

Adrenaline coursed through her, lighting up her nerves. She was buzzing with energy, like she could run for miles and miles without stopping. She had the Night Guard's patrols memorized by now, and it was easy enough to avoid them as she crept to the academic wing, padding silently towards the labs. And if she got caught? Well, she'd come up with something then. She always did.

The hallway was dark, deserted. The only sound was the faint scuffing of her sneakers, and her own breathing. She thought of Hedy Lamarr in *My Favorite Spy*. She flattened herself against a corner, peeking around the last turn. There was nowhere for anyone to be lying in wait to trap her. It was kind of fun, honestly. Hedy would be proud.

She waited for three breaths, but no one was there. She crept toward the last laboratory, as sneaky as a cat.

"Hello," a voice said behind her.

"JESUS H. CHRIST," she screeched, then clamped a hand over her mouth. She spun around, tensing to flee.

It was Jaxon. And he was laughing at her.

"I appreciate your stealth," he said, walking past her, hands in his pockets. "But it is not necessary. Come on. There's no one else here." He inclined his head, indicating that she should follow him into the lab. She narrowed her eyes at him, then after he'd disappeared inside, she entered.

"Sophie," a calm voice greeted her. "Welcome."

"Oh, come on," Sophie said, putting her hands on her hips. There was only one other person in the lab besides the lanky J'nai prince. There, leaning back against the countertop, was Dean Prasad. Even at this hour, her uniform was pristine, her black hair pulled back smoothly, her eyeliner immaculate. The Dean, *really*?

"Is this a setup?" Sophie said, eyeing Jaxon. He shook his head.

Next to the petite dean, he was practically towering. Still, he looked at ease, calm, just as he had the first time she'd met him, and perhaps slightly more well rested, even under the harsh glow of the overhead lights. Like nothing at all could ruffle him. Sophie certainly felt ruffled, which wasn't something she was used to.

"No, it's not a setup," Dean Prasad said, and — surprisingly — she smiled. "Have a seat. We have a lot to discuss."

"Like... how you're about to expel me for breaking curfew? Send me back to Earth? Chain me up in the dungeons?" Sophie said, and didn't budge. She considered leaving, but what good would that do? The dean and Jaxon had already seen her. They probably had the lab bugged too, for all she knew, to lure students into some kind of misstep. This was entrapment — but before she could voice her indignation, the dean shook her head. Not a single hair in her braid dared break free of her coiffure.

"Ms. Bauer — Sophie. First off, you know that we don't have dungeons. You've hacked the blueprints for Ganymede Station enough times to know that. Secondly," she said. "Nora came to me, before she left."

That took a little of the wind out of her sails.

"Where is she?" Sophie demanded, crossing her arms. Jaxon and Dean Prasad shared a glance.

"Terra Prime. We hope," she said. "Her ship carried a portable device similar to the technology on the Star Ports. They were to go to Terra Prime, investigate, and return. Only..."

"Only they haven't returned," Sophie whispered, horrified. A portable Star Port? How was that possible? And why hadn't Nora told her? It felt like a betrayal. She was sure that Nora had been sworn to secrecy — but that didn't mean she could keep it from her best friend. She swallowed, the movement sticking in her throat.

"We don't know anything for sure," Dean Prasad started. Sophie's stomach turned. The woman already had top-secret security clearance, didn't she? Why didn't she know? Nora's ship could have broken down. They might have been caught by the Qaig. They might still be floating around in the Current, unable to get home. There were a million possibilities, each one more terrifying than the last. She looked up at the petite woman and the teal J'nai, the only two beings in this universe that had access to the information she wanted, and that could get her the answers she needed.

So, Sophie sat, ungracefully, on the lab stool that the dean offered.

"Now," the woman said, and pulled up her own chair so that her eyes were level with Sophie's, which were beginning to blur with frustrated tears. "Let's get you caught up with what's *really* going on."

CHAPTER 5
ZOE, GANYMEDE
STATION

She was wakened not by the blaring of her alarm clock, but by Raina, thumping on the side of her bunk, letting her know that it was time to get up. Her eyes were hazy, unfocused for a moment. *Have to stop staying up so late*, she thought, but smiled, and smacked her alarm clock into silence. To her surprise, Sophie was still in bed. Her alarm chirped cheerily, but Sophie slept — and snored — on. Not that she'd ever admit to snoring. Zoe got up, went over to the other bunk, and shook Sophie by the arm.

"Hey. Sleeping Beauty. Time to get up," she said, and yawned, stretching. Her muscles felt tight, unused. She was really missing her time in the gym. The J'nai conflict and curfews were really grating on her, and some time working out her frustrations on the weight bench or in "Fight Club" would have been welcome. She'd snuck a few of the free weights into their room though, and so she started putting her muscles through a series of curls and chest presses. As usual, the exercise woke her up better than any Terra Prime coffee, getting her heart pumping and clearing the fog of sleep from her mind. She did squats and a series of stretches. Raina joined her for a two-minute plank, though both girls' arms were shaking by the end. She'd finished her routine by the time the other girls had showered, and while they dressed, she rinsed off and threw on her uniform before Sophie had even finished applying her eyeliner. When Sophie went to adjust some pins in her hair in front of the bathroom mirror, Zoe ran a hand through her own cropped black hair, which was still damp — and this completed her daily grooming.

The four remaining occupants of Room 10013 made their way quietly to the cafeteria for breakfast. Zoe dropped back, to see if Raina would too, but instead she kept pace with Sophie. Zoe frowned a little to herself, but soon enough the awesome smell of bacon — who cared if it was just chemical additive to their veggie-based proteins? — and coffee hit her nose, and her stomach gave a leonine growl.

The rest of the day passed quietly too. Raina didn't look her way much and said even less than usual. This made Zoe grumpy, but she'd noticed Raina, too, was on edge, like a plucked guitar string, just vibrating with suppressed energy. Zoe tried to focus on her work on the hangar, fetching things that needed fetching, providing a little extra *umph* of muscle at the behest of her task-mates, who were actual engineers instead of officer-track students. By the end of the day, the strain of trying to covertly keep an eye on Raina while also working was making her dizzy.

"Hey," Sophie said, popping up at her elbow out of seemingly nowhere. Zoe, startled, looked down at her.

"What are you doing here?" she asked. It wasn't like Sophie to frequent the hangar. It was too messy, too smelly. It was a massive white dome, usually filled with dozens of PJs, usually as busy as any major airport terminal back on Earth. It seemed oddly empty, as many of the ships hadn't returned after the Qaig attack on Terra Prime. Still, there was a ton of activity. Cleaning bots and engineers and ships' crews scuttled about, some lugging along carts and trolleys loaded with parts and tools, all trying their best to make the remaining ships space-worthy.

Sophie's eyes darted around, and she lowered her voice to a whisper. Zoe fought to keep from rolling her eyes. Even for Sophie, this was dramatic.

"Hey," Sophie repeated. "Get Raina. I need you guys to hide somewhere until curfew is called. Then dodge the Night Guard and meet me in the chemistry labs."

"The *what?*" Zoe asked. She wiped a grimy hand across her brow.

She laid down the tools she'd been working with — repairing a heat shield on one of the damaged PJs — and looked at her roommate as if she'd finally gone completely bonkers.

"Shh!" Sophie said. A pair of da Vincis — Leonardo da Vinci clones — walked past, eyeing Sophie, who winked and waved at them. When they were finally far enough away, Sophie whispered again.

"Chemistry labs. The furthest one. As soon as you can after curfew. There's something … someone I need you all to meet."

"Who?"

"Shh! I can't say it here, are you crazy? There are cameras and microphones all over this dome. Just come!" Sophie said. She gave Zoe's arm a meaningful squeeze. That extra time spent on her eyeliner had really paid off, Zoe had to admit — she'd really nailed the cat's eye look. And Zoe never could resist Sophie's crazy ideas. She sighed, nodding. Sophie gave her a mega-watt smile and sauntered out of the dome.

"So, she didn't even give you a clue as to why we're doing this, instead of just hotwiring the door after curfew?" Raina said, scratching her neck. Zoe and Raina were huddled in a classroom, waiting on the curfew. Zoe had gone to meet Raina, like she usually did when they clocked out, and had told her about Sophie's request. They'd made their way down here as surreptitiously as possible when their shift was over.

"Not even the slightest hint. She wanted us to meet someone," Zoe said.

"We know everyone on this rock," Raina muttered. "It's not that big."

"Yeah," Zoe agreed. The classroom was cold; the corridor, dark. Since classes were suspended indefinitely — a fact that usually Zoe would have loved — no one was coming down this wing much anymore. She figured they'd hang out here until curfew, then make their way down the halls to the chemistry labs. The only other time she'd had reason to be down there was Sophie's crazy Halloween party last year. It had been a toga party, complete with moonshine that had left half the station with a hangover. She grinned at the memories. Raina had worn a very short toga that had really shown off her legs.

"What are you thinking about?" Raina asked. She was sitting on the edge of a desk, swinging those toned legs.

"Sophie's toga party," Zoe said, a wide grin splitting her face.

"Ugh," Raina said, making a face, but she smiled, too. "Remember how segregated everyone was? The only Original who came anywhere near a Fax was Greg."

"Yeah," Zoe said, frowning. She hadn't seen much of Greg lately. He'd been infatuated with Nora from the start, but after the Qaig attack, she'd only had eyes for Bastian. Not that Zoe blamed her — he was handsome, in a blond, broody kind of way. Plus, he'd been Zoe's mentor, along with Olivia, during "Fight Club," and was one of the few that could consistently knock her on her ass. Not even Olivia — the Nordic model who was also Bastian's ex-girlfriend or something — could make that claim. Zoe looked up to anyone who could take her down.

"I think things are getting better," Zoe said.

Overhead, the curfew alarm sounded. Well, here they were. They were committed to Sophie's crazy plan now. Zoe could only hope that there were no cameras in this classroom, or at least that no one was watching them. The station was short-staffed, after all. Why waste a pair of eyes watching deserted classrooms? She wasn't sure what punishment would be meted out for breaking curfew — more work hours? What could they do, ground them? The reprimands for Sophie's prior infractions had barely been a slap on the wrist, largely in part to Dean Prasad, she thought.

"Things are not getting better," Raina said. "Originals and Faxes will never get along. We're too different."

"That's not true," Zoe said slowly. "Greg might have been like ... a catalyst. Getting the snowball rolling, you know? And Sophie and Ty are getting along pretty well, don't you think?"

Raina frowned. "Yeah."

"Besides, right now the Admiral needs everyone he can get, Fax or

Original, to help the J'nai. Strange times make strange bedfellows and all that."

Raina didn't answer, but she glowered. She had always felt everything so intensely, taking personally every barb to every Fax.

"I hear he's demoting MacGregor," Raina said at last, looking at Zoe from the corner of her eye. Zoe sat up straight. The XO was the highest-ranking Fax on the station, which was widely regarded as a sort of 'affirmative action' ploy. Still, it was nice having a Fax like him there, looking out for their interests. He'd stood up for Nora before, so in Zoe's book, he was okay.

"Where did you hear that?" Zoe asked.

"Around," Raina said, shrugging. "The official rumor is that it's because MacGregor wants to make peace with the Qaig, and Savaryn says he's too soft — but we all know it's because he doesn't trust Faxes," she said. She picked at something on the desk, scratching at it with a fingernail.

"And the Board's okay with this?" Zoe asked. Raina looked up.

"Savaryn's basically a dictator out here. What are they gonna do, reprimand him from a million miles away?" Raina spat. "We're on our own, and they'll just keep holding us back so their precious 'original' selves can stay in power and do whatever the hell they want. They don't like us any more than we like them."

"So, there's no Originals out there then who've caught your eye, Raina?" Zoe asked, as nonchalantly as she could. Raina flushed and didn't meet her gaze.

Well, that was basically a confirmation, Zoe thought. Raina was tight-lipped, that much was true. Was there an Original she was interested in? Was that why she'd been so uptight? Zoe would have to do some investigating — better yet, she'd get Sophie on board. Even Raina couldn't withstand a Sophie Bauer inquisition.

"Let's go," Raina said suddenly, and hopped off the desk, effectively breaking Zoe's musing. She peeked out the door, her dark braid swinging, and then motioned for Zoe to follow.

It was time.

W hen the assembly was called to order, about a dozen people were crowded into the lab. There were the four girls from Room 10013, along with Dean Prasad — Aditi, she'd now insisted. Also, an Alpha J'nai named Jaxon who apparently had been her room-mate Lara's crush, and six more humans. Two she recognized, students from a year or two ahead of them. The other four, she thought she'd seen around. They were engineers maybe, and she thought one was the chief botanist that ran the greenhouse. Sophie, it seemed, had insisted that all of her roommates be made a part of this clandestine society. It didn't seem like Jaxon was so happy about it but wasn't that just too bad. If he wanted Sophie, he'd get the rest of them, too. Faxes forever.

They all stood quietly in the lab. There were cabinets and tables with sinks along each wall, complete with racks of drying beakers and test tubes. In the center were several black rectangular tables with stools. Aditi and Jaxon were near the center, the heads of this group.

"Ok, let's get everyone up to speed," Aditi said, shortly after the four girls had entered the room. She clasped her hands together, scan-ning and meeting the eyes of everyone in the room. Zoe and Raina exchanged a glance. Cat, she noticed, looked absolutely scared stiff. Sophie must have literally dragged her here. She could see the girl's fingers twitch, searching for a tablet that wasn't there.

"Jaxon and I have been communicating with some of the J'nai on Terra Prime — or we were, before the Qaig attack. There are concerns that the alliance between Queen Iyle and our Admiral Savaryn is not as well-intentioned as it might appear.

"Of course, we all know the story. The Qaig attacked years ago; J'nai were stranded near Jupiter; the administration on Earth received the distress signal, et cetera, and here we are. Now, the question is — why did the Qaig attack?"

"Because they're murderous slimy bastards?" one of the engineers said, raising a hand. He was maybe in his thirties, already with a receding hairline. The man with him — who was a little younger, also dressed in a grease-stained flight suit — chuckled, but no one else moved.

"Clearly," Aditi continued, fixing her teacher's glare on the two, "there are discrepancies about the reasons behind the original attack, all those years back. What we know now is that the Qaig are in possession of extremely advanced supraluminal flight capabilities that outmatch the J'nai. The Admiral would have you mount an all-out assault with the best weapons we have to offer and reclaim Terra Prime. That's the strategy you all have been working for, in your own ways, since the attack."

"This will not work," Jaxon said coolly. He leaned back against one of the lab tables, arms crossed. He was a strange complement to Aditi, Zoe thought — relaxed where she was stiff, tall where she was petite. His long white hair hung loose, whereas hers was back in a severe braid. The intensity on their faces though, that was exactly the same.

"The Qaig are crafty. There could be millions of them for all that we know. And, whatever their faults, they are not stupid. We do not know the status of Terra Prime yet, though some reconnaissance is already underway."

"If they're so advanced, why haven't they come to Ganymede? Why not take us out here?" Raina asked, frowning. It was a possibility they'd all considered. Those first few days after the attack, it was a cold chill down everyone's spine, just waiting for the Qaig fleet to pour through the Star Port. Many had clamored to Admiral Savaryn to destroy the Star Port, to eliminate it as a possibly entryway. He'd refused, and kept it open, in case any J'nai ships needed a refuge. As time had passed, that chill had eased a little, though the possibility still remained. All eyes turned to Aditi and Jaxon, wondering the same thing.

"If they don't need to use the Star Ports, what are they waiting for?" Raina continued.

"No idea," Aditi said. She wiped a bead of sweat from her brow. "It could be that humans pose no real threat to them. That what happened at Terra Prime was purely to wipe out the last pockets of J'nai civilization."

"We need answers, and a lot of them," Jaxon said. "We've asked you all to be here to help. We need your skills and your discretion. I am young, in my race," he said. "But there are those who came before me, who remember a time that was different than what is passed down as truth now. A time when the Qaig were not enemies, but slaves. Files that were long buried in the archives, discovered by my tutors long ago, and revealed to me when I reached adulthood. Files that showed the Qaig being used as test subjects on newly terraformed planets. I believe the analogy you use has something to do with canaries in a mineshaft. When the Qaig were used and their lives, disregarded."

"No," Cat whispered, horror-struck. Zoe couldn't even form the word herself.

"It's possible that the relationship between the two species goes back hundreds of Earth-years, or more," he said. "After the Star Ports were cut, the few of us that were left made it to Terra Prime. The J'nai empire was so big, so spread out, that no one knew the whole story. We still don't. There might be pockets of J'nai out there being attacked on other planets, just like at Terra Prime, if the Qaig can access the whole Current. We need to know more about the Qaig if we wish our species — and yours — to survive."

The thought of 'their species' — humanity as a whole — being under threat was not something Zoe liked to consider. If the Qaig came through the Star Port, what was to stop them from moving on to Earth? Only Ganymede Station stood in their way. It was a point that Admiral Savaryn had made before. If it had been propaganda to get the Faxes and Originals and J'nai on the station to work together toward his end goals, it had been an effective route to take.

"The 'truth' was what Queen Iyle told us — that the Qaig were evil, only intent on eradicating us and absorbing our technology," he said, shaking his head, "Clearly, they have no need for our tech. But we need to figure this out before Savaryn sends us all on a suicide mission to Terra Prime, and before we endanger your homeworld as well."

"What can we do?" Sophie asked. She stood, straight as a post, chin up, the picture of patriotism. Zoe would later swear that the ferocity of her gaze could have melted tungsten.

"Well, first we need to communicate more openly with Terra Prime. I have friends there, those who are trying to get to the truth behind the façade. We've been trying to send signals on the Current through the Star Port. It can take days or weeks to reach them, but it's all we've got," Aditi said. "We need something more effective, and preferably encrypted, so that the Admiral and the Qaig can't intercept or interpret it."

"But the Admiral is monitoring all transmissions. Everything's been blocked," Raina said. There were murmurs of agreement. "There's no way to get a message off Ganymede to Terra Prime. And we don't have any satellites to bounce it off of."

"We could use Callisto," Zoe said, frowning. They'd all heard rumors of the dead station, now derelict for years. "If we were on Callisto, could we send a signal from there?"

"We can't even send a *transmission* off Ganymede. Now you want to take a little trip across half a million miles without anyone noticing?" the sarcastic engineer said. His partner again silently nodded his agreement.

"Besides, there's just the teeniest problem of Callisto being Chernobyl'd. If you want your skin peeled off by all that loose radiation, be my guest. Besides, any tech would have been fried long ago," he continued. Aditi frowned. There was silence for a long moment, as everyone thought.

"No, it's not," Sophie said suddenly, then again, louder, "No, it's not!"

Everyone turned to look at her. There was a bright spot of pink on her cheeks, and a wild look in her eyes. She punched the air with one hand.

"It's not what now?" the engineer said, rubbing his chin. Jaxon and Aditi leaned in.

"Go on, Sophie. What are you thinking?" Aditi prompted.

"Callisto. It's not radioactive," Sophie said, her eyes shining. "I'm betting that story was made up, too, to keep us from being too nosy."

"Soph, what on earth are you talking about?" Zoe asked, putting a hand on the girl's shoulder. Sophie grinned and looked over at Cat.

"Well, Cat, go on," she said. She waved her hand, prompting her. Cat froze, obviously uncomfortable at being the center of attention. Her fingers twitched again, and she knotted them together in front of her.

"Um, well…" she said, confused. Sophie took over.

"Cat was tasked with fixing the telescope in the observatory. Some of the sensors were off. The one she couldn't get back online was the radiation detector. Do you remember, Cat?"

"I remember," she said slowly, as realization hit her. "I remember!"

"Cat couldn't fix the radiation sensor, don't you see?" Sophie said. Blank expressions stared up at her. She huffed.

"She said the radiation sensor didn't work. All it picked up was noise. When she aimed it at Callisto? Nada. She figured the sensor was faulty, because there should be a *ton* of radiation coming from there. You know why the sensor didn't pick up anything? Because all it was sensing was the Cosmic Microwave Background, or something low-level from Ganymede. *No radiation* from Callisto," she said, and smiled, pleased. "I should have realized it sooner when Cat told me she couldn't get the sensor to work. Cat knows *everything,* if there had been an actual problem with the sensor, she would have found it," she finished.

Stunned silence blanketed the room.

"I mean, it could work," Jaxon said slowly. "If that's true. If we could get someone to Callisto, the equipment might still be functional. The Bridge would have been sealed on evacuation, yes? Just like the protocol on Ganymede? From there, they could re-establish the communications with Terra Prime, maybe set it up to relay back to Ganymede somehow."

"Again, just the tiniest problem," the engineer interrupted, raising a finger. "You're going to have to, one — steal a ship," he said, ticking the issues off on his hand. "Two — hope something works on that station and that you can get a signal out, three — hope it's not actually radioactive, four — get back to Ganymede undetected and, five — well, I can't think of a five, but I'm sure there is one."

"Oh, come on, gents," Sophie said, tossing her hair. Zoe tried to resist rolling her eyes. "We've got the most brilliant, capable minds in history here. Surely we can figure something out."

"Not to mention, there's one thing Room 10013 is better at than just about anyone else you'll meet," Zoe said, grinning.

"Kicking ass?" Raina asked, but she grinned, too.

"Being fabulous?" Sophie said. Zoe looked at Cat for a response, but the girl just shook her head, mute.

"Shenanigans!" Zoe shouted, pumping a fist in the air.

"Shen — what?" Jaxon asked, clearly confused. He looked to Aditi, who shrugged. Zoe thought for a moment, then rattled off something in the J'nai language. Jaxon blinked, but that was the extent to which he showed his surprise. He nodded and responded in kind. They held a short conversation in J'nai, and more than a few jaws in the group had dropped at the exchange.

"What?" Zoe asked, when she caught Raina staring at her, though maybe gawking was a better word. "The great Septimia Zenobia Augusta had a knack for languages, so I do, too. J'nai's not that hard to learn, but just you try wrapping your tongue around the Qaig language, that one will really make your mouth cramp."

Raina's gaze drifted to Zoe's mouth, as if considering, before looking away.

CHAPTER 6
NORA, THE
RAPSCALLION

Nothing happened.

She blinked. The countdown was over. She could still hear Bastian's heartbeat in slow, measured beats. Could still feel his flight suit curled in her fingers.

She wasn't dead. The ship was still — more or less — in one piece. Relief coursed through her, like a wave of warm water, melting away her icy fear.

And yet, there was confusion, too. She looked up and caught Bastian's eyes. He was looking down at her with a strange expression, no trace of his usual smirk on his face. She was still wrapped in his arms, so close she could feel the warmth of his breath on her forehead. He looked up, peering down the hall, as if he could see to the engine room at the aft of the ship. She felt his arms tense around her then, and he pushed back; the sudden warm feeling evaporated like a puff of smoke, leaving Nora cold and uncertain. What was going on? Why hadn't the ship exploded? What did Bastian know that she didn't?

"*Et merde,*" Bastian said. He jumped up and ran from the Bridge. Nora could hear him yelling for Thalia, followed by more screaming from both of them. And the sound of things clattering — things being thrown, she guessed. She exchanged a look with Donovan, who sat stunned, then pushed his glasses back up on his nose. Asher and Soren exchanged a long glance, before Soren rose, and stalked off the Bridge as well.

"Well," Donovan said, watching the Qaig ship approach. They were close enough to make out details now: the antennas of communications equipment, the scrapes in the dark paint.

"What... what happened?" Nora asked, not taking her eyes from the front view screen.

"Thalia cancelled the self-destruct," Asher said softly. He sat slumped in his chair, a gray shadow of his usual self.

"What... how?" she asked in a whisper.

"Does it matter?" Asher asked sullenly. "We survived. Yay. Now the Qaig can tear us apart limb from limb until they get what they want from us. The P2? They'll take it. Location of Earth and its defenses? Already theirs. Whatever they want. And we will beg to give it to them before they are done."

Nora's mouth was so dry she couldn't swallow. Donovan, at least, seemed to have woken from his stupor, and his hands were flying over the controls at his station, a blur. More shouts erupted from the cargo bay down the hall. Nora went to stand, but Donovan shook his head, nearly dislodging his glasses.

"I don't recommend it," he said. "Going to be ugly. Sit tight."

She sat. She'd never felt so helpless in her life — well, except in the previous five minutes. She twisted her hands together in her lap, wringing them so hard that they turned red. What was going on down there? What exactly had Thalia done to the ship? Could they still get out of here? Did Thalia think they had a chance? Nora glanced out the front view panel at the assembled monoliths beyond — if there was a chance of getting out of here, she couldn't see how. Especially not with a fried P2 drive. She hoped Thalia knew something she didn't.

Soren came back in a moment. Her face was flushed and sweat plastered strands of her white hair across her face. She moved calmly though and sat back down in the captain's chair.

"Donovan, status," she said. Her speech was steady and composed. She could have been asking about the weather for all the emotion in her voice.

"Well," Donovan said, stopping his frantic task and turning to face her. "I've got most of the good stuff erased or buried under mountains of encryption. They won't be getting anything useful off the *Rap* except the raw materials it's made of. Databanks, comms records, flight plans, the whole bit. Gone, or hidden."

Soren nodded. Nora assumed this sort of data purging was trained into them, one option to prevent anything from falling into the Qaig hands. Like they were about to. She shivered.

What could she expect once they were captured? Would they be ransomed? Tortured? She rubbed the goosebumps that had formed on her arms — her brain couldn't even comprehend what was about to happen. She knew too little about the Qaig, too little about their capabilities. Then again, maybe they all did. No one had suspected they had tech similar to the P2, that would let them jump and off the Current at will.

Bastian came back to the Bridge and stood behind Soren rather than returning to his seat. Nora continued to knot her hands in her lap. The screen in front of her, where she'd usually handle the flight, was blank.

"Soren," Bastian said, putting a hand on the captain's shoulder. She nodded, understanding whatever unspoken question he'd asked.

"If we must," she said. The words dragged out of her, slow, and Nora had to strain her ears to hear them.

"Must... what?" Nora asked into the silence. Soren fixated her grass-green eyes on her. The usual laser-focus of her gaze rippled with unshed tears.

"Plan C," she said, and stood, brushing the grime from her suit jacket. "Captain Benoit, lead on."

CHAPTER 7
CAT, GANYMEDE STATION

She opened her eyes, and the nausea that hit her threatened to overwhelm her. It was a tidal wave of bile, slamming the back of her throat. She shut her eyes, but the holographic zigzags in her peripheral vision remained, even in the dark. She groaned, curling up in the bunk as her consciousness registered the pain of the migraine, digging at her skull like a thousand shards of glass. There was nothing beyond the pain; no roommates, no station — no universe, nothing, nothing, nothing but pain.

"Cat?" Sophie asked softly. The sound barely registered. Cat felt a cool hand on her forehead, then her shoulder. "Cat, you okay?"

"Mmmph," she murmured, peeling one eye open. Sophie's face swam in her vision, but Cat could tell she wasn't happy.

"You look awful," Sophie said, straightening, her hands on her hips.

"Thanks," Cat croaked, and shut her eyes again, blindly reaching for the medicine bottle at the top of her bunk.

"I'm serious," Sophie said, grabbing Cat's tablet. Cat's eyes shot open — taking her tablet away from her was like removing a limb.

"I'm telling *them*," Sophie said, jabbing her head toward the door to the hall, "that you're sick and heading to the medical wing. You can't work like this," she said, typing furiously.

"How... did you know my password?" Cat said, confused. She

struggled to sit up without puking. Each tablet was locked to its owners' specific code, and Cat's was extensive, with sequences of symbols and numbers and letters she changed every 48 hours on the dot. Sophie merely arched an eyebrow at such a preposterous question, then triumphantly hit the power button 'off' and handed the tablet back.

"Done," she said. "Come on. Let's go."

C at and Sophie made their way into the crisp whiteness of the medical wing. The area was so clean and bright, it made spots of brilliant pain dance in Cat's vision. She swayed, but kept walking, somehow. *Potassium, Calcium, Scandium...*

"I can do this on my own," Cat said at last, embarrassed by Sophie's attention. It was at least 49.4% true. Sophie had her arm around Cat's shoulders and gave her a squeeze.

"I know."

Sophie settled Cat into a chair in the waiting room, then went over to the check-in kiosk and entered Cat's information. This early in the day, they were the only ones there. Cat had just closed her eyes, trying to block out the brightness again, when she heard a door open and someone called her name. She tried to stand, but her legs didn't want to respond properly. She plopped back down into her seat, the jarring motion making her gasp as pain rocketed up her spine into her brain. She curled into a ball and tried not to moan.

"Wes, you remember Cat?" Sophie said. Cat had closed her eyes again, nauseated with pain. She didn't see Sophie and Wesley, one of Ty's roommates, exchange a worried glance.

"Well, I'll let you get to it then," Sophie said. "See you, Cat."

Cat couldn't open her eyes, so she nodded, waving a blind hand in the air in farewell.

"Come on," a softly accented voice said in her ear after a moment. Before she could react, warm hands were lifting her from the plastic chair she was trying desperately to cling to. "Let's get you feeling better."

He carried her through a door and into a long bay lined on either side with medical cots and partitioned off with flimsy curtains. She felt like a baby but was in too much pain to protest. He took her to the farthest one before settling her down. She opened one eye, and found a tanned face peering at her, close to her own, and frowning. She winced.

"*Lo siento,*" he said, standing. "Let me get you something. I will be right back."

Moments later he returned with a tray that had several small syringes on it.

"This is something for the pain, and the nausea," he said. He donned a pair of disposable gloves and cleaned the skin of her upper arm, before giving her two injections in quick succession. She hissed through her teeth, then sighed, leaning back on the cot as the medication took rapid effect.

"Now, that's better, no?" he asked, and offered her a smile as he placed a small bandage over the injection sites. Cat nodded, swallowing. She vaguely remembered seeing him before, usually with Ty and Greg in the cafeteria, though usually she was too shy to talk to them. Sophie had said he was handsome, Cat recalled — well, 'devastating' was the word she'd used — and 'a genius.' If Sophie thought he was smart, that was really saying something. She could be in worse hands, she thought.

"Better," Cat breathed, relaxing. She could feel the migraine, like a panther stalking her at the edges of her consciousness, but it no longer had its claws in her. Her entire body sagged in relief, and she looked over at Wesley, grateful. He wore olive-green scrubs, like the other medical personnel, and the short, white coat that marked him as a trainee. Somehow, despite the relative lack of UVB rays on the station, he maintained a natural tan, complemented by tousled, dark hair and a brilliant white smile that had to be the product of extensive dental manipulation.

"Now," he said, sitting by the cot and crossing his ankle over his knee, leaning back as if he had all the time in the world. The movement revealed bright orange socks — those were definitely not station-approved workwear. Cat shook her head a little, clearing out the drug-addled thoughts. She was an observant person at baseline — it was in her genes.

"So, what happened this time?" he asked.

"This … This time? You … know about the others?" she asked. She tucked a curl back behind her ear, feeling her face heat.

He nodded. "Your friend … Nora. She asked me to keep an eye on you. You have quite the file, you know. And your friend, Sophie? She has been telling Tylajah of your migraines, and he told me, too."

"I have a file?" Cat said. She recalled Nora saying something similar, long ago. She reached for her star-shaped earrings, fiddling with them as she thought. She didn't like that so many people had been talking about her. It was rude.

"Well, you *are* one of the few Curies we have, you know," he said with a smile. Devastating, indeed. "We'd like to have more — but the radiation, you see. It made the cloning process tricky, messed with the DNA on a molecular level. It failed more often than it succeeded."

"Are the others… are they like me? Do they have migraines too?" she asked. He shook his head, leaned forward, and she made note of how that made his hazel eyes seem to glow as they fixated on hers.

"No. No, you are unique," he said, as if that should make her feel better. She felt tired suddenly, so very tired, to her bones, as if all the coffee in the galaxy wouldn't keep her up. She yawned, and he stood.

"Ah. I see the side effects of the medications are kicking in. Take some rest, Catherine. I will check on you in a bit," he said, but she was already closing her eyes. She barely registered the blanket he tucked in around her, before she was drifting away into a foggy — but pain-free — sleep.

She woke later to the sound of the curtains rattling around her, as Wesley peeked in to check on her. He smiled, as if relieved to see her awake.

"Ah, *mi diamante brillante*," he said, coming over to her. She felt heat rising to her face again.

"How long was I out?" she said, pulling off her glasses to rub her eyes. They felt sandy.

"Not long," he said, sitting next to her once more. "How are you feeling?"

"Better," she said. "The pain is there but... dulled."

"I'm glad. I'd like to examine you and run some tests, if it's all right with you," he said. She nodded.

"Ok," he said, standing again. He put her through a brief barrage of maneuvers, checking the strength and reflexes in her arms and legs, asking her to raise her eyebrows and stick out her tongue. She felt ridiculous, but he did each maneuver with utter professionalism, assessing her the same way she might look at a complicated equation.

"Good," he said, when he was through. "One last thing. Let's get an MRI to look at your brain, and if everything's okay and you're still feeling well, I'll let you go back to work."

"Deal," she said. She swung her legs over the edge of the cot, and he held his hand out to her, helping her up. She flushed again — she wasn't disabled — and found that her gait was unexpectedly wobbly. His hand tightened around hers.

"Careful, Catherine," he murmured. "The medications can leave you a little off-balance for a while."

He led her to the end of the Medical Bay, down another small hall, and into a room with the large, ring-shaped MRI machine. He didn't let go of her hand until he had her settled on the table.

"Hang on," he said, raising a finger. "This may take a little time. Try to think of something pleasant. Or nap, your choice," he said, then headed out of the room. Overhead, the machine whirred to life, a giant, pulsating donut, a magnet so big it was going to realign all of the protons in her brain. With a hundred trillion atoms or more per neuron, the number of protons involved was staggering. With that pleasant thought dominating her consciousness, she decided on another nap instead.

I t did take a while, after which Wesley walked her back to the bay with the cots.

"Just rest," he said. "I have to get my attending to look at the films, then I'll come back, and we can come up with a plan."

"Ok," she said, and gave him a small smile. She nearly asked him for more medication — the pain was returning, the claws flexing, probing for an opening. She didn't want him to think she was here for the meds, though, like she was some kind of addict. She hated taking the meds. What she wanted was a solution. She closed her mouth again. He left, and she settled back onto the thin mattress of the cot.

A while later, another boy came in. He was ushered in by a different medical trainee, a girl with blond hair that Cat thought was a year ahead of them. Penny, or Jenny, or something. Cat blinked her eyes, trying to focus through the blossoming pain and the lingering side effects of the medicines. The boy was holding a cloth to his nose, and there were streaks of blood on it. Cat recognized him after a moment through her pain-addled haze — the tall, dashing, deceptive Raphael. Once he'd been settled onto the cot next to hers, the girl dashed off to grab supplies.

When Cat realized who he was, she ducked her head under the blanket. Her heartbeat hammered in her ears. Thoughts of what she should say to him — what possible explanation she should give for her being here — were suddenly pushed aside as another thought came to the forefront — what had happened to his perfectly arched nose?

"That bitch," he muttered to himself. Cat tried to tune him out. He didn't appear to have recognized her as the shape cowering under the thin blanket, or else didn't care.

Her head pounded. The medications were wearing off, had worn off — how long had it been? A few hours? She couldn't tell. Claws of pain scraped down her temple, bringing with them a wash of nausea. She closed her eyes, silently willing Wesley to hurry up. This time, she'd ask him for another dose, no problem. She moaned as the pain tore into her. She didn't care what Wesley or Raphael thought anymore, she just wanted the pain to go away.

"Hey, you okay?" Raphael asked. She stuck her hand out from under the blanket and gave him a thumbs-up, as she didn't trust herself to speak without vomiting. *Iron, Cobalt...* She curled up on her side, pulling the blanket over her head.

Thrrrrum. Thrrrrum.

She cracked open an eyelid. Raphael was drumming his fingers against the metal rail of his cot as he waited.

Thrrrum. Thrrrrrrrrrrum.

She curled up tighter. Stop stop stop, she thought. Please stop. She just wanted quiet. Quiet and dark and quiet and ...

Thrrrrr......

BANG

Her eyes flew open, and a shower of sparks drifted from the ceiling, where a light had just exploded.

She sat up, momentarily unable to process what was going on. Raphael shrieked and jumped up, running away from the sparks. They drifted like snow down to where he'd been sitting, just moments earlier.

"Catherine, come on," Wesley said, appearing out of nowhere, his face paler than she remembered. "Come on," he said again, tugging on her arm, pulling her off the far side of the cot and leading her to the other end of the bay. She tried to look over her shoulder at the scene — several people were converging on the space, flipping switches, trying to isolate the short in the circuitry.

Wesley sat her down and peered at her, checking her over for injury.

"Are you okay? Are you hurt?" he asked, looking over her arms. She shook her head, then stiffened. It didn't hurt. Her head didn't hurt when she shook it. She blinked, realizing that the stalking pain was entirely gone.

"I'm... fine," she said, smiling brightly. "I'm fine!"

He looked at her strangely, but before he could speak, an older man in a wheelchair came over. The smooth mechanical movements of his chair were controlled by minute motions of his fingers over a panel on the arm rest. It was impressive technology, even by Ganymede standards.

"Well, you seem to be all in one piece," the man said. "I'm Doctor

Adebayo, Wesley's supervising attending today. He tells me you've been suffering from migraines, yes?"

She nodded, glancing at Wesley. He deferred to the older man, nodding as Dr. Adebayo spoke.

"Fortunately, your MRI looked fine. Perfect, even," he said, smiling, revealing even, bright teeth in his dark face. "And you are feeling better? Good, good. You know, stress can be a trigger for migraines. Tell me, have you been under any excessive amounts of stress lately?"

She gaped him, thinking, *of course I am stressed, we are all stressed* — then realized he was teasing. He raised a hand in apology.

"I jest, I'm sorry. You are free to go, but come back if the migraines bother you again, yes?"

She nodded. Wesley motioned for her to stand, and she followed him out of the medical wing. Just once, she glanced over her shoulder. In the back, where she'd been just minutes before, a hole the size of a plate was blasted in the ceiling, wires and tubing still sparking within. Then the door to the long Medical Bay shut behind her, and she couldn't see it anymore. Wesley stopped, tapping away on his tablet for a moment.

"So that's it?" she asked, as Wesley sent a work excuse note to her tablet.

"That's it," he said, then frowned, looking down at her. His hazel eyes were intense, focused on her like a problem he couldn't solve. "Unless you want to tell me what in God's name happened back there?"

Cat looked at the door to the medical wing, as if she could see through it to the light that had burst. She couldn't explain it. Faulty wiring? Should have taken out the whole half of the bay, not just one light. Faulty bulb, then? Must have been some fault to explode like *that*.

She shook her head. It didn't make any sense. He nodded, crossing his arms. He seemed disappointed.

"Ok then," he said.

She thanked him and turned to go.

"Catherine," he called. She turned, and he caught up with her. "Has anything like this happened before?"

She thought for a moment. She thought of the time the lights in her room had flickered, and when she'd been repairing the telescope and the piece she was straining for just broke. Both times, her headache had mysteriously disappeared. She nodded, slowly. Wesley frowned.

"Ok, look…"

"Wesley, get back in here and show Jennifer how to do a proper running suture," Dr. Adebayo called. Wesley ran a hand through his hair. The motion made it stick up at crazy angles.

"You need me, you let me know, okay? Send me a message. I can help, I can…"

"Today, Wesley, or I'll have you cleaning the leech tanks after your shift!" Dr. Adebayo did not seem to be a patient man. Cat shivered.

"I will, thank you. You'd better go," she said, nodding towards the door. Wesley nodded.

"Yeah. He's all bark and no bite, though," he said, grinning. "Listen. Please. You can trust me."

Cat tried not to roll her eyes — what, was he going to ask her for 'help' with his work, too? He'd be nice to her now, sure, but then he'd start asking for favors. It always happened.

"*Escuchame*," he said, and the intensity of the word reached her, if not the meaning. "If you need help, you let me know. Okay? Okay. And take care, Catherine."

He was so earnest, the pleading in his bright eyes so intense, that she almost believed him. And then he disappeared, back through the door into the medical wing.

CHAPTER 8
RAINA, GANYMEDE STATION

That morning, Cat's migraines had been so bad that Sophie made her go to the medical wing. Raina thought it was about time. They were all tiptoeing around her like she was made of eggshells, like she might shatter at any moment. Raina blamed this Raphael character. She knew he was shady, but she hadn't realized that her quiet little roommate had been silently crushing on him all this time.

Raina took a deep breath — in through her nose, out through her mouth. Steadying herself. If she'd been back home — back on Lanai, the idyllic Hawaiian island she'd grown up on — she would have spent the first hour of her day meditating. Instead, she and Zoe went to the cafeteria, like they did every morning; Raina missed the peace she'd known back on Earth. She'd known since she was old enough to talk that she'd been adopted. She bore no resemblance to the Japanese American couple she'd been raised by — but she had loved them, in her way. Even after they'd told her who she was, what she was, on the day she turned thirteen. Why she was being raised by a couple of yogis on a small island in the middle of the Pacific.

Since that birthday, she'd felt herself distancing from them. It was as if by pushing them away before they could send her away, she was the one making the decision to sever all contact. She'd brought nothing sentimental from the island — no pictures like Nora or stuffed animals like the one Cat tried to pretend she didn't have.

Still, she missed the quiet mornings together on their lanai — not just the name of their patio, but the name of their island — when the three of them would roll out their mats, stretch, and center. Listen to the chirping of birds, the distant roar of the ocean that she loved to swim and surf in, the feel of the sunshine on her face and the wind in her hair. She'd give anything to feel that again, to feel something other than the recycled wafts of air that blew through the station. To feel sand instead of metal beneath her feet.

Zoe was uncharacteristically quiet as Raina brooded, but she was grateful. She didn't feel like talking. Too much time thinking about Earth usually put her in a bad mood.

They went through the breakfast line and got their coffees and food — eggs and a protein bar for Zoe, fruit for Raina — and sat down. A few moments later, they were joined by Dean Prasad, right on schedule.

"Good morning Raina, Zoe," she said pleasantly, sipping on her tea. "Tasks going well?"

"We're headed to the Hangar Bay again today," Zoe said, around mouthfuls of food. "Glorified grease monkeys."

"Mostly I help with the wiring. Zoe does the heavy lifting," Raina said. "There's a lot of damage to some of those ships."

"Yes," Dean Prasad — Aditi — said, tracing the rim of her mug with one finger. "A few of them will be headed out in a few days, I hear. They must be working hard to be ready to go asteroid mining again. The day of the next eclipse, I believe. I heard it from MacGregor," she said innocently, and sipped from her mug. Zoe and Raina exchanged a glance, then looked up at Jupiter's mass, looming above the cafeteria like an all-seeing eye. An eclipse might just provide cover for their craziest plan yet — hijacking a PJ and going to Callisto to belay a signal to Terra Prime for Jaxon.

"Will many ships be going?" Raina asked. Aditi shrugged.

"There's always room for one more, I'm sure," she said, and winked. "Especially if you have, say, upper-level clearance to alter the flight paths in the Bridge's tracking system."

Raina frowned.

"What if there's not enough pilots for all the ships," she said, fighting the urge to just spit the words out plainly, and be damned if anyone overheard them. Cat and Sophie going on this crazy adventure was one thing — but neither girl could maneuver the complex ship. It was too bad that Nora wasn't there. Raina wasn't sure she'd trust anyone else.

"I'm sure we'll think of something," Aditi said, and stood to go. She beamed a smile at them.

"Have a lovely day, girls, and thank you for all of your hard work."

If anyone was listening in, Aditi's act would have fooled the best of them. Raina hated this sneaking around, hated that those in control of Ganymede had kept them all in the dark. The whole thing made Raina irritated, on edge. Like a bomb just waiting to explode.

Which is probably why, when she ran into Raphael later, she'd broken his nose without a second thought.

L ater that evening, with Cat tucked away in her bunk, asleep, Raina filled Sophie in on the morning's conversation with Aditi. Sophie nodded and punched a few things into her tablet.

"And how was your day?" Zoe asked. "Break any hearts?"

Raina grinned to herself — hearts, no, but noses…

"Not yet, but the day's not over," Sophie said slowly, chewing on her bottom lip. She looked back at Cat's bunk from her seat at the big table dominating their room and lowered her voice. "A panel in the ceiling blew out in the medical wing today. Right over where Cat was."

Raina frowned. Cat had looked shaken when she made it back to the room, but there hadn't been any obvious scrapes or burns on her. She'd assumed the pallor was from her migraine, like usual. Cat certainly hadn't mentioned any equipment malfunctioning.

"That's weird," Zoe said, leaning her chair back on two legs. "She okay?"

"I think so. She said she feels fine, actually. Her migraine is gone. She's just tired."

A moment later, a knock sounded on their door. Sophie grinned and bounced up to get it.

Ty's bulk filled most of the doorway as she opened the door and ushered him in.

"Curfew's in ten minutes," Ty murmured, his eyes taking in the other girls seated at the table. "Um, Soph? What's going on? You wanted to talk?"

Sophie took him by the arm and led him to the table, sitting him down across from Zoe and Raina. He looked very uncomfortable. Raina looked at Sophie — she wanted to know what was going on, too.

"Ladies," Sophie said with a flourish. "Meet our pilot!"

Silence. A series of glances exchanged. Zoe's chair slammed back down on all four legs, rattling the table.

"Seriously?" Raina said. "You're going to have this guy fly you over to Callisto? He's barely had any training!"

"Wait, what?" Ty said, stuttering. His dark eyes went wide, and his mouth literally fell open.

"No offense, dude, but have you ever actually piloted a PJ? I don't mean in the Sim Gym, I mean a real one?" Zoe asked.

"Sophie, please tell me what the hell is going on," he begged. Sophie sat by him, one arm on his sleeve, and filled him in. She summarized the whole crazy scheme — Raina could see his eyes widening even further, but he kept his mouth shut. Good. She liked that about him. Raina cracked her knuckles loudly as Ty thought things through.

"So, you want to steal a PJ..."

"Borrow," Sophie corrected, raising a finger.

"Right, right — borrow a PJ, fly it out of the hangar and to Callisto without anyone noticing, break into a radioactive station, turn on the radio, and fly you home without getting caught. Is that it?"

"It's not radioactive," Sophie said calmly. "It's a lie. Another one. But to the rest, yes. That's what I want."

"Uh huh," he said. He leaned back and crossed his massive arms. He was one of the few, Raina thought with a little rush of pride, that could keep up with Zoe in the gym.

"And we want to do this because some J'nai royal told you to," he said. Sophie nodded.

"Aditi too. She'll mask our path from the Bridge on the scanners.

And we're going during an eclipse, so no one will be able to tell whether we're there or not in the dark."

"Shenanigans," Zoe rumbled. Raina elbowed her lightly, but grinned.

"Why not just go to MacGregor?" Ty asked. Raina frowned — the XO, a Charlemagne clone, had been friendly to the Faxes in the past. He'd undermined Savaryn, publicly, in the past. He could be an ally.

"Aditi and Jaxon aren't sure of his allegiance yet. We just need more information from Terra Prime, for Jaxon and for us," Sophie said, her eyes pleading. "We may be able to find out what happened to Nora. We can't get anything out with Savaryn's stranglehold on things here."

He considered, then sighed, and stood.

"Curfew's in a minute," he said, and made for the door. Sophie deflated. He opened the door, then paused.

"Let me think about it," he said, then left. It was like all the air in the room got sucked out with him.

"That went well," Raina hissed after a moment. "And how do we know we can trust him?"

"I trust him," Sophie said, her eyes gleaming and chin lifted. "He'll do it."

The next morning, all four of them headed to the cafeteria. Cat looked better than she had in days and smiled as she collected her peach pancakes. They sat at their usual table, the cafeteria starting to fill up with cadets and graduates, humans, J'nai, Faxes and Originals. She watched Admiral Savaryn walk by, looking down his hooked nose at — well, everybody actually. A cloud of other officers trailed behind him, his willing little Original lackeys. Raina despised them all and turned back to her own group. All getting ready for another day of preparations, repairs, computing … and plotting.

"Good morning," Wesley called, taking a seat by Cat. He was joined shortly by his roommates, Greg and Ty. The other roommates, Raina recalled with a lump in her throat, had died in the Qaig attack, like Lara. She couldn't remember their names. For Originals, they were generally an all-around good bunch, though something about Greg made her skin prickle. It was probably his eyes, one brown, one blue. Nora had had a thing for him at the start of the school year, but that had fizzled once she'd started working with Sebastian Benoit, the heartthrob of Ganymede. She wasn't sure Greg was quite over it, though. He still turned red whenever her name was mentioned.

"Catherine, you're looking well today. Feeling okay?" Wesley asked. She flushed and nodded, focusing on her breakfast. He grinned, but didn't push any further.

"You too, ladies," Greg said with a bow. "All of you, lovely as ever."

Raina rolled her eyes. Zoe flicked a bit of scrambled egg at him.

"Ouch," he said, but he grinned, his mismatched eyes lighting up. "And seriously, Sophie, are you *tan*?"

Sophie tossed her hair. Raina narrowed her eyes and looked her over. She *did* look tan. A group of medical trainees was passing by, and one of them almost stumbled over his own feet when he caught a glimpse of Sophie.

"More cocktails from the chemistry department? Self-tanning lotion?" Zoe asked. The medical trainee — a tall blond boy, wearing a long white coat over scrubs — seemed to have recovered his composure, and caught back up to his friends. She might have been imagining things, but she could have sworn that Wesley was glaring after him.

"Oh no," Sophie said, putting out her arms, admiring the slight golden glow. "I just exchanged the bulbs in my bunk for UVB light. My own personal tanning bed."

Raina had to admit, that was brilliant. She missed the sun, missed sitting all day in its glow back on her quiet beach in Hawaii. Sudden homesickness seized her, and she shoved a piece of melon in her mouth to distract herself.

"Best part is," Sophie said, raising an eyebrow and looking impishly at Ty. "No tan lines."

Greg choked on his coffee. Wesley patted him on the back, laughing. A flush stained Ty's dark face, but he remained quiet. Still thinking about their conversation from last night, Raina guessed, or Sophie's bunk modifications. It was hard to tell with him sometimes.

The remainder of their breakfast passed without incident. As they stood to go, Ty took Sophie's arm, and Raina could just hear him say in her ear, "I'll do it."

CHAPTER 9

NORA, THE RAPSCALLION

The crew assembled on the Bridge — save for Thalia and her team, who were locked up. Soren stood in front of the captain's chair, arms crossed. Standing there, she resembled a golden statue — elegant, immobile.

"We're out of options," she said, and her words rung out like a gunshot across the Bridge. No one answered. A faint *bzzz* sounded overhead as another wire short-circuited. The lights flickered red briefly, the emergency backups, before returning to normal.

"We can't run. We can't restart the self-destruct — *she's* completely disabled it," Soren said, nodding her head towards the cargo bay. There was no question who she meant.

"Our only option is to go calmly. Benoit will take the lead as acting captain. The Qaig won't be too keen on seeing J'nai, but with a human in charge, they might listen to us. They're a primitive, backwards people — but they don't usually go after those who've offered them no offense first."

"Unlike the J'nai," Asher mumbled. Nora had gone cold. Numb. Bastian stood next to her, as straight as if he were made of steel. His hand gripped hers, but she barely registered it. They were captured by the enemy. The best they could hope for was that the Qaig wouldn't execute them on sight. The reassuring part was, they hadn't blasted them out of the sky immediately. That meant they had some interest in them — what *that* was, Nora shuddered to think. At best, they'd be prisoners of the Qaig. At worst … Her hands were clammy, and she hoped Bastian didn't feel the trembling. As if in response to her thoughts, his grip tightened, ever so slightly. It was a reassuring gesture, and she focused on it, on the feel of their palms, touching, instead of contemplating whatever fate awaited them.

She might vomit.

"About three minutes," Asher warned, glancing at his console. Through the front view panel, the Qaig ship loomed, stark and bristling. Their doom, hanging over them, coming inexorably closer with each passing heartbeat.

Pop.

For a moment, no one registered what had happened. The bulk of the Qaig cruiser was just … gone. The entire fleet before them — gone, as their ship sailed onto the Current. The *Rapscallion* lurched then, like a stone skipping on a pond, and dropped back out of the Current into normal space.

Ten seconds. Ten seconds at faster-than-light speed, which meant they'd traveled literally millions of miles. Put millions of miles between them and the Qaig fleet. For now.

"*Zut,*" Bastian said, and launched himself at the flight controls. The *Rap* was listing, badly — the artificial gravity seemed to be holding, but everything was tilting, the entire ship now approaching 45 degrees from level. Nora clutched at her chair, which was bolted down now like the others for just such a purpose. She heaved herself into it before her brain could even process the jump.

"What was that?" Soren asked, once more seated in her captain's chair. She was pale now, as if the jump had leached some of her golden color from her skin, save for two spots, furious pink on her cheeks. Donovan muttered a string of curses, the screen before him blank as he tried to reboot it.

"No idea. I purged the databanks, remember? I have no idea where we are. I could try a manual reboot, but…"

"Are you idiots ready to listen?"

Thalia's voice boomed over the intercom, and the room froze. Bastian had hastily regained control of the *Rapscallion* and the listing sensation had nearly leveled. There was nothing in front of them — or around them, based on limited sensor ranges — for as far as they could tell. Just black, empty space.

"Thalia, what have you done?" Soren asked, her voice clipped.

"Saved your asses, that's what," came the reply. "Had to hotwire the doors on the cargo bay and I may have fried the keypad to engineering, but hey, you're welcome."

Soren sat a moment, as still as ice.

"What do you need," she said through the intercom. "To get the P2 working again. To get us home to Ganymede. What do you need."

"Time," came the reply. "And an apology for trying to blow me up."

Soren pursed her lips, contemplating a response. Nora didn't dare to breathe. She felt cold all over, and she didn't know if it was in relief from not being hauled into a Qaig ship or if maybe the ship's heater had stopped working now, too. She thought it was probably the latter.

When Bastian turned to look at Soren — the two of them having a wordless conversation — Nora reached over to his control panel and brought up the temperature controls. Usually, the *Rap* was kept warm from the surrounding vacuum by dispersing some of the energy from the Xenon drives — energy that Thalia was apparently re-routing; to where, she couldn't tell. As she moved her chilly fingertips to swipe down and investigate — to make sure that they hadn't left Qaig territory only to freeze to death — a proximity alert sounded, the claxon blaring overhead with the pitch and intensity of a fire engine.

In front of them, where moments ago there had been only space, half a dozen blocky Qaig ships now appeared. They were in a less friendly mood this time — lasers were already being fired. They were seconds from impact. Soren slammed a fist onto the communication button on her seat.

"Thalia, I'm sorry. And you have about fifteen seconds before those Qaig catch up to us so if you can get the P2 fired up for another jump, do it now," Soren shouted through the comms.

Pop. They returned to the Current, for only a second or two this time.

Before them now loomed an immense fleet, the ships immediately lighting up on Bastian's console like so many fireflies.

Qaig.

Surrounding a blue-and-green marbled planet.

Soren sat down, hard, the air leaving her body in a *whoosh* as hundreds of ships launched red laser-fire directly at the *Rapscallion*.

Pop.

Bastian reacted immediately on re-entry to normal space, sending the *Rap* into a steep dive, narrowly avoiding a collision with an asteroid the size of a building. The burst had lasted only two or three seconds again this time, a fact which had Nora's heart seizing in her chest. Was that all that the drive could handle? She gripped the armrests of her chair and hung on desperately as Bastian maneuvered the ship in this veritable minefield.

"Was that… what was that?" Nora stuttered.

"Terra Prime. And two thousand Qaig ships. Asher, a little steering next time please," Soren said through gritted teeth.

"Still rebooting," he said, hands flying over the screens in front of him. He swiped across one screen, then back, muttering something under his breath. Back and forth, from screens to keyboard, his hands moved independently, as if controlled by two different people, as he fought to recover the systems he and Donovan had encrypted or shut down.

Nora's mind spun. She'd had only a glimpse of Terra Prime on her last mission. With that many Qaig ships stationed in orbit, who knew what the citizens below were experiencing? Were the J'nai and humans there still alive?

Her chest ached as the *Rap* weaved again, throwing her against the restraining harness in her chair, which bit into her skin with a nasty pinch. There seemed to be a number of asteroids around them, some small as bullets, which should bounce harmlessly off their shields. The bigger ones though, giant craggy, gray ship-destroyers, plowed through the field essentially unimpeded. But then Bastian saw an opening and took it, a sharp ascent, pulling more than a G of force that made Nora's stomach plummet. The *Rap* cracked and screamed around them, and the overhead lights dimmed, before turning red again.

A few bone-shattering seconds later and they were free of the asteroid belt, or at least above it. They were in between two large gas-giant planets — a blue one with rings, and a smaller red-orange one. An orbit of asteroids hundreds of miles wide stretched out before them.

"Well, that was fun," Donovan remarked. His screen came back on, and with a whoop of excitement he began typing at a speed faster than Nora could comprehend.

"Comms up," he said. "Aaaaaand — Asher, you up?"

"Nav up," Asher said, something like awe in his voice.

"Thalia, how are we doing?" Soren asked over the intercom.

"There's only so much I can do in here," she said. Even over the intercom, she sounded irritated. "I'm not sure how long I can keep it engaged and keep us in the Current. A few seconds at best."

"So, we're going to hop back to Ganymede in ten-second intervals? That will take..." Asher said, sweating. He wiped at his face with one hand while the other continued its frantic movements.

"Too long," Soren said. "Keep working. Let us know if you need anything."

"Coffee?" Thalia asked. Soren laughed, a short, barking sound, but didn't reply.

Nora looked at the controls. Bastian was gripping them so tightly, his knuckles were white.

"Know where we are?" she breathed. He shook his head, then let out a deep breath, and the grip he had on the controls eased a bit. Any space but the space in their own solar system and that of Terra Prime's might as well have been on the other side of the universe — it was all uncharted, as far as they knew; any information that prior generations of J'nai had had about it was long gone, dissolved with destruction of the Star Ports. She could see Donovan running through the Earth databanks, trying to pinpoint any familiar stars in their view to get an idea of where they were.

"You okay?" Bastian asked, looking at her from the corner of his eye. Was she okay? She'd nearly been blown up, nearly been captured by Qaig, and was now drifting in uncharted space with a wonky supraluminal drive and a ship that might fall apart around her at any second. If she didn't freeze to death first. Her thoughts spun in a million different directions — was she okay? No. But could she function? Yes, yes, she could. She would.

She nodded.

"You?" she asked. His lips were a tight line, his entire body taut with apprehension.

Before he could answer, two Qaig ships appeared in front of them. Donovan groaned loudly, slamming his hands against his console. The sensors on the *Rap* screamed a proximity warning, just as the enemy unleashed a barrage of laser fire at point-blank range.

Bastian dove, the ship plummeting in negative G forces that made Nora gag.

Back into the asteroids.

CHAPTER 10
ZOE, GANYMEDE STATION

"Y ou've been wound up tight," Zoe said, as Raina heaved her alarm clock across the room. Zoe leapt down from her upper bunk, peeking her head into Raina's. Raina gave a mumbled reply that she couldn't make out and buried her head under her blankets.

"You know what you need?" Zoe asked, and at her tone, Raina peeked out from her covers, suspicious but intrigued.

"Get up. Let's do some sparring before we go," she said. Raina groaned, but the sound was truncated by an *ooph* as a pair of gloves landed on her stomach.

"Come on," Zoe said, rolling her head, loosening up her shoulders. "Burn off some of that steam. Your right hook's been looking a little wimpy lately."

Raina glared, her hair still messy from sleep, but she got out of bed. Zoe grinned. Raina stretched, smoothed back her long braid, and strapped on the sparring gloves. Zoe already had the thicker mitts on, ready to receive Raina's pent-up fury.

"Seriously," Zoe said in mock-exasperation, after Raina threw a few punches while yawning. "Tighten that core. Move those feet." Raina glared but picked up the pace. After a few minutes, they were both sweating, and Raina had started grinning.

"Atta girl," Zoe said. Raina wiped her forehead as Sophie finally emerged from the bathroom.

"My turn," Raina shouted, and disappeared into the steamy bathroom. Zoe grinned, her mood lighter, too, and took the sparring gloves. She worked on a speed bag, her hands moving with swiftness and precision.

"I'm glad you both have an outlet for your frustrations, but does it have to be so … sweaty?" Sophie asked, grabbing her blow dryer.

"And what's your outlet, then? Ty?" Zoe said wickedly. Sophie arched an eyebrow, but didn't reply.

"You think he'll be ready by tomorrow?" Zoe asked, quiet and serious. Sophie paused.

"If he says he'll be ready, then he will be," she said finally. "Aditi has taken care of the tracking and the flight manifest from the Bridge. Do you have the distraction finalized?"

"Nearly," Zoe said, watching as Raina emerged from the bathroom. "Just ironing out the details."

"When you said, 'ironing out the details,' I didn't realize that meant that you *had no plan at all*, and we're only 36 hours out from …" Sophie hissed over their table at breakfast.

"We could let Raina go after some of the engineers. A few black eyes might do the trick," Zoe said, half-kidding as she sipped her coffee. Raina jabbed her elbow hard into her ribs.

"I'd prefer not to be locked up when they come back to Ganymede," Raina said. "If they can meet back up with the returning shuttles, they may be able to get by unnoticed. I was thinking a failure or near-failure of the force field in the hangar bay would set off enough alarms and panic that people might not look too closely at a couple of cadets sneaking off one of the PJs. I can't do that if I'm in detention, or worse."

"Not bad," Sophie said, tapping a fingernail against the table. "Can you really do that?"

Raina nodded. "I've been doing nothing but electrical repair and wiring since this whole thing started. I can do it. We can cover up your return. The trick will be getting you off the station in the first place.

Also," she said, taking a big bite of an apple. "Do you know how many monitors are around this station? Because it's a *lot*."

"Did you mean motion sensors, heat sensors, audio, or video? Because there are over ten thousand ..." Cat asked, then frowned. "Or were you just asking hypothetically?"

"There *are* sensors everywhere..." Zoe said, thinking. "Could we like, pull a fire alarm?"

"Where? The Hangar?" Raina asked, frowning.

"The Bridge?" Sophie asked.

At that moment, the overhead intercom crackled to life. Cat jumped at the sound.

"*Attention, Ganymede Station,*" a woman's nasally voice intoned. Everyone in the cafeteria paused to listen — except one poor medical trainee, who'd been so startled he dropped his coffee. Sophie merely arched an eyebrow.

"*Attention, Ganymede Station,*" the voice boomed. "*Effective immediately, the location of all personnel is hereby limited to one's workspace, and task space, with exceptions made for mealtimes in the cafeteria. Movement beyond such locations must be with the accompaniment of a Ganymede Station officer, or with their express verbal and /or written permission. Failure to comply with this regulation may result in house arrest not to exceed a maximum of thirty days, with the potential for court martial. Thank you for your attention and have a nice day.*"

"What in the hell?" Zoe said. In the silence of the cafeteria dome that followed the message, her voiced echoed. Sophie frowned. Raina was turning as red as a tomato, gripping her seat with both hands hard enough to make her knuckles blanche.

"Do you think he suspects something?" Cat whispered. She was as pale as the white plastic table they were sitting at, and beginning to tremble.

"Who?" Zoe asked.

"The Admiral, duh," Raina said.

"Please," Sophie said, stretching, catching the eye of most of the male population in the dome, including the coffee-stained medical trainee. "He'll have to do better than that."

"What's got his panties in a twist, then?" Zoe asked.

"Ugh, let's not talk about the Admiral's panties, please. I don't want that mental image." Sophie said, wrinkling her nose.

"So maybe it's a preventative measure, instead of a response to Jaxon's activities?" Raina said, looking to Zoe. "Like he's getting suspicious?"

"We have no time to lose, then," Sophie said resolutely.

"We could release some of the greenhouse bees into the Bridge," Zoe said, lighting up. Raina smothered a laugh. "For a distraction, when you guys need to take off."

"I hope he's allergic," Raina muttered. Sophie rolled her eyes.

"What if," Cat said slowly, and Zoe realized it might have been the first time she'd spoken up without them directly asking her a question. "What if we sounded a Qaig proximity alert?"

"A what?" Raina asked.

"If," Cat said, then looked around. No one paid them any attention. She lowered her voice anyway. "If a Qaig ship breaches the Star Port, the station goes into an emergency mode. If we time it right, after a few PJs have taken off, then you can turn on the *Desiderata* and fly out with the rest who go to investigate. There'll be a lot of chatter on the comms and some of the PJs will head to the Star Port to investigate, even once they've confirmed that it's a false alarm. It should generate enough confusion for you to slip away, undetected. Especially with Aditi watching your back," she said.

For a moment, they were silent, exchanging glances as each thought their way through the possibility.

"What about the actual crew of the *Desiderata*? Won't they get suspicious when they get the call-to-arms and discover their ship is missing?" Raina asked.

"We'll have to have Aditi tell them that the ship has a core leak or something, temporarily reassign them to other ships," Zoe said. "It could work."

"And could... could we do that? Access that alarm without anyone noticing?" Raina asked.

"Child's play," murmured Sophie, nodding her head as Ty and his roommates approached their table.

"Good morning, ladies," Wesley said, taking a seat by Cat.

"Good morning yourself," Sophie said. The other girls were quiet — too quiet — as the rest of the boys took their seats.

"Everything... okay?" Greg asked, his brows drawing together over his mismatched eyes.

"Oh, I was just trying not to notice that my *friends* here," she said, meeting the eyes of her roommates, "had questioned my hacking capabilities. I am offended. Truly offended," she said, frowning. The boys collectively rolled their eyes.

"People just assume that because I'm gorgeous and actually spend time with my grooming, that I'm stupid," she said, but she winked at Cat, who grinned back at her.

"We know," Greg said, his hands up to halt her tirade. "The only one smarter than you is Cat. Good thing she's not as much trouble."

Cat exchanged a glance with Sophie, but didn't say anything. Zoe caught the glance — Cat was plenty of trouble, all right. They just didn't know how much yet.

"*No one* is as smart as Cat," Sophie said, tossing her hair over her shoulder, deflecting attention from Cat, who was turning quite red. "I can't be dissatisfied with second place."

"So ... what do you think about it? The announcement?" Greg asked, chomping down on a mouthful of cereal.

"We'll just have to get a little more creative, that's all," Sophie said. Zoe wondered about the gathering of Jaxon's "Mutineers" — speaking in code was fine, she guessed, but it was already hard enough to meet up.

Zoe watched Cat, who squirmed a bit — whether from Sophie's praise or the strain of keeping their secret, it was hard to tell. Zoe wasn't sure if Ty had clued his roommates in on their plan yet. They didn't need any more people than necessary to be in the loop at this point. Sophie looked at her roommates from the corner of her eye, then fluttered her lashes at Wesley. She put her chin in her hands and changed the subject.

"So, Wesley, tell me, is it true that Savaryn puts birth control in the water supply?"

Greg snorted coffee from his nose. Wesley chuckled and handed his roommate a stack of napkins. Greg wiped the dribble from his face and dabbed at his jacket.

"It's true," Wesley said, sipping his own cup of coffee elegantly. "We're just not equipped to handle prenatal care here. Or babies."

"Interesting," Sophie purred, tapping her scarlet fingernails on the table. Ty kept his gaze firmly fixed on his cup, as if assessing the compounds within.

"Well, that's just ... you know, not everyone needs..." Raina started, turning red and heated. Zoe could practically see the steam rising from Raina's head.

"Oh please, Raina," Zoe intervened, swiping a piece of pineapple from Raina's plate. "This is one idea of Savaryn's I'm on board with. Even teenage geniuses are complete idiots when it comes to sex. Can you imagine a station full of screaming babies?"

Raina grumbled, but agreed, though her lips remained tightly pursed. Another Raina-explosion averted. Zoe was starting to get good at it, if she did say so herself. She helped herself to another piece of fruit from Raina's plate as a reward and nearly got stabbed with a fork as a result. She grinned, looking past Raina to check on Cat, who was sitting as quiet and still as a statue. Wesley bent his head a bit to talk to her.

"So, Sophie, are you going to be joining us for our next poker night?" Greg asked, grinning wickedly. Sophie scoffed.

"Not unless you promise me that Tesla kid — which one was it last time, James? — won't be counting cards again," she said.

"Eh, hard to enforce," Greg said with a shrug.

"Then make him an offer he can't refuse," Zoe said in a horrible mock-Italian accent. Greg looked startled, then laughed.

"Hey, I'm the one with the movie quotes, remember?" he said.

"Yeah, yeah," Zoe said, slurping at her coffee. "Aren't you about out of grams this month anyway?"

"No way! Who told you that?" Greg asked, clearly offended.

"That guy down in the printing lab," she said, grinning. They were all allotted five hundred grams of 3D-printing weight each month in place of monetary compensation. As a result, these grams were often traded — or gambled — like currency.

"More resistance bands, Zo?" Ty asked. She shook her head.

"Did a speed ball with this month's pay. Works pretty good. You can borrow it sometime," she said. He nodded, considering.

"Well, I have so many grams, I don't know what to do with them all," Greg said, winking. "I could print a Lamborghini with all my grams if I wanted to."

"No matter that there's no place to drive it," Wesley said, raising an eyebrow. Greg shrugged again.

"Listen Soph, next eclipse, you want in on the game, you message me, all right?" Greg said. No matter that Sophie wouldn't even be on the station that day, Zoe thought. She watched Sophie give a noncommittal answer. She probably would have liked to go gamble with them, but she had more important super-spy things to do.

"Zoe?" Greg asked hopefully. Zoe shook her head.

"All out of grams this month, my friend, remember?" she said. He sighed dramatically. Wesley, Zoe noted, was pretty much ignoring their whole conversation now, and was strictly focused on Cat, and not trying to hide it. Zoe took another sip of her coffee — too much, too fast, singeing the roof of her mouth — and tried not to be too obvious about eavesdropping.

"How are you feeling?" he asked. He watched Cat carefully, like she might shatter like glass at any moment. "Any more ... problems?"

Cat shook her head, then got up. Her silverware clattered loudly against her tray as her hands shook, and the rest of the table turned to look at her.

"I've... got to go," she said, and walked away. Wesley jumped up, grabbed his mug of coffee, and walked out with her, placing a hand momentarily on her back. He whispered something, but Zoe didn't catch it. She exchanged a glance with Sophie, who again arched an eyebrow, but didn't say anything.

"So..." Greg said, watching the pair walk off. "That was weird. That was weird, right?"

"Cat's ... been stressed," Raina offered, pursing her lips again. She dared Greg to challenge her. Greg, fortunately for him and his nose, did not rise to the occasion.

CHAPTER 11

SOPHIE, GANYMEDE STATION / THE DESIDERATA

The next morning came after the longest night Sophie had ever experienced. She'd barely slept at all. She'd checked and rechecked her bag, made sure she'd packed every bit of hackware that she thought she'd need, and triple-checked to make sure she'd packed her spare lipstick. Ty had stashed three EVA suits on the ship they were taking. Everything else should already be on board. After all, there was no telling what condition the station was in after so much time. It was thrilling, really. And terrifying, of course. Maybe mostly terrifying, and just a little thrilling. It was hard to say. Her emotions were running so fast through her head that discerning the difference was close to impossible.

They'd gone over the plan with Aditi and Jaxon before curfew. They'd done it in bits and pieces — Sophie nonchalantly talking with Aditi in the cafeteria line; Cat and Jaxon chatting over her newest chemistry-lab project. The piece-meal conversations were a hard way to communicate, but they all agreed it was safer than trying to use the messaging system on their tablets — those were definitely being monitored. At least this way, they could find places where the audio sensors didn't quite reach. Cat had even installed a program on each of their tablets, with an alert when they entered dead zones on Ganymede Station. They'd mapped them all out over the past few days and utilized them for their covert meetings.

But morning, at last, did arrive, and when the curfew was lifted and the door lock clicked off, Cat and Sophie were ready to go. Cat, she thought, looked pale, but quietly determined. Sophie smiled to herself. Cat had more courage than she'd given her credit for. Cat would never dare so much as cheat on a test or sneak out past curfew — and here she was, getting ready to hijack a spaceship, fly it to another moon, set up a broadcast station, and fly back, all without getting caught. Just thinking through the whole thing was making Sophie giddy — Cat must have been scared to death, but she didn't look it. Cat's resolve gave Sophie a little more confidence in their mission.

Zoe and Raina followed them to the cafeteria just like it was a normal morning, where they all ate a silent breakfast. Cat barely managed a nibble of toast, and it was all Sophie could do to sip on her coffee. Her hands shook as they grasped the mug — she really didn't need the caffeine, she thought, sleep or no sleep. Adrenaline was making her jumpy enough.

"*Attention, Ganymede Station,*" the intercom droned. Raina snorted and rolled her eyes.

"*Attention, Ganymede Station. Effective immediately, no gatherings in groups equal to or larger than six persons will be permitted within a single location, exceptions again made for the cafeteria and task spaces. Thank you for your attention and have a nice day.*"

"Do we know whose voice that is?" Raina asked. "Because I'm tempted to ..."

"Oh, no," Zoe cut her off, but she grinned. "No violence. We can't have you locked up right now, remember? We need your electrical wiring genius-ness to help us pull this off."

"Fine. After, then," Raina muttered.

After breakfast, no goodbyes were said, no hugs or fanfare. Just a knowing glance, exchanged between them. Cat touched her ears, where her star-cluster earrings sparkled. Raina and Zoe had theirs on, and Sophie pulled her long hair back for hers to catch the light, too. They exchanged a nod and left the cafeteria dome.

"Faxes forever," Sophie whispered.

She and Cat made their way toward the hangar bay. She soon

became aware of a giant shadow behind her — Ty. Just having him there made her less anxious. As it was, her heart rate was probably approaching critical. Damn the caffeine, she thought. She wondered if she should have swiped some sort of sedative from the Medical Bay. Or learned Raina's calming yoga techniques, the deep breathing. She tried it as they walked — breathing in, breathing out. Again. And again. It was working, maybe. She tried matching her steps to her breaths — three steps breathe in; three steps breathe out.

"What are you doing?" Ty asked. She could hear the amusement in his voice, and it rankled her a little.

"Breathing, obviously," she said, but she gave up on the attempt at calming her nerves. She felt like all she was doing was hyperventilating anyway.

The crowds thinned as they made it through the airlocks and into the hangar bay. Not too many people were there yet, just some yawning mechanics and a few of the cadets who would be helping at their assigned tasks throughout the day. A dozen large, sleek, black crescent-shaped ships dotted the hangar, which used to hold nearly fifty. The PJs were massive up close — each as large as a gymnasium, with four xenon drives at the back. Or aft, she corrected herself. She hadn't set foot on one since arriving at Ganymede — it felt like eons ago.

A few moments later, Zoe and Raina came into the hangar and gave them a nod.

"What're you doin' here?" a tired voice mumbled. Sophie nearly jumped out of her skin.

"Oh," she said, fluttering her lashes at the disheveled mechanic, his jumpsuit splotched with grease. She wondered if he'd been working all night. He eyed her, and the pack she carried.

"So sorry," she said. Cat and Ty stood mute behind her. She could only hope that her face wasn't flushing with the extra shot of adrenaline. "We're here to install the new software updates on the PJs. Could you tell me which one is the *Desiderata*? They all look the same to me," she said, giving him her best movie-star smile. And kept fluttering her lashes for good measure.

He rolled his eyes but nodded his head back and to the right.

"Don't touch anything else," he called, and wandered off. Cat let out a long breath.

"Thanks," Cat said. Sophie nodded, her entire body pulsing with excitement. Infiltrating the hangar bay was going to be easier than she thought. No one was looking twice at a couple of cadets wandering around.

They headed to the ship — Ty had known which it was, of course. Asking for help was a part of her cover. Playing dumb was a cinch. Sophie Bauer, super spy.

Up close, the ship was enormous. The gangway was down, as it was with all of the other ships, since repairs were being done. The scheduled departure for the asteroid run was in two hours. Crew — Originals and J'nai — were starting to filter into the hangar. The *Desiderata* was not scheduled to be a part of the departure. Its crew was being utilized elsewhere on Ganymede, on a Rover expedition to the glaciers to replenish the station's water supply. Hence the lie about updating the software; no one else would be on board.

It was a clever cover that Aditi had helped them construct. She could only hope that the code she'd given Aditi would sufficiently mask the ship's movements in the chaos to come. Aditi was supposed to plug the thumb drive into a computer on the Bridge, and the virus would upload the false coordinates. There shouldn't be much computer security in there, anyway. The Bridge was secured physically — no one allowed in or out who wasn't cleared — but the computers were barely password protected. She'd have to remember to thank Savaryn sometime for his arrogance.

They walked into the cargo bay of the ship, an enormous, empty cavern with ladders leading up to the deck and engine rooms. The xenon engines — those subluminal monstrosities capable of jettisoning them to Callisto, the hopefully-not-radioactive-deathtrap — loomed around them, quiet sentinels. She shivered despite herself.

"Ok. Let's do this," she said, hiking her pack up higher on her shoulder. She gestured to Ty to lead the way. She was glad he was with them. She followed him up the ladders, then down a hallway past bunks and the kitchen. She thought back to her own trip to Ganymede, to what she'd left behind on Earth. Surprisingly, she noted a lump in

her throat. She didn't think she'd ever miss those she left behind —
and she didn't, really. But she missed the sun, and the feeling of a
breeze through her hair. She missed going to movie theaters. Not to
mention she'd *kill* for a real cheeseburger these days, instead of the
plant-based proteins and fish sticks they were served. Even the
thought of fish sticks made her stomach roll. She swallowed hard and
kept moving.

Once at the Bridge, Cat got to work immediately, plugging her
tablet into one of the consoles and uploading the coordinates to
Callisto. Ty took a seat with controls similar to those she'd seen in the
simulation room. Nora had spent enough time in the Sim Gym's
"mockpits" last year that Sophie had become somewhat familiar with
their layout.

Now, with Cat and Ty seated at the consoles, the captain's seat was
left open for her. With a smirk, she sat down in the central chair.

"What are you doing?" a voice called. Sophie jumped. Cat flushed
crimson.

"Software updates!" Sophie shouted, then took a deep breath. The
accusation had come from another mechanic, this one a woman, in the
same kind of besmirched jumpsuit as the other mechanic they'd run in
to. She also looked tired — her hair was a mess, her skin, gray.

"All of you?" she said, raising an eyebrow. Her hands were on her
hips, a scowl across her face. Sophie gave her a mega-watt grin.

"Oh, no," she purred, and sauntered over to where Ty sat, silent as
a stone. She licked her lips, which had suddenly gone very dry. She
knew she had enough confidence to pull this off — she just wished she
could have warned Ty. She sat on his lap, wrapping her hands around
his neck, and gazed into his eyes. His bottomless dark eyes, with the
longest, curliest lashes she'd ever seen on anyone. He froze, looking up
at her, a silent question on his face. She ran a finger over the dark
brown skin of his cheek. He swallowed, his Adam's apple bobbing.

"I'm just keeping them company," she said huskily, not looking at
the woman.

Then, without further ado, she kissed him.

It wasn't exactly how she'd planned her first kiss with Tylajah, but
desperate times called for desperate actions. She could feel his

surprise, and then to her delight, she felt his response, kissing her back, his muscled arms coming up around her, holding her to him. She felt like a movie heroine in his arms, safe and adored, as their lips met. After a moment, breathless, she broke the kiss, and tossed her hair over her shoulder, looking back at the mechanic. The woman rolled her eyes, but there were two pink spots on her cheeks.

"Just … don't touch anything, okay? Takeoff is coming up, and … I don't need any cadets caught in the thrusters," she stuttered. Sophie winked at her. The woman groaned and left.

"Whew," Sophie said, disentangling herself from Ty. She pushed her hair back from her face, and headed back to the captain's chair, where she re-acquired her discarded tablet.

"Um…" Cat said, blushing. "Was that necessary?"

"What? People get uncomfortable around PDA. I figured it would be an easy way to get rid of her without too many questions," she said, feigning innocence. But she couldn't keep the smirk from her face as she glanced back at Ty.

"Right," Ty said, his expression dazed. "Right. Good plan."

"All right, now get your head in the game, Casanova," Sophie said, snapping her fingers. "We have a job to do."

"Aye, aye," he said, pivoting back to his console. But she heard the low chuckle that escaped him before he turned.

Cat mumbled.

"What?" Sophie asked.

"I said, *I'm* uncomfortable," she said, flushing to the roots of her frizzy hair.

"I swear, it won't happen again," Sophie said. Ty flashed her a look, eyebrows raised. She grinned wickedly. "For now."

Time crawled. No one else came up to the ship. Cat and Ty had more or less figured out their flight plan and it seemed to Sophie that they were both satisfied with the setup. By some stroke of luck, this full eclipse — time for shenanigans — had Callisto and Ganymede nearly aligned. A few hours there, a few hours to assemble their transponder, a few hours back, and it would be like nothing had happened. Zoe and Raina were covering for them — Cat had a migraine and was sleeping, and Sophie had been re-assigned to work in Aditi's office, 'updating her computer's security.' Ty was 'helping Wesley restock the medical ward.' It was foolproof.

Right?

And then all hell broke loose.

Sophie was nearly dozing in the captain's chair — it was much more comfortable than she'd first thought — when a blaring horn shrieked through the hangar bay, an ear-piecing squeal that had Cat slamming her hands over her ears. Sophie cringed. Outside, the hangar resembled nothing so much as an ant hill that had been kicked over.

"Qaig alarm?" she asked. No one responded, the sound of her voice drowned by the alarm, so she repeated her question, louder. This time, Ty nodded. Cat tried to crawl under her console.

The overhead lights in the hangar had changed to a blood red. Mechanics and crew scrambled about, disappearing into PJs. Cadets streamed from the hangar, crowding into too-small decontamination chambers and pushing while they waited their turns. Around them, the pulsing alarm was nearly drowned out by the roar of a dozen PuddleJumpers, screaming to life. The blinding blue of the Xenon drives drove back the red overhead lights.

"Ready to do this?" Sophie asked, loudly this time. Ty nodded, and a *thrum* went through their ship as Ty hit the ignition. Sophie had never been so simultaneously terrified and turned on in her life.

"So far, so good," he muttered.

"*Qaig alarm, I repeat, Qaig alarm. Qaig have breached the Star Port. Proceed immediately to the Star Port. This is not a drill, I repeat,* NOT A DRILL."

Sophie wasn't sure who was screeching over the intercom, but the panic in their voice was undeniable. So far, so good. She hoped Aditi had the thumb drive installed — the virus would take a few minutes to work, to mask their departure. Although, if the rest of Ganymede was in as much of a tizzy as the hangar bay was right now, she probably had ample time. Sophie felt a sudden twinge of regret. She wondered what was going through the heads of the other cadets right now, the clueless ones mindlessly following their orders. Were they all panicking? Probably. She made a mental note to feel guilty about it — later.

PJs around them started lifting off, hovering a few feet above the ground before streaking out of the hangar's opening. From here, it looked like a wide-open maw covered by a translucent glittering veil, the force field that kept their atmosphere in. The *Desiderata* lifted. Sophie could feel it in the pit of her stomach. The ship vibrated lightly — was that normal? — as Ty paused, seeming to wait his turn in the queue of ships. A slow hum passed through the ship, which she assumed was the landing gear retracting.

Slowly, haltingly, the *Desiderata* made its way to the opening. Sweat poured from Ty, gleaming on his face as he concentrated. Sophie gripped the armrests of her chair so hard that her hands were hurting, and her knuckles had gone white. She hurriedly strapped herself in, motioning to Cat to do the same. The girl nodded, speechless.

"Here we go," Ty said, increasing his acceleration — and then, they were free.

For a moment, Sophie nearly forgot about the Qaig, and Savaryn, and everything. Ahead of them loomed the gigantic mass of Jupiter, darkened but somehow not entirely blackened by the eclipse. The outer edges gleamed in a halo of smoke. And beyond — infinite blackness and glittering stars.

The line of PJs streamed away from the station. Ty gradually increased his distance from the pack, before veering off. Sophie couldn't see Callisto in the forward viewing panel, but the screen attached to her chair charted their course. Callisto gleamed, a tiny green dot.

ETA: 2 hours.

CHAPTER 12
CAT, THE DESIDERATA / CALLISTO

She'd never been so terrified. And yet — she felt alive, like an electrified wire, humming with energy, every atom vibrating. She'd gone over the flight plans in detail several times. Ty had checked them too, and as far as either of them could tell, the plans were sound. It was nearly 600,000 miles to Callisto — and that's only because Ganymede and Callisto were aligned. With a period of 16.4 days to Ganymede's 7.2, and with the eclipse, this was the best chance they'd get for days, if not weeks. Since the moons were moving, their path would take them on a roughly parabolic course. She hadn't spent much time on the PuddleJumpers, but Nora had told her a lot about them, and she'd read up on the engines and software specifications. The J'nai tech that allowed them to build these ships was amazing. She hoped one day she'd have the chance to study their tech more. Assuming of course the J'nai civilization survived. And that she survived.

The Bridge was a relatively large area at the front of the crescent-shaped ship, with a short hallway behind it branching off to various rooms. The hall led back to stairs and ladders, where the larger cargo bay and engineering areas were. The subluminal drives were really impressive — the kind of thrust generated by the xenon drives was many times what the old Earth shuttles were capable of. She wished there was a whole course devoted to J'nai tech — maybe she could suggest that to Dean Prasad. If classes ever resumed. If she wasn't expelled for this. But Dean Prasad was on their side, right? So it couldn't be that bad, what they were doing.

As long as Dean Prasad covered their tracks… she didn't want to think of what the consequences would be if they got caught. She didn't know if Ganymede had a jail, exactly, and she didn't want to find out. Could she be expelled and sent back to Earth? She had nothing left there, no "family," not since her handlers died in a car crash two years ago. Her admission to Ganymede had been sped up by a year as a result, making her the youngest cadet in their year, and one of the youngest on the station. Sometimes — like today — she definitely felt the age difference. Another year of study and she would have been ready for something like this, or readier, at any rate. She shuddered, then turned her gaze back to the console in front of her, re-running the calculations for their trajectory. It was too late for regret now.

She tried not to glance out the front viewing panel too often. It gave her vertigo, like she was standing on the edge of a cliff, staring down into an abyss with no railing between her and falling. They were flying away from Jupiter, so after takeoff the only thing she could see was the vast emptiness of black space in front of her, speckled with distant stars. She tried not to think about what would happen if they were hit by space debris, or lost control of the shuttle, or … She rubbed at her right temple, where a headache was starting to form. She squeezed her eyes shut, hard, and blinked several times. The ache receded.

All in all though, she was pretty impressed with Ty's flying. Nothing fancy, not taking any chances. Just smooth, calm movements. He seemed to relax a little, now that Ganymede was shrinking into the distance behind them. They'd left the comms on, and the chatter of the PJs and Ganymede Station sounded like rain on a tin roof — a background noise, nothing more. An hour into the flight, and it seemed that they were starting to get the idea that someone had cried wolf. No one could find the Qaig on any of the sensors, and the PJs stationed at the Star Port reported no activity at all.

Sophie wasn't talking, which was unlike her, but her fingers drummed against the armrests of the captain's chair she'd claimed. She rested her chin on her other hand, her gaze fixed on the view panel.

There were three consoles on the Bridge; Cat's was on the right next to another for the communication's officer, Ty's was on the left. The captain's chair had its own screen from which they could view which-ever console they needed to. It was an impressive network, linked to a quantum computer in the nose of the ship for cooling purposes. She comforted herself with thoughts of the technical aspects of the ship during their journey. It didn't take long for them to approach Callisto though, and they watched silently as it loomed closer and closer.

Callisto looked very different from Ganymede. This moon was harsher, sharper. It was a gray hunk of rock peppered with so many craters that there was hardly any untouched ground visible. She knew there were 140-odd already named, mostly from Norse folklore, from Adal to Valhalla. Unlike Ganymede though, Callisto didn't have any tidal forces to smooth out the impacts; there were no palimpsest. Those collision marks remained as stark and jagged as they had been on the day they formed.

The edges of the craters glimmered in the scant light they could see, a network of interconnected rings in varying sizes. As Ty brought the *Desiderata* around the moon, she could see that it was frosted with ice. Like Ganymede, this moon was tidally locked, meaning that the same face was turned to Jupiter at all times, just like with Earth's moon. And like Ganymede, the initial J'nai and humans had built their station on that side, away from prying eyes. However, the similarities stopped there.

The station on Callisto was a dark, small structure, not even a quarter of the size of sprawling Ganymede Station. There were no lights. One of the larger domes had caved in, now looking like a roaring mouth filled with jagged canines from the exposed struts. They'd assumed, from what little they were able to glean about the station, that there would be no atmosphere, no oxygen, and likely no power in most of the station. They'd have to wear the EVA suits — extra-vehicular activity, a term leftover from early human space explo-rations — the entire time and be quick and careful. The suits were marvels of design, meant to withstand all of the conditions they might encounter in space, while remaining flexible and mobile. Still, one rip in the suit, one puncture in the air tank, and they'd be dead in seconds

— but not before their eyes boiled in their sockets, among other equally horrible things.

Cat swallowed hard. Her mouth was so dry, her tongue stuck to her teeth. She wished she'd skipped breakfast entirely that morning, as it was not settling well in her stomach.

Ty circled the station several times, trying to find what looked like a landing area or hangar. One of the smaller domes must have looked promising, because he took the ship towards it, hovering like a hummingbird at its entrance. Cat looked down at her scanners — no beeps, no alarms. No radiation present. She met Ty's and Sophie's eyes and nodded her head. Sophie let out a breath and pushed a strand of hair back from her face.

After a moment, Ty took them down. The entrance to the dome had partially collapsed, but the remaining space was more than large enough for a single ship to pass. Inside, the hangar was illuminated only by the faint glow from Jupiter above, and the lights of the *Desiderata*. Cat felt like she might vomit again. She rubbed at her temples, where the familiar ache was returning.

There were no ships here at all, just a few machines and parts, and some beams that had fallen in from the ceiling. It was eerie. Cat couldn't help the feeling that something was watching them. None of them seemed to want to talk first, to break the stillness of the tomb of Callisto Station.

They landed and exchanged silent glances. Cat ran a few diagnostics from her console, but Sophie had been right — there didn't seem to be any radiation at all. The Geiger counters were silent. There was a fusion reactor here, of course, but it appeared to still be well-shielded.

"Let's do this," Sophie said at last. It sounded like Sophie was talking to herself, convincing herself to go forward with the plan. If Sophie was nervous, Cat was terrified. They unbuckled their harnesses and headed to the back of the PJ, to the cargo bay where they'd stashed the EVA suits. Cat's was a little snug, especially around the middle, but she could move fine. It smelled like the inside of Zoe's sneakers, though.

The suits were highly technical pieces of equipment, one of the first things they'd been required to learn how to use on Ganymede. Cat guessed this was something like having lifeboat drills on a ship back home — the suits could protect the wearer from the vacuum of space for an extended period of time. The material was thick, though not as bulky as the space suits of the 1960s. Her joints could bend nearly to their full range of motion. Her fingers carefully connected the little hoses and wires she'd been drilled on — some for the portable oxygen tanks, ready to be worn like backpacks, complete with carbon dioxide scrubbers that would keep them going for several days, theoretically. Cat swallowed hard, and moved on with her suit — with any luck, they wouldn't be on the station for more than what, an hour? Maybe two if Sophie had trouble hacking the system?

She pulled at the neck of her suit, where the itchy turtleneck of the suit was stained a disturbing shade of brown from the sweat of previous wearers. When she was ready, the helmet would attach seamlessly with the suit. Both would provide them with protection from the vacuum, the cold, and limited amounts of radiation. She'd carry a Geiger counter with them, just in case. If they came across any radioactive hotspots, the suits would provide only minimal protection. They'd have to be careful and move quickly if they encountered any major radioactive sources.

Sophie flexed her fingers in her suit, checking the maneuverability. She was going to have to type and potentially re-wire some circuitry, so she had a bag of tools with her. Ty, looking even more massive in his EVA suit, would carry the heavy portable battery unit. They hoped they could rig it up in the Bridge, with enough power to help them get a portion of the computer systems back on-line. The fusion core was still active and hadn't been breached, that much was certain — probably, but they didn't know what state the Bridge would be in. Likely the power to the computer system had been mostly shut down as the inhabitants left. If they followed Ganymede's protocols, though, the Bridge would have been sealed, like a time capsule, hopefully preserving everything they'd need inside.

"You good?" Sophie asked. Cat nodded and put on her helmet. It was clear all around, and she felt like she was wearing a fishbowl on her head. Still, the visibility was impressive, as was the shielding, single-atom-thick coatings of various materials to keep her safe. But any puncture in the suit could be fatal, and if she wasn't careful and snagged it on a broken piece of metal, or if …

"Great. Let's go!" Sophie said and gave them both a thumb's up. Her voice now came over the earbud Cat had placed in her left ear. She could hear herself breathing heavily in the helmet and hoped the others couldn't hear it.

Ty went first, opening the gangway of the PJ. There was a hiss as the air in the ship left — the hangar bay had been sealed after they entered, no point depriving the *Desiderata* of all her air — and a fine mist initially obscured the view.

Inside the hangar bay it was dark and silent. The lights from their ship pierced the inky space, casting long shadows. There was no dust on anything to mark the passage of time. The exodus of Callisto Station could have happened yesterday. Only the decay of the support beams and domes marked the passage of time.

"All right. Seems clear. Let's go," Ty said. Cat and Sophie followed him, silent. They skirted their way around fallen tool chests, abandoned trolleys, and discarded pieces of equipment she couldn't identify. They walked single file, trying not to disturb anything or touch anything if possible.

The end of the hangar bay had a place where sealed doors for the airlock would have been, just like Ganymede — but these had been blown outwards by the decompression of the station. Ty took them through the doors, picking his way carefully — as large as he was, encumbered by his suit, he still moved with impressive agility. He had to stop a few times to move large bits of debris from their path. Cat remembered Sophie saying he'd played football back on Earth, but she couldn't recall exactly what position. She did remember how Sophie's eyes had glowed when she'd described meeting him the first time. Sophie might have tried to pass herself off as a flirt, but Cat knew her better than that. Sophie was smart, and confident, and if there was anyone in the universe that Cat wanted to be in this crazy situation with, it was her.

A headache throbbed in her left temple. She went to rub the spot, her glove bouncing off the helmet instead. Sophie shot her a glance, one eyebrow raised, but didn't say anything. Cat blushed, grateful for the darkness. Usually, she'd be grateful for the quiet and the dark with a migraine — now, though, it was like walking through a graveyard. She shivered despite the sweat rolling down her back.

They all switched on their flashlights. Now that they were through the hangar, the lights from the ship couldn't reach them. While there were some shadows from dim amounts of Jupiter's glow passing through windows and broken ceilings, it was still eerily dark. One false step, one scratch in their suit from a pointy piece of metal they hadn't seen, and…

"Smooth steps Cat, remember," Sophie's voice said into her ear. Cat focused on the back of Sophie's EVA suit, following in her footsteps, trying to remember to breathe as she did so. Her vision blurred as another burst of pain pierced the left side of her head. She stopped — she couldn't risk falling if the pain persisted — but it did let up, quickly, and she continued on.

She swiped the beam of her flashlight from side to side. They were in a corridor just like at Ganymede. The walls were gray, any paint or color leached by time. On their approach, they'd guessed that the Bridge was to the right of the hangar bay, taking a left at a crossroads, before getting to what must have been a Recreation Dome, now shattered like a dropped snow globe. The distance had seemed so small then, the work of just a few steps.

The reality was much more grueling. She was sweating in her suit, and panting. She wasn't an athlete like Zoe or Raina. She was soft, and squishy. She wasn't used to walking this kind of distance, toting her heavy equipment, wearing an EVA suit. She was supposed to be in a lab, working equations. And she still couldn't shake the feeling that they were being watched.

She'd have sworn they'd walked at least six or ten or twenty miles before Ty finally stopped. The light from his flashlight illuminated another door, this one sealed. He turned to Sophie, his eyebrows raised in question.

"Let me see," Sophie said. There was a touchpad beside the door, that had probably once had numbers on it, presumably for a password, but the power to the door was long gone. Sophie pried off the covering for the box and went to work with her tools and the battery Ty carried.

The minutes ticked by, each one lasting at least an hour. Cat, at least, had a moment to catch her breath. She could hear Sophie swearing softly through the earpiece every time her hand slipped. She was so careful not to cut herself with the edge of the screwdriver she used, or puncture her suit on the wires, but her attention to detail came at the cost of time. Ty watched her, poised, ready to jump in if needed.

He wasn't needed.

Sophie got the power back to the panel by connecting it to the battery, and soon the device and the door were bathed in a red glow. A few more minutes, and she'd hotwired the door, the same way she'd hotwired their dorm door back on Ganymede to let her sneak out after curfew.

"Lady and Gentleman," she said, pressing the now-green panel button with a flourish. The door groaned, some mechanism unlocking with a sticky sound — but it only inched open. Ty took over then, placing his shoulder on the door and pushing. After a moment, it opened fully, sliding on its track, exposing them to a narrow chamber with another door at the other end — one that would provide an airtight seal to the vacuum outside. A thin row of lights ran down both walls, casting an icy glow over them.

They dragged their suits and equipment inside and re-engaged the door. Now that the power here was back on, something hissed and spun to life overhead — the pressure seal. Hope fluttered in Cat's chest.

The door at the other end opened.

Inside, the Bridge, though dark, appeared undisturbed. Tablets and chairs, and even empty coffee cups, seemed poised just as though the occupants had planned on returning, only they hadn't. Ty found a light switch on the walls, and soon the room lit up in a cold white glow.

And there was air pressure here. The readings on Cat's monitors showed that, though it was cool by human standards, this room had not been breached. She'd have to do some more testing, but...

Sophie reached up and disconnected her helmet. Cat heard Ty shout over the earbud, but Sophie just looked back at them, grinning. Her dark hair was matted with sweat, her face glowing with excitement. Ty shook his head. Cat wasn't sure if Sophie was brave or reckless. Maybe both. Sophie took off her gloves and wiped her face before looking around at the computers.

Cat and Ty slowly removed their own helmets. Cat gulped at the stale air, relieved to be out of the fishbowl. It was so cold, her breath formed little puffs in front of her face. The air had a tang of metal to it, but her monitors reported a good mix of oxygen in the room. It had been well designed and well preserved. The computers, she saw, appeared to be operational. Despite the passage of time, they had not been damaged. She assumed the Bridge was well built and protected, even more so than the rest of the station, for situations just like this. Ty let out a low whistle.

"How long has it been since anyone's been in here?" he asked, picking up a discarded tablet.

"Fifteen years," Sophie said, walking to the main computer in the center of the room.

"Actually," came a crisp voice behind them. Cat's blood froze. The voice was not coming from Sophie or Ty, who were in front of her. There was no way anyone else should have been in this room. No one could have survived on the derelict station this long without outside assistance — could they?

"It's been fourteen years, eight months, three days, six hours, fourteen minutes, and twenty-six seconds. Approximately."

CHAPTER 13

NORA, THE RAPSCALLION

Bastian leaned hard, and the *Rapscallion* dove down, staggering G-forces plastering Nora back into her chair, her hair swinging wildly behind her. Then, like a roller coaster, he swooped them back up again. Looking at the console, she could see the two Qaig ships, as small green dots, following their every move flawlessly.

"Why aren't they firing anymore?" Nora whispered. Bastian appeared not to have heard her. Sweat trickled down his face despite the cold, dripping from his chin, and his long, tanned fingers were gripping the steering apparatus so hard that the tendons stood out in sharp relief.

"They don't want to kill us," Soren muttered, and slammed her hands against the armrests of her chair. Nora jumped. Soren slouched back in the chair, her lips a thin, hard line. She kept checking her console, her gaze flicking back to the front view panel every few seconds.

Bastian corkscrewed the *Rap* around a pair of asteroids. There must have been mere inches separating them from certain cataclysmic doom, but again, the Qaig followed. Like white on rice.

"*Zut*," Bastian murmured, and spun them again, this time in a hard left-hand loop. Nora felt the bile in her stomach burning the back of her throat. She swallowed hard, trying to repress the urge to vomit.

"They're playing with us?" Nora gasped, putting a hand over her mouth. Bastian shook his head, a slight movement only, not daring to take his concentration from his work. Behind them, the Qaig ships flanked them, and she noticed that because of their positions, Bastian's choices in maneuvers were limited.

"They're *herding* us," she muttered. "They're herding us!"

"Oh sh..." Donovan shouted, his voice trailing off as just above them, maybe a few kilometers out and just meters above the top of the asteroid ring, two of those giant skyscraper Qaig crafts popped out of the Current. They could barely see them on the view screen, but their signature immediately appeared on their consoles as glaring icons.

"Thalia, jump, now!" Soren screamed over the intercom.

"Uh, negative!" came the clipped reply, then, "I need a few more minutes. Or fifteen maybe."

Nora groaned, her stomach clenching. Could they last fifteen more minutes against the Qaig ships? It again seemed like capture, rather than destruction, was their goal. Bastian dove, trying to get behind one of the larger rounded chunks of rock, but one of the Qaig ships outflanked him, funneling him back into an intercept course with the larger ships.

"You have two minutes," Soren replied, then cut off the intercom.

"Donovan, they're not hailing us?" Soren asked, turning to the communications officer. Sweat darkened the T-shirt he wore, and his hand shook badly as he stuffed his glasses back up on his nose.

"Nothing, not on any frequency, not in any dialect or code we've heard," he said, removing an oversized headphone from one ear. "It's silent as the grave out there."

Soren cursed then, or so Nora guessed. Asher repeated the sentiment. If they got back — *when* they got back — she'd really have to brush up on her J'nai. And French. It would be useful to be able to curse in three languages for situations like this; not that she planned to be in another situation like this. Ever. If she even got out of this one.

Nora turned to Soren. The J'nai woman was leaning forward in her chair, her eyes like green lasers, focused and deadly.

"Bastian, take us further down," she said quietly. He did — and then the *Rap* was rocked by a series of laser shots. As Nora had said, they were being herded. As long as they remained on an intercept course with the larger ships, the two small ones would not fire. Those had been warning shots across their bow.

"Asher, time until we're within reach of their traction beams?" Soren asked.

"Four minutes, maybe less," he said. The *Rap* wasn't moving particularly fast. The xenon drives had been badly damaged. Nora expected that they could normally fly circles around the clumsier Qaig craft — then again, they'd underestimated their enemy before. No one would have guessed that the Qaig — so often portrayed to them as an ignorant, primitive race — would have supraluminal capabilities that far outshone the J'nai. It gave Nora a real idea of just how little she knew of the universe, beyond what she'd been fed by the Admiral and the J'nai leadership.

"Bastian, can you lose them?" Soren asked. His jaw clenched, sweat clinging to the blond stubble on his upper lip.

"The *Rap* is barely holding together. I might be able dodge them behind that large one coming up," he said, highlighting an asteroid on his console. This also highlighted it on the front view panel, outlining it in eerie green.

"Just buy us time, as much as you can," Soren said. Bastian nodded, too absorbed to spare another moment talking. Nora had never experienced fear like this before — it was something primitive, the response that a mouse had when being pursued by a cat. It made her pulse race, her breathing quicken, as every muscle in her body prepared for either fight or flight. She watched Bastian's motions with heightened focus, the way he dove and maneuvered, using the asteroid field to his advantage, for cover, rather than viewing it as an obstacle.

"THALIA!" Soren screamed again over the intercom.

"Captain," came Sun's clipped voice. "Ms. Jones asks for your patience, please. What we are doing is incredibly delicate and ..."

And then the intercom faded out, and nothing but static issued from the speaker in Soren's chair. She smacked the armrests, hard.

"Okay, okay," she said. "Bastian, as much time as you can. Our only hope at escape is that Thalia can re-engage the P2. We've got to give her that time."

His grip tightened, then relaxed, the tendons no longer quite so prominent in his wrists. It was a fighters' stance — ready, and aware. He kept the *Rapscallion* on an intercept course for the larger Qaig ships, but just a bit to the right, towards the large green asteroid. Their flanking Qaig ships didn't seem to notice. He shot a glance to Nora, and she must have looked terrified, because he gave her a small smile, one that didn't quite make it to his eyes.

And then his gaze flicked upwards.

Between one heartbeat and the next, his arm shot out, faster than any punch she'd ever seen him throw, and struck the back of her chair. The force caused the locks that kept the wheels anchored on the floor to disengage, and she slid across the Bridge, her neck whipping to the side, the wide straps of her restraining harness straining to keep her in place. With her back to him now, she used her feet to spin back around, mind reeling, and —

Overhead, a ceiling panel fell. A snarl of wires, sparking like the fires of Hell, were restrained by a single corner of the panel still adherent to its mooring. She watched it swing on that corner, as if in slow motion.

And then that corner gave out, and the whole tangle of wires and metal ceiling grating and sparks fell with a grating, screeching sound, knocking Bastian from his seat and burying him in an avalanche of debris.

"BASTIAN!" she screamed. She flailed at the straps holding her to the chair. She couldn't get up. Her fingers trembled as she fumbled with the fastenings. She couldn't tear her eyes off the scene, couldn't see him underneath the carnage. Couldn't hear him over the screaming — and not all of it was coming from her.

The final buckle gave way at last, and she stumbled over to the mess, the Qaig ships momentarily forgotten. She reached for the nearest wire, and her arm leapt with a shock as the electric current tore up her nerves. Her fingers felt numb — but they responded to her mental command, flexing and extending normally, so she ignored the sensation and kept going. On the other side of the wreckage, Donovan yelped as he grabbed a bit of fabric — the arm of Bastian's green flight suit. He pulled, and Asher grabbed another arm, and then a torso, as

Bastian emerged. His head hung limply, rolling to the side as they yanked him free. The left side of his face was a mess, blood obscuring his eye and ear, pooling on the floor in crimson puddles. There was at least one deep gash on his cheek, where a dark ooze seeped from mangled flesh. Asher nearly lost his footing as he stepped in the blood, cursing as he readjusted his grip. Nora stood paralyzed, nauseated at the sight but unable to turn away.

"Is he..." the words died on her lips. She couldn't lose him — he couldn't be dead. He couldn't be. She looked up, watching the sparking wires, flexing fingers on her hand that feeling was gradually returning to. Had he been shocked maybe?

Donovan put two fingers to Bastian's blood-soaked neck. He nodded and frowned.

"He's alive. But unconscious," he said, then swore, trying to use his hand to stanch the flow of blood from Bastian's scalp. "We've got to stop this bleeding."

Soren and Nora moved the rest of the debris off Bastian as Asher and Donovan pulled. Nora's gaze flickered to the front panel — the green asteroid was nearly on them. The *Rap* was staying on a straight course for it; their two small Qaig attendants seemingly unperturbed.

"You two, take him to his quarters, do what you can," Soren said. Asher and Donovan heaved Bastian's limp form between them, his arms slung over their shoulders. Blood ran down the side of his face, onto his collarbone, forming an ever-widening stain on his chest. And that was only the injury she could *see*. Whatever had happened to his skull, his chest, had he been crushed —

"*Nora*," Soren barked. Nora snapped her head around and met the laser-focused eyes of her captain. She felt like a deer in headlights — unable to move, unable to process anything beyond that gaze. Her hands trembled, hanging loosely at her sides, as if they too had forgotten how to do anything constructive at all.

"It's on you, now," Soren said curtly. "I'll move this mess. You dodge those ships, buy Thalia as much time as you can."

"But..." Nora said and stopped. She wasn't sure what she wanted — to go with Bastian? Then who would fly the ship? Could Soren do it?

"*Now,*" Soren roared. Nora's cerebellum fired before she even realized she'd heard the command, and she found herself leaping through the tangle of metal to the chair — *Bastian's* chair — and sitting down as best she could. She swept her arm across the console, clearing the mess, trying to avoid any sparking wires. Soren heaved the panel aside and began hauling the larger pieces of pipe away, clearing the console but surrounding Nora in a nest of metal.

She breathed deeply. Her hands were shaking so hard she could barely grip the steering — so she searched her pockets, finding the hard square and two small earbuds in the one over her left chest, nearest her heart. She put the earbuds in and clicked the metal square.

Even over the crackling of the exposed wires, and the shuddering of the *Rapscallion* all around her, she could hear the smooth tones of Debussy, the piano drowning out everything. She took another breath, and her trembling stopped. This is what she was trained to do. This is what she was good at. No one else on the ship could handle the *Rap* like she could. She, Eleanora Clementine Clark, would do this. And if Bastian woke up — *when* he woke up — he'd be proud of her, of how she'd implemented all those hours of his training.

She took hold of the steering and dove the *Rap* behind the green asteroid.

CHAPTER 14
SOPHIE, CALLISTO STATION

Sophie winced when she heard the terse voice behind her. So much for being alone on this rock. She sighed — had this whole thing been a setup? Some really elaborate way of finally catching Sophie 'in the act' of rebellion? She wouldn't put it past Savaryn — he was a real dick sometimes.

However, when she turned around, the voice was not coming from a person, but from a projection. A hologram, a floating head, larger than life-size, sat above a table in the back of the Bridge.

The face was a bland, human face, just a pale man with short hair and a long chin. She was reminded of the disembodied head of the wizard in the *Wizard of Oz*. He blinked — which was disconcerting. Holographic projections didn't really need to blink, did they? Was this some sort of programmed affect to make him seem more human? He also moved — or rather, rotated — his eyes going to each of them, as if *looking* at them. What kind of sensors did this thing have built in? Motion detectors, thermal scanners? It almost seemed aware, sentient. It was really creepy.

"And you are?" Sophie asked, crossing her arms. The head bobbed, as if nodding on an invisible neck.

"You can call me Adam," the face said. Ty approached it cautiously, then put out an arm and waved his hand through the hologram, not meeting any resistance. She thought she saw him shudder, though it was hard to tell with the EVA suit. The face looked at him, expressionless.

"The station is unstable. You should not be here," Adam said. His gaze drifted uncomfortably across the three of them, evaluating them.

"Yeah," Sophie said, rolling the tension from her shoulders. "Anyway, Adam, are you plugged into the station's mainframe?"

"I am," the hologram said. Cat moved until she was behind Ty, her helmet gripped tightly in both hands.

"The station is... somewhat smaller than it was the last time I was activated. In fact, outside of the Bridge, I am getting no feedback from any of my sensors. Why is that?" Adam asked.

"The station is dead, Adam. Now, can you help me bypass these security codes?" Sophie asked. The initial shock at Adam's presence had worn off, so she went back to work. She'd plugged Ty's portable generator into the Bridge computer system, and the extra power had awoken nearly all of the electronics.

"I cannot," Adam said. "You should not be here."

"Look, Adam," Sophie said, fingers flying across the keyboards. "You can help, or you can be unplugged. Your choice."

The AI hologram frowned. The fact that it could do so made Sophie chortle. He remained silent, though. She let out a sigh and got back to work. The encryptions on the Bridge computers weren't that sophisticated — after all, they were fifteen years old. They'd been cutting-edge at the time, and would take her some time to crack, but she had no doubt that she would.

"How's it going?" Ty asked, crouching by her. His presence both calmed and thrilled her. She liked the sensation. She shot him her movie-star smile, then doubled down on her hacking efforts.

"I'll be in momentarily," she said, and sneezed. The musty air in the Bridge was a welcome change from the EVA suit, but that didn't mean it was pleasant.

The screens scrolled in front of her, lines of green glowing text faster than most eyes could follow. Her fingers flew over the keys, bypassing the antiquated security measures.

"Cat, get ready," she said, extending one hand to the other girl. Cat rubbed at her temple but came over.

"Ok," Sophie breathed. A desktop opened on the screen in front of her, dozens of files neatly splayed across a blue backdrop. She tracked down the communications equipment, and when she activated them on her computer, a row of machines whirred to life at the back of the room. Cat jumped, one hand still rubbing at a spot on her neck.

"Headache?" Sophie asked, viewing her in askance. It would not do to have Cat collapse on her now. Not when they were so close. Cat jerked her hand away from her neck, and a guilty flush stained her face.

"I'm fine," Cat said. "What's that?"

"What?" Sophie asked, tracking Cat's finger. A file was set a little apart from the rest, and when she clicked it, there was another layer of security she had to bypass. Sweat dripped down her nose despite the cold. Her fingers moved nearly of their own volition, conditioned to the kind of work she had been doing since she was a small child, when she'd cut her teeth, so to speak, on systems just like this one.

"*Tabula rasa*," she whispered.

"What?" Ty asked, leaning closer, his hand on her shoulder. Sophie was too engrossed to make a flirtatious comment.

"A theory that all humans are born without any mental constructs, that all knowledge comes only from experience and perception. We are blank slates," Cat said. Sophie and Ty shot her a look, then Sophie opened the file. "I've heard it used as a counterargument to the cloning program. That it's not worth the cost and risk, since we don't have any of our host's attributes."

"I hate that term," Sophie muttered. "It makes us sound like parasites."

She kept scrolling, then paused, half-way down one of the Word documents.

"Can it mean something else? Because I think this means something else," Sophie said. Her heart started fluttering in her chest, and her hands felt suddenly stiff, and clumsy, as if they were no longer a part of her. This was unbelievable.

"Cat," she breathed. "Get me the portable drive."

Cat handed over the thumb drive, and Sophie plugged it in to the console. She dragged the file over, and a countdown began as the file began transferring.

"Whatever you are doing here, I suggest you hurry," Adam said. Sophie turned. The AI was frowning at her again.

"We'll leave you alone in a moment. We could move a lot faster if you told us how to access the outgoing communications," Sophie said, glancing back to her screen. On a whim, she dragged a second file over, and the countdown to transfer increased — five minutes remaining.

"When you opened the doors to the Bridge, you destabilized the dome. I estimate no more than three minutes before the entire structure collapses," the hologram said, in his eerie, monotonous voice.

They looked up. Cat rubbed her temple again, frowning. Nothing happened for a long moment. Sophie's eyes flicked back to her monitor — four minutes.

"Put your helmets back on," Ty said, fixing his own into place. "If there's a crack, I don't want us caught off-guard."

Sophie and Cat followed suit. Sophie tried to work on the computer with her gloved hands, but it was futile. She could barely grasp the external drive, let alone type.

"Adam, where did you say the weakness was?" Sophie asked. Come on, move faster, she willed the bars to move but they only crept along. They were at fifty-two percent … Fifty-three.

"The outer door. The … airlock … depressurization," he stuttered. The hologram flickered, then disappeared.

"Uh, Adam?" Sophie asked. But nothing happened. Well, good riddance. He'd been pretty useless, as far as AI went. Still, she swapped out the drives, and the second file began to transfer.

"Sophie, have you been able to isolate any of the communications equipment? Are any of the antennae still operational?" Cat asked through her ear buds.

"Doesn't look like it," Sophie muttered, her hands moving like oven mitts over the mouse. This whole trip had been pointless. She was tired, and hungry, and needed a shower, and they didn't even have an antenna to hijack. She let out a long breath in frustration, hands on hips as she considered their options.

She squinted, then paused — the Bridge was silent, not a single creak or groan to signal impending collapse. Adam was probably just malfunctioning. His sensors were old, probably frozen or worse. She let out a sigh and went to unbuckle her gloves again. She might as well double-check the —

Ty's hand shot out, clamping down on her wrist. She glared at him but stopped when she saw the whites of his eyes, visible all the way around his dark irises. Something scared him, and that scared her.

"What?" she whispered. An icy trickle made its way down her spine. Ty shook his head, waiting. He grabbed Cat's glove with his other hand, pulling them both to their feet. Sophie grabbed at the thumb drive —

"Wait, just a few more seconds," she said, yanking back. *Ten, nine, eight…*

Crash.

The table that had been Adam's platform toppled over, as a wave like an earthquake shook the Bridge. Ty grabbed her and Cat around the waist, one of them under each arm, and dashed for the doors.

They never made it.

A massive strut fell from the ceiling, a wedge of metal a dozen feet long, landing just feet in front of Ty, bringing with it an avalanche of debris. Particulates flew through the air, creating a thick cloud they couldn't see their way through.

Ty backed up, letting Cat and Sophie down, but they stuck close to him. Sophie glanced over at the computer — dead. The machinery was all dead. Not in low-power mode, or the hibernating state they'd been in when they arrived. Dead dead. Dead as a doornail dead. She tapped a key, clicked the power button, checked the portable battery — nothing. At least this was just an internal support structure — her sensors told her that the airlock hadn't been breached. There was still oxygen and gravity in the Bridge. She grabbed the external thumb drive and shoved it into a pocket on her suit, hoping that there had been at least enough time, that the file had downloaded without corrupting. They might not be able to get a signal to Terra Prime, but what she'd found …

"Is there another way out of here?" Ty asked, breaking her focus. She looked around — no, there wasn't. Great.

"Not unless you can break through the wall there," Sophie said, indicating the direction with a nod of her head. "But there's a double layer of insulation before the outer hull. It would take a bulldozer to get through that."

Ty looked back to the door, now blocked with the strut and other smaller pieces. He bent, placing the elevated end of the beam under one shoulder, and pushed.

Nothing happened.

He shifted his stance, like it was a push sled at football practice. He threw his weight against it. Even through the helmets, Sophie could see the strain on his face, the sweat pouring down his cheeks, fogging the glass.

The strut wouldn't move. Cat went to help him, putting her own meager strength to the middle of the beam. Sophie shook herself from her idleness and joined, but even together, they could not move the beam. They pushed and pulled, panting, until they sat, slumped together, silent except for the ragged breaths they drew.

"How long will our oxygen last?" Ty asked quietly. Sophie sighed. Her own meter was no longer quite at 'FULL', and she had to imagine that Ty, being larger, had consumed more already.

"A few days, maybe," Cat said, just as quiet. "If we conserve our energy and don't move too much."

"Won't do any good. No one knows we're here. No one is coming to help," Sophie said. She leaned into Ty, grateful for his solid strength. He put an arm around her, pulling her close. He bent, the dome of his helmet touching hers. She refused to give in to despair — but it lurked there in her chest, its icy tendrils trying to gain purchase. Maybe, when they didn't return, Aditi would send someone after them. It would mean jeopardizing all of the Mutineers though, their secrets — would Aditi take the risk? Would Jaxon?

Another tremor, this one smaller, went through the dome. More debris fell from where the beam had dislodged, but no more large pieces came off.

"Can we get through there? Maybe Cat will fit?" Ty asked, gesturing to the hole in the ceiling above where the beam had been.

"If it's built like Ganymede, that space doesn't go anywhere. She'll just get stuck in more insulation," Sophie said.

"We have to try something," Ty said. It wasn't accusatory — just a statement of fact. She looked at Cat — the girl had her eyes closed tight, and she had drawn herself into a ball, as compact as she could be in her suit. Sophie felt a pang of regret, dragging them all out here on this fool's errand. Now she'd gotten them all killed, and for nothing. Her hand strayed to the pocket where the thumb drive lay protected. She wondered if anyone would ever see it. A whole host of regrets played through her head — she'd never see Nora again. Never yell at Zoe again for leaving her boxing equipment laying around. Never see Raina change from a boiling kettle of rage to calm yogi again, like a little chameleon. Never kiss Ty, not for real.

And then, Cat stood up.

Sophie looked up from her shelter under Ty's arm. She barely recognized the girl in front of her. She stood tall, as tall as she could be anyway. Cat's eyes were positively blazing, and her face was stone. Any trace of the prior panic or migraine was gone. She strode to the beam, placed both hands on it, and *pushed.*

The beam flew, as if propelled, smashing through the inner and then outer chamber doors, tearing through them as if they were nothing but tissue paper. The beam continued on and on, out of sight. Sophie could hear the groans of other structures in the distance as the strut crashed through them, and the ground under her shivered with the impact. The air was sucked out of the Bridge in a *whoosh,* and the room went pitch-black save for their flashlights and suit sensors. Sophie didn't dare breathe — beside her, she could tell Ty was in just as much shock.

And then, Cat fell.

CHAPTER 15
NORA, THE RAPSCALLION

Within the same microsecond that Nora started to move the *Rapscallion* off-course, the two smaller Qaig ships behind her immediately started firing again. A few of the laser shots hit their rear shield this time — no more warning shots. Soren had diverted power to the shield, but it was running dangerously low, the sensor on her console glaring yellow. Nora now had to avoid getting shot, avoid getting pulled into the traction beams of the two larger Qaig ships looming ever closer, and buy Thalia and her team as much time as she could.

Easy.

She licked her lips, which were bone dry, despite the sweat that made her flight suit stick to her chest like it was adhered. All of her focus bent to the task before her.

"Thalia!" Soren called over the intercom. Nothing but static answered. She said something else, but Nora didn't catch it. The soft strains of Debussy were still whispering in her ear buds, keeping her heart rate at a steady pace. She flexed her hands on the steering, grateful for the repetitive patterns Bastian had drilled her on.

Bastian.

Her chest squeezed, and if she'd had a single neuron to spare, it would have instantly thought of Bastian, if he was okay, if she should go see if she could help…

But she had no spare neurons at the moment, so on she flew. She corkscrewed around the asteroid that he'd highlighted before the … accident. She came out nearly on top of the smaller Qaig ships and flipped the *Rapscallion* over the top of them in a gut-wrenching maneuver. She fought to keep the *Rap* in between the two ships. She wagered they wouldn't fire on her if she stayed between them, when they might have a chance of hitting each other.

She was mostly right. At least the frequency of the blasts settled down. She tried every trick she knew and invented a few more on the spot. She threw the *Rap* into a hard reverse. The engines screamed, and the metal vibrated around her like a plucked guitar string, but the ship obeyed. She thought she heard voices from down the hall behind the Bridge, but she couldn't be sure, and she didn't have the energy to pay attention to them. Her single focus was keeping her ship away from the asteroids, between the two small ships, and away from the large, rapidly approaching Qaig skyscraper-ships. It was a deadly dance, and the *Rap* was not the most agile partner at the moment.

Before her, a giant asteroid tumbled end-over-end, bigger than a football field. It was approaching too fast. She slammed the *Rap* into reverse again, hard, and this time the rattling was ten times worse. Metal creaked and protested around her, and she felt hot sparks showering her back from the panel above — but it was like it was happening from a great distance. The pain barely registered.

Pop.

Nora jerked in her chair — Bastian's chair. The smoothness of the Current spun around them, and the *Rap* purred now like a contented kitten.

"Okay," came Thalia's voice from behind her. Nora pulled the ear buds out.

"Okay what?" Soren asked. Her laser eyes had Thalia pinned. Even Thalia couldn't help but squirm. Thalia's gaze shifted though, to the debris around her, to the bloodstain on the floor near Nora's feet.

"Where is everyone?" she asked softly. Nora shot a glance to Soren

—

"Benoit was injured when that panel fell. Asher and Donovan are taking care of him," she said.

Thalia's hand went to the base of her neck, eyes wide. Then she cleared her throat.

"So, I guess I have you to thank for that crazy-ass flying back there? Knocked me across the engine room. Thanks for the bruises."

"You're welcome," Nora said, biting her tongue. They stared at each other.

"So… the P2?" Soren prompted. Thalia shrugged, as if she didn't care about it, any of it.

"It'll hang on for a few more minutes, or an hour, probably. But then we're going to be out of luck. I need parts, Soren. I need deuterium and tritium. The core was damaged, I need to replace that too. Oh, and a bourbon."

"Unfortunately, I can't help you. With any of that," Soren said, returning her attention to her own console, effectively dismissing Thalia. "Let me know when you have a realistic request, and I'll see what I can do."

"Can't you rewire the setup to the old supraluminal drive instead of the P2?" Nora asked. Thalia's withering glare would have made her blush, if she wasn't so exhausted.

"First thing we tried," she said, fluttering her hand in Nora's general direction. "We had to sabotage some of the original hardware when we installed the P2. Not going to work, unless you have a way to contain literally a 10-megawatt-per-meter-squared thermal load. Or a way to shield us from getting blasted by a gazillion alpha particles."

"What if…" Nora said, then cut herself off, biting her lip.

"Yes?" Soren asked. Nora swallowed hard.

"The Qaig seem to be able to jump on and off the Current like the P2," Nora said. Thalia rolled her eyes.

"Yeah. I noticed."

"So… would they have those things you need on board? If I could hit one — disable it without destroying it — you could go on board and get what you need?" Nora asked. Thalia raised an eyebrow, but no snarky comment followed.

"You spent the last ten minutes flying like a drunk pigeon just staying away from them," Thalia said after a moment. "You really think you could avoid them *and* disable them?"

"I can handle the weapons," Soren said slowly. "Nora, if you can get us lined up, I can do it. I can hit them where it would cripple them but not obliterate them."

"Teensy little problem of all those Qaig on board," Thalia said, crossing her arms. Soren shook her head.

"Shouldn't be more than two or three. They're only sending small scouting craft after us. I'm willing to bet they calculated our last trajectory and sent them in all different directions. The larger ships waited until the small ships found us, then the small ships signaled back, and then they jumped as well."

"So given that we're currently on a longer jump, we could presume that the larger ships would take longer to reach us?" Nora asked, thinking. "If we're on the Current for an hour, and we disable the ship soon after it reaches us, we should have, what, three or four hours until the larger ships follow, maybe?"

"That sounds right," Thalia said, and Nora could hear the fatigue in her voice. She didn't feel at all sorry for her, she just noted the fatigue.

"Got any better ideas?" Soren asked. Thalia thought for a moment, then shrugged.

"Think you can take out a Qaig or two once we board them?" Thalia asked. Soren grinned, her teeth gleaming.

"It would be my pleasure."

Thalia estimated the P2 would hold for another forty-five or fifty minutes, so Nora took the opportunity to visit the head, grab a protein bar and a cup of coffee from the galley — and stop by the captain's quarters. She swallowed hard — the protein bar, dry at the best of times, had turned to ash in her mouth. She took a sip of coffee, stashed the bar in a pocket, and opened the door.

Bastian lay on his bed, his torso bared. Asher and Donovan were winding long strips of white cloth bandage around his head, holding a larger bandage in place over the left side of his face and ear. Blood plastered his bronzed hair to his head, formed dark pools on his collarbone, smeared on the sheets. Dripped on the floor. His clothes had been cut away and lay in a tangled heap at the foot of the bed, matted with dried and drying blood.

She didn't move from the doorway. Couldn't move. Donovan saw her, but didn't say anything to her. He and Asher were involved in a deep conversation, whispering hurriedly.

She crept a foot closer. They'd started an IV in Bastian's left elbow. Hung on a makeshift stand behind his head were three bags of fluids: one milky white, one clear, and one yellow. A blanket had been pulled up to his waist. Over his chest, the skin was already darkening into what looked to be massive bruising. She wondered how many ribs he'd broken. His left side was starting to swell, distorting the muscles of his chest.

"Please don't faint again," Donovan said, looking back at her. Nora narrowed her eyes at him. How dare he joke at a time like this. On their last flight together, she'd fainted at the sight of her own blood from a relatively minor head wound. What was before her now was infinitely worse.

"What? I've got enough on my hands without you syncopizing. Basic life support training doesn't exactly cover enucleation," Donovan said.

"Doesn't... what?" Nora breathed. Her chest constricted.

"He's going to lose that eye. Maybe both," Donovan said, rubbing a hand over the back of his neck. "And he's got a concussion, at the least. Broken ribs. Broken collarbone. Um, maybe electrocution? Shit, I don't know."

"He's going to... lose his sight?" Nora asked. The words barely made it past her throat.

"If he survives, yeah," Donovan said. Asher must have stepped on his foot — hard — because Donovan glanced quickly up at her, whispered a 'sorry,' then returned to his ministrations. She swallowed — well, tried to swallow, but her mouth was too dry, so she cleared her throat instead. It was a nightmare, unfurling right before her eyes. This wasn't possible. Not Bastian. Not the Ace, the best pilot in the entire fleet. Not her mentor, her friend. Not the man who meant more to her than she dared admit. Even if they somehow made it home, he'd never be the same.

Nora drifted to his bedside, like she was pulled in by Bastian's own gravitational field. This couldn't be happening. For a pilot to lose their sight? Lose the ability to do what he was born to do, what he lived and breathed for? Her breathing became rapid, shallow. Her vision clouded, narrowing, like she was looking down a tunnel.

"Oh, sit down, for the love of …" Donovan said, grabbing the chair by the desk and placing her in it. She felt numb, barely felt the pressure of his hands on her shoulders but obeyed. Her vision gradually cleared. Donovan and Asher were applying more gauze over the side of his head, where his ear was. Or where it had been, anyway.

"Can he… can he hear us?" Nora asked quietly. Asher shrugged. He tied off the last of the bandage.

"Who knows?" Donovan said. "We've got him sedated. Probably have to keep him down until we can get him back to Ganymede. Maybe intubate him? Shit."

"We … *are* going back to Ganymede, aren't we?" Asher asked. Donovan startled, his glasses nearly falling off his nose.

"The P2 is only going to last a few more minutes. But I've got a plan," Nora admitted, rubbing the back of her neck, where a tightness the size of a softball had formed. Donovan rolled his eyes.

"I feel better already."

"We're going to disable a Qaig ship. Board it, loot it. Take whatever we need," Nora said, too numb for Donovan's sarcasm. "Thalia thinks she can get us home if we get her some of their parts."

Donovan let out a long, low whistle.

"We don't have many options. It's that or get stranded out here," Asher said. Donovan grunted.

"Well, Bastian called you his North Star. Let's hope you live up to his expectations."

E ither she *was* lucky, or maybe Soren was just that good. She suspected it was the latter.

As if on cue, shortly after the *Rap* emerged from the Current, two more small Qaig scout ships appeared. Nora licked her lips, feeling them crack in the dry, recycled air.

"Steady," Soren said. She'd taken Asher's place and was managing the weapons controls. They didn't have much left — Thalia had had to remove the ventral cannons when the P2 was installed for weight issues. That left only the smaller laser turret on the aft of the ship. Soren would have to be very precise in her targeting — otherwise, the lasers wouldn't do much damage. Plus, they'd have to be close — way too damn close — for them to be effective.

But what choice did they have?

Nora readjusted her grip on her own controls. They'd talked it through. She hoped to separate the ships — to knock out one and maim the other.

But these ships were crafty, and this time there were no asteroids to hide behind, just wide-open space and a distant black hole, which she was very careful to keep in her sights. A black hole, though a relatively small one, less than a hundred miles across, was the kind of pint-sized killer that formed when a star burned out and collapsed under its own weight. Nora could sympathize, she felt similarly ready to implode. Her mind barely registered the immensity — she really had no idea where in the universe they were, or what they might encounter the next time they fell off the Current. They could have fallen immediately *into* the black hole. They were way, way off the beaten path — here, there be dragons. Big ones.

She decided to go on the offensive, swooping into a tear-jerking backwards loop that had the edges of her vision starting to cloud from the G-forces. Then she threw the *Rap* into a teeth-chattering spin, sliding across space. She had the nose of the *Rapscallion* lined up with the Qaig ships as they passed. Soren hadn't fired a shot yet — didn't want to be too hasty, otherwise the ships might realize what she was up to and retaliate. As it was, and as before, it seemed they were more interested in keeping her from escaping than they were in destroying them. They were biding their time until reinforcements arrived.

Then Soren took out one of the ships with a single blast, right where the engines joined the back of the blocky ship. It exploded in a bloom of sparks, and the debris rattled against their shields like gravel on a windshield. An entire ship, gone.

Now the other ship was angry. It started firing on its own — stronger laser pulses, designed to maim, but it wasn't being all that careful. A single shot could tear right through their hull like tissue paper if the rapidly dwindling shields were down. And they were getting too damn close to that black hole, that gaping maw, darker than the surrounding space.

The ship had gotten behind her, and she was having a hard time avoiding the onslaught of laser fire, much less being able to get Soren lined up for a shot of their own. Each heartbeat felt like an eternity, inching them closer to the time when the larger ships would arrive. There was no promise that Thalia would be able to make another jump with the P2 drive this time.

She feinted right — the ship followed, and she swooped left, skidding again. The *Rap* rattled around her like an old station wagon instead of the sleek spacecraft that she'd known, but the ship held.

Soren saw her chance, and with unerring accuracy, fired another single bolt. Like a shooting star, it gleamed across the inky blackness of space, a brilliant red beam — and then it contacted the shield of the Qaig ship, where Soren had said there would be a weak spot, at the shield generator itself. The beam tore through the ship — and instead of exploding, the engines winked out, and the ship started drifting at an angle to them.

Right towards the black hole.

"Why do I have to go?" Donovan whined. "I'm ... being the medical officer."

"You're the only one fluent in Qaig. I need you to read whatever is on their engines, so we don't blow us all up," Soren said. Everyone was up on the Bridge — everyone except Bastian, who had not regained consciousness. Nora fidgeted in her chair, keeping an eye on the drifting Qaig ship as Soren outlined their plan.

"Right, right. Valid point," Donovan said, pushing his glasses back up his nose. His T-shirt was plastered to his chest with sweat, and he stunk. Nora sniffed — well, so did she, for that matter. Even the air scrubbers of the *Rap* couldn't carry that stale stench away. She rubbed her nose and tried not to breathe too deeply.

"All right. Donovan, Thalia, Sun, you're with me. The rest of you, get ready to bolt. If those Qaig destroyers show up and we're not back, you take off. That's an order."

"And if you get too close to the event horizon?" Nora asked. She rubbed damp palms against her legs. The flight suit was starting to chafe. She yearned for a shower and clean clothes — and a nap. A long, long nap.

"You take off," Soren articulated, meeting her gaze. "You keep fighting. Understood?"

"Yes ma'am," Nora said, swallowing hard. Not that they'd have much of a chance without the P2, but she'd try.

Nora watched the team leave the Bridge and head to the cargo bay. Asher peeled off and went back to take care of Bastian. Daven — the enigmatic gray J'nai scientist — silently made his way back to work on the P2. He'd felt confident he could have it ready by the time Soren and the rest of the crew returned.

Nora could see the security camera in the cargo bay on her console and brought up the window to the corner of her screen, keeping one eye on the Qaig ship and the black hole. The crew got into their clunky EVA suits. Donovan was given a blaster about the size of a handgun; Soren's looked more like a grenade launcher. Where it had been stashed, Nora had no idea, but she was sure she'd never seen the thing before. Somehow, the sight of it made her feel better.

Soren waved at the camera. Ready. The ship-wide intercom was still down, but the crew had ear buds and microphones in their EVA suits. Nora now had similar ones connected to the same frequency. Bluetooth technology — she couldn't help but grin. Sophie would love that. She missed Sophie and her roommates so much that for a moment, her vision blurred, and she had to blink rapidly to get herself back on task.

She nudged the *Rap* towards the disabled Qaig ship. The *Rap* had a docking door in the cargo bay, a small thing barely large enough for them to crawl through single file. It had been designed with other J'nai ships and PJs in mind. However, as the Qaig ships were supposedly based on old J'nai technology, they hoped it would work. None of them had heard of it being done before. Then again, you could say that about most of what Nora had been through in the past few days.

She used the smaller thrusters, and, with agonizing slowness, the *Rap* approached the blocky ship, which was only slightly larger than their craft. She identified what looked to be a docking hatch on the ship's aft and targeted it with her computer. It was a delicate maneuver — she doubted any neurosurgeon in the history of the universe had ever had to make movements so minute and precise. Centimeter by centimeter, the gap between the ships closed. Nora used the computer's docking assistance program to help match the other ship's speed, spin, and trajectory, before extending the docking clamp.

She missed. Metal grated on metal, sending tremors through the *Rap* like nails scrabbling down a chalkboard. She ignored Thalia's taunting voice coming through the earbuds and took a deep breath.

On the second attempt, the latches caught, the seal was made, and the walkway extended between them. The ships were joined with a startlingly flimsy umbilical cord. A twist of the ship, a single piece of space debris, and the cord would be severed; the occupants, jettisoned into space with no hope of rescue.

She swallowed hard.

"*Rapscallion* to Soren, come in," Nora said. A crackle, then —

"Loud and clear, Nora. See you in twenty minutes. Prepare for immediate departure," Soren said.

Even through the shoddy connection, Nora heard Thalia *hmph*, then, "We'll see. You can't rush perfection."

Nora sighed and rubbed the space between her eyebrows. She'd set a countdown clock on her console, based on the amount of time they'd spent in the Current, how long it would take the Qaig scouting ships to send a transmission back, and then the time it would take the larger ships to appear. They had less than two hours now, at best. It was an educated guess, but it would have to do. They were all out of options.

She watched the camera in the shuttle bay as the crew entered the airlock, one by one, and scuttled across the latch to the Qaig ship.

Soren had gone first, cutting open the hatch with a handheld blow-torch, and since there weren't any immediate gunshots or explosions, she was quickly followed by Donovan, Sun, and then Thalia.

"Entering what seems to be their cargo area," Soren narrated, her voice thick. She was panting in the heavy EVA suit — or possibly because of the size of the weapon she carried. Nora was alone now on the Bridge, perched like a hunched bird of prey over her console with its countdown and various screens — the cargo bay, the view screen with black hole. A cup of coffee cooled by her left hand. She was too intent on her task to remember it.

"Stairs — doors, and — nope, no, wrong turn," Soren muttered. There were some hushed sounds, then:

"The Bridge. It's sealed. Can't — well, doesn't matter. Moving on."

Minutes passed in silence. Each minute, they inched closer to the black hole and its point-of-no-return, the infamous event horizon. Not even the P2 could save them once they passed that mark. It was coming up on the front view panel now, not just on her sensors, as a brilliant orange glow, like a sunrise — but at the center, instead of a sun, was a well of deepest midnight.

"At the engine bay," Soren narrated. "Donovan, you're up."

For many long minutes, Donovan and Thalia and Sun worked, mostly grunting and occasional mumbles as Thalia must have pointed at various things she needed.

"Soren, we're down to an hour before the Qaig ships arrive, slightly less until event horizon," Nora warned.

"Understood. Thalia and Sun are returning now. Donovan and I will carry the larger pieces next, and..."

Boom.

Nora's eardrums vibrated, even though the noise was muffled somewhat by her ear buds. Out the front view panel, she could see sparks flying out of a giant hole in the side of the Qaig ship. Pieces of metal and something soft and dark flew by, too fast to recognize.

Worse still, the impact of whatever had exploded had sent the Qaig ship into a twisting motion. Nora fought to keep the *Rap* in sync, but she could *feel* the connections on the walkway tearing.

"Soren!" she shouted. "HURRY!"

She glanced at the cargo bay camera, her hand poised over the 'emergency detach' command for the airlock. Sun and Thalia stumbled through, their arms full of various tools. Donovan came next, with a massive bowl-shaped object that looked like it weighed a hundred pounds from the way he staggered. He dropped the item to the deck, and the *clang* reverberated all the way up to the Bridge.

"Soren?" Nora asked, heart thudding in her throat. Donovan rushed back into the airlock. Seconds later, he re-emerged, carrying a long, heavy item. Then he rushed back again — and he wasn't met by Soren.

Instead, a massive shape, clothed in dark material that must have been the equivalent of an EVA suit, came through the small tunnel. It had to be seven feet tall, its head shielded with a darkened dome. It was hard to see more detail on the small camera, but there was no mistaking the hulking creature. Behind it came Soren, her weapon trained on the thing. Something inside of Nora contracted, a squeezing sensation in her thorax like a vice.

"Soren," Nora whispered, her words barely making it past her lips. "Please tell me you didn't bring a Qaig on board."

"I brought a Qaig on board," Soren said, panting heavily. "Now get us the hell out of here."

Nora slammed the detach command, and the Qaig ship spun out of reach. She took the *Rap* into a steep acceleration, to put some distance between them. She glanced at the countdown clock — thirty minutes, give or take.

"Thalia, thirty minutes," Nora said, then took off her headset. She flung it across her console, and wiped the sweat from her face, fingers trembling. A Qaig. There was a *Qaig* on this ship with them. What was Soren thinking!?

"Not bad, cadet," Soren said, striding onto the Bridge. She dropped her weapon with a *thunk* against her captain's chair, and sat, heavily.

"Soren, what...?" Nora said, turning towards her. She couldn't even find words to express her incredulity. Her mouth just gaped open.

"It was lurking in the halls. Thought it might be useful to actually talk to one of these things, maybe we can find a weakness. Or get some information on their tech, and their ability to jump on and off the Current at least."

Soren ran a hand over her face, her usually lemon-colored skin covered with a layer of sweat and grime. She looked haggard, years older than — however old she was, anyway.

"So, what was that explosion?" Nora asked. On the screen, the Qaig ship dwindled, spiraling towards the black hole. She could hear a scuffle in the hallway behind them and shuddered. It seemed their prisoner did not want to come quietly. Soren glanced back at the hall before checking something on her console.

"Another Qaig holed up in the Bridge. Came after us in the engine room, guess it realized what we were after. It got a few shots off before I got it back," she said, patting the weapon beside her. It was then that Nora noticed a smear of black and red ichor across Soren's left arm, up to her shoulder. The sounds in the corridor intensified briefly, then were cut short by a *thunk*, and a clanking of chains that Nora could only assume were some sort of handcuffs or other restraining device.

"You — you're injured," Nora stammered, getting up. "Let me get, um…"

"Oh no, cadet, I know how you get around blood," Soren said with a smile. Then, of all things, the J'nai woman started laughing. She laughed and she laughed, until tears streamed from her green eyes. And Nora couldn't help it, the sound was infectious. It felt so good to laugh, to let the tension of the past few hours out. The entire situation was absurd. They were floating in a ruined ship. Their only hope of returning home involved hotwiring their own jerry-rigged P2 to bits of an alien supraluminal drive and doing it quickly. And they had a goddamned QAIG on board their ship.

They were still laughing when the Qaig destroyers showed up, a full twenty minutes ahead of schedule.

CHAPTER 16
SOPHIE, THE DESIDERATA

Sophie wasn't sure how they were going to make it back to the *Desiderata*. She was standing in the remains of the Bridge. The air lock had been decimated by Cat's projectile. The air had been sucked out of the room in a great gust, knocking her and Ty to the floor. Ty had recovered first, helping Sophie up and then getting Cat. He'd turned her over — her head lolled to the side, but she was breathing. Her breath fogged up the glass of her helmet where her mouth was closest. She could have been sleeping. She didn't appear hurt; she hadn't been under any of the falling debris. Sophie called her over their earbuds — nothing.

"CAT!" she yelled again. Ty winced, but Cat didn't flinch.

Around them, the station shuddered and groaned. She met Ty's eyes — wide, unblinking. She nodded and got up. He hefted Cat into his arms, leaving the battery behind. Sophie checked her pocket for the thumb drive — it was there, safe and sound in its little locked compartment — and grabbed her equipment. They'd have to leave Cat's sensors and the battery behind, there was no way to carry them and Cat — and it didn't appear that they'd have time to come back to get them, either. Another tremor shook the station, gently, like the aftershock of an earthquake.

Ty picked his way over the chunks of wall and shattered stumps of the support beams. The station's gravity emitters must have been damaged by Cat's actions, as they suddenly found themselves bounding over the mess instead of having to crawl over. Sophie's experience moving in a low-G scenario was largely limited to simulations in the Zero-G dome. The gravity on Callisto now seemed to be about equal to that on Ganymede, from what she could tell. Even small movements threatened to send her careening into walls, which were studded with all kinds of sharp ends, ready to tear into her EVA suit.

"Careful," Ty muttered. At least this meant Cat was lighter, too — Ty didn't seem to have any trouble, cradling her like a baby in his arms as he moved, bounding over the rubble, whereas before he'd been carefully threading his way through.

If it had seemed like days to make it from the ship to the Bridge, then it was weeks getting back. Instead of helping, the lack of gravity hindered them. Even Ty was having trouble — with his muscle bulk, he smacked his helmet on the ceiling more than once while simply taking a step forward. She didn't think he'd cracked his helmet, but each impact had her heart racing. A single crack, a single hairline fracture, could spell doom.

They were finally back in the hangar bay when another shudder went through the station, like a gently rolling wave. The motion set the loose materials in the hangar dome rattling — and sent a toolbox spinning into her.

The metal box only hit her gently, but it was enough to tip her over. She fell to her hands and knees, scrambling against the floor to steady herself.

And that's when she heard the rip.

A small corner of a metal floor panel was sticking up, barely noticeable. And it had caught the suit near her shin, snagging it, and then tearing.

A pinhole-sized puncture in her suit. She could see oxygen leaking out, like mist. An alarm blared in her ears, but she barely heard it. Her gloved hands scrabbled against the material, trying to stanch the flow of air, like blood streaming from an arterial wound.

Her palms were slick with sweat inside her gloves. Adrenaline surged through her, and her breathing became fast and ragged, just when she needed to keep it slow and steady to conserve what air she had left. She had to stop the leak. She had to — what could she use? She tried pinching the hole shut, but it barely helped. She looked around, for tape, or a bandage, or anything. She turned over the toolbox where it had fallen near her, opening drawers furiously, but all she found were screwdrivers and bolts and wire cutters. Where was the damn electrical tape? Maybe that would work, if her gloved hands could manage it. She bet there was some sort of patch material on the *Desiderata*, but that was so far away, so very very far, and she was suddenly so tired, and so cold…

And then she was being hoisted up around the waist. Ty tucked her under his arm like a football, aided by the low gravity, and leapt. While she'd been trying to fix her suit, he'd gotten Cat back to the ship and then come back for her. Despite the panic pulsing through her like molten lava, she felt like she was flying. Like he was Superman, and she was Lois Lane, as he leapt across the hangar bay in three great strides.

He crashed into the back of the ship, jarring her, rattling her head around inside the helmet. Her vision was turning dark; her fingers and toes were numb. Was this what it was like to die from hypoxia? If it was … well, she had a few regrets.

She faintly registered the door of the cargo bay closing. And then Ty was ripping her helmet off, and his own, calling to her as she gasped for air like a fish out of water. The recycled air of the ship, now re-pressurized, was sweet and warm. Gravity again surrounded her, like a blanket, a soothing weight, pressing her into the floor. Relief flooded her system, bringing with it a stinging sensation in her extremities. She coughed, inhaling deeply again, filling her lungs as if they could never be filled enough.

"Breathe, Sophie, breathe, that's it," he said. He sat on the floor with her, cradling her head in his lap. His dark eyes were rimmed with red, his skin shiny with sweat, but he had never looked more perfect to her. She coughed again, clearing her throat, and tried to look around.

"Cat?" she said, surprised at the hoarseness in her voice. Ty lay her down, letting her head rest gently on the floor, and moved to Cat, who was motionless a little way away from her. He took off Cat's helmet, and Sophie propped herself up on an elbow, still breathing hard. A tremor shook the ship, like a wave in a storm. The ship creaked softly around them. Ty put a hand on Cat's neck and nodded.

"She's breathing. And her heartbeat is strong. Cat?" he said, shaking her. Cat's head lolled to the side, like a broken doll.

"I got her," Sophie said, crawling over. "Can you get us out of here?"

He nodded and stood. Sophie knelt by her friend, and brushed strands of sweaty hair back from her too-pale face. Cat breathed softly, as if asleep.

"I... Jesus, I don't know what to do," Sophie said. "I don't know how to help her." Sophie was at a loss — Sophie, who had an answer for everything, was staring down at her friend's still face, completely baffled.

"Get her out of the suit. Get her warm. I'll come back down once we're en route," Ty said. He had turned to go up the stairs to the upper hall, which would lead him back to the Bridge.

Then he stopped. He came back and lifted Sophie to her feet by the front of her EVA suit. She squeaked in surprise — but the sound was cut short, as Ty bent his mouth to hers. He kissed her as if he were the one starving for air, holding her to him as if he were afraid she'd be ripped from him. She melted into the kiss, warmth filling her all the way to the tips of her still-tingling toes. He kissed her and kissed her, as if he could never have enough of it. And then he pulled back, panting, after a moment, pressing his forehead to hers, and sighed.

"Don't you ever scare me like that again," he said.

She nodded — for once, she was speechless.

CHAPTER 17

RAINA, GANYMEDE STATION

Despite her bravado, Raina was a little nervous about her plan. They hadn't heard anything from Sophie and Cat. She could only hope everything had gone according to schedule, and that they'd be returning just as the other PJs returned from their trip to the asteroid belt.

"Steady," Zoe murmured. They were sitting in the recreation dome, poised over their tablets, for all intents and purposes just two students, diligently at work. They shared a bench, like any park bench on Earth, and the Astroturf rolled out before them. Curfew had just been lifted for the day, so they had the place nearly to themselves. It could have been romantic, in other circumstances. Raina took a deep breath, filling her lungs, letting her entire body exhale the negative thoughts spinning through her.

Raina glanced upward. The rec dome and the hangar bay were attached by a series of airlock doors. They could see into part of the hangar bay as both domes had large, clear panels in parts of the ceiling. Overhead, Jupiter's eclipse was ending. It was a stunning display; the gas giant loomed over them in just the slimmest crescent of red and orange.

A PJ landed, but just one, not the small flotilla that had left for asteroid mining or whatever. A group of people disembarked and crammed into the airlock chamber. The crew of the shuttle emerged —

several Originals, she didn't know their names — followed by two girls and three boys, about their age or a little younger.

"Who's that?" Raina asked, frowning. Zoe leaned back, as if she were sun tanning — though, of course, there was no sun, just simulated sunlight and the reflective surface of Jupiter, twenty times as bright as a full moon.

"New recruits," Zoe murmured. "Since we're so short-staffed, Savaryn's bringing in all the Faxes he can, anyone that's close to being ready, without waiting for the start of the academic year since, you know, we have no idea if we'll ever be back in an academic year."

Raina considered. The five new cadets stayed with one of the officers, obviously waiting for something. They each had damp hair, freshly starched uniforms, and a backpack or duffle with them. Raina remembered the smell of the coma couch goo — the blue material that she was immersed in for over a month to make the trip from Earth to Jupiter, so that her body could withstand the massive acceleration forces. Forces like her friends were now undergoing on their trip to Callisto — fortunately, their trip was so short that any adverse effects should be minimized. Theoretically. They'd probably feel like they were hungover for a while if they got back. When they got back.

A pair of officers in crisp uniform came over, one J'nai and one human. They stood in front of the girls, arms crossed.

"Yes?" Raina asked. "Can I help you?"

"No loitering at any location except your room and your task space, Admiral's orders," the human one — a Xerxes clone — said, his handsome face contorted in a snarl.

"Relax, cupcake, I have permission," Raina said, and pulled up Aditi's message on her tablet, handing it to them. The J'nai officer didn't bother to read it, just glared at the girls with unblinking dark eyes.

"Everything appears to be in order," the Xerxes grumbled after taking way too long to read the brief message. He tossed the tablet back to Raina, then turned on his heel and left, the J'nai trailing after him.

"Good thing Aditi sent us those messages," Zoe murmured, watching their retreating figures. This spot in the Rec Dome was one of the "dead zones" in the station, where no sensors or monitors would pick up their words. Aditi had sent each girl a few excuses in case they were out and about — and just in time, too.

Raina snorted and looked back at the new group of cadets.

"So, what do you think," Zoe said, propping herself up on her elbows, eyeing the group. "Faxes or Originals?"

Raina looked them over. There was a girl who might have been Egyptian or Arabic, who stood straight and imperious. Two were definitely Einstein clones, with their bushy dark hair. They were being approached by a group of older Einsteins — the second largest Fax group on the station, behind da Vincis. The Einsteins liked to dye their hair crazy colors, for two reasons — one, it helped people tell them apart; two — they liked the attention and since hair color was not specifically addressed in the uniform guidelines, they pushed the limits. Two of the older Einsteins appeared to be graduates, and one younger one Raina knew from class, with bright pink hair he wore in a short spiky cut.

"What do you think? Cleopatra?" Zoe asked, eyeing the dark girl. The other girl and boy appeared to be Originals — they stood apart a little from the others, not talking, mostly just looking around themselves, gawking at the station. Raina remembered how that had felt — how cold, compared to her home; how foreign. It was only minimally better now, almost a year later. At least she had friends here. She remembered how it had felt, lining up in the giant hangar somewhere in northern Canada, seeing a PJ for the first time — how she'd been thrust into days of training before liftoff with a few other clueless cadets, one of whom had turned out to be Zoe. Even then, Zoe's optimism and work-ethic had impressed her. They'd been put through a battery of testing, physical and mental and psychological, before being told exactly who they were, and what their purpose was. She wondered if the crazy-haired man who'd instructed her and Zoe was still there, scaring class after class of cadets with his talk of the coma-tank goo and effects of gravitational forces on the human body. Still, once he'd mentioned they'd be going to a top-secret station on Ganymede and — oh yeah, meeting *aliens* — every single one of them had volunteered to go.

Sometimes, Raina wondered what the Board would do if someone backed out or changed their mind. What would happen if Earth knew about the Board secretly cloning the most brilliant minds of the past — to build the future. She suspected there were severe measures in place to make sure that didn't happen — after all, both Cat and Nora's host families had "conveniently" died when they attempted to keep the girls on Earth, to give them a little more time, or a chance at a normal life.

"I didn't think they made any Cleopatra clones," Raina said after a moment, checking her tablet — the rest of the PJs should be returning from their mining mission momentarily. "DNA was too corrupted, or something." Her mind was still buzzing — would she have been content staying on Earth, if she knew something like this existed, that she had a chance to be a part of it?

If she had known that Zoe existed?

"Maybe," Zoe said, startling Raina out of her thoughts. Then, she jumped up and strolled over to the new group, waving. Raina rolled her eyes but followed. The last thing she needed right now was a distraction.

"Hi!" Zoe said, extending a hand for the new girl to shake, the one she thought was another Fax from the way the other Original students seemed to be avoiding her. "I'm Zoe. I'm a Fax — uh, a clone of Zenobia, third-century Syrian bad-ass. This here is Raina," she said, slinging an arm around her, which Raina didn't shrug off. "Raina is a Rani Lakshmibai clone, an Indian Queen. Welcome to Ganymede!"

The girl looked them over, then shook Zoe's proffered hand.

"I'm Aziza. I'm a clone of Arsinoe IV, sister to Cleopatra," she said. Her voice sounded raspy, and the acrid scent of the blue coma couch goo clung to her.

"Good guess, Raina!" Zoe said, beaming. "We thought you might be a Cleopatra."

"Well, you're still another queen anyway, if I remember my history," Raina said. The girl gave her an appraising look.

"You do," she said simply. "Are you the ones who are supposed to show us to our rooms?"

"Uh, no," Zoe said, shaking her head. "We just saw you all

standing here and wanted to introduce ourselves. It can be a little over-whelming being a Fax here."

"Why do you call yourself that?" Aziza asked. The girl did not smile at all. Zoe was trying her best to be welcoming, but the girl was not cracking.

"You know, copies. Clones. Facsimiles. We're Faxes, and your friends over there," Zoe said, pointing at the boy and the girl who stood apart, "we call Originals."

"Cute," Aziza said, running a hand through her damp hair. A wash of goo smell — akin to vinegar — hit Raina's nose, and she sneezed.

"Well, anyway, nice to meet you," Zoe said, as Raina grabbed her arm, nodding back to the bench. Aziza nodded, returning her attention to the other new students with her.

"Come on, it's almost time," Raina hissed, looking down at her tablet. Just a few minutes now. "Besides, she didn't want to talk."

"She will," Zoe said, sitting back on her bench, watching the small group meet up with another cadet, who led them out of the dome. "Being a Fax here — being a girl here, hell just *being* here is hard. I can't imagine going through it all without friends."

"Yeah," Raina said, rubbing at a smudge on her tablet screen. "Did you see how the Originals stood apart? Like it's already been ingrained into them."

"Maybe they're just shy," Zoe said, cocking an eyebrow. Raina shrugged.

"Yeah, maybe."

"Is it really so hard to believe that someone wouldn't want to talk to you clones?" a boy's voice drawled. "Maybe they're tired of all your 'high and mighty' attitudes."

Raina's face flushed with anger, and she gripped the tablet so tightly that the frame cracked. Zoe put a hand on her arm. Raina took a deep breath — the boy was one of the Originals in a class or two above theirs, she couldn't remember his name. He was stocky, with sandy hair and freckles. He had his hands stuffed in his uniform pockets and walked with two other friends, one of whom was tossing a football around. People always came to the rec dome for some space and activity. It just so happened that teasing Faxes — and Faxes teasing Originals, if Raina was honest — was a favorite pastime to many.

"You're right," Raina said, giving him a big smile. It probably looked creepy, judging by the strange look on his face. "Why would anyone want to talk to a boring old clone like me when they could talk to someone as stimulating as … what was your name again? John? James?"

"Russell," the kid mumbled. "Just what we needed — more clones," he said, eyeing the newcomers who were just leaving the dome. Zoe shrugged, and leaned back again on the bench, hands resting over her belly, eyes closed like she was so bored that she was napping. Raina fumed but continued to give the kid her silent creepy smile, staring him down. Eventually, he shrugged and left.

"That was a new one," Zoe said after a moment.

"Channeling my inner Sophie a little," Raina said, checking her tablet — any second now.

"You still want to hit him, don't you?"

"Oh yeah," Raina said, glaring at the boy, who was now tossing the football back to his friends.

"Here they come," Zoe said, sitting up. Raina looked down at her tablet — the command for the virus she'd planted in the hangar bay doors was a glowing red button on her tablet screen. She'd set a small receiver into the wiring for the door. One touch, and the wires would short out. She glanced into the hangar dome, where a couple of PJs were landing. A flurry of activity was taking place on the hangar floors — crew and cleaning bots all rushing to the ships.

"And here we go," Raina said. She looked up, locking eyes with Zoe. She took another deep breath and pushed the button.

A dull thud boomed through the dome. The lights in the hangar bay dimmed, flickered — then went out. Red emergency lights came on, and a pulsing alarm sounded.

"Oops," Raina said. Zoe was already up and running toward the hangar bay. Raina tucked the tablet into her jacket and followed, annoyed at Zoe's speed.

People were piling out of the airlocks. She struggled to see into the hangar — the red lights blinked, then stabilized. The alarm was so loud, she couldn't hear anything else. PuddleJumpers landed awkwardly on the hangar floor, some skidding and leaving trails of sparks in their wake. Crews mostly stayed onboard their ships — it was safer there, since the ships were pressurized, but the hangar workers were scrambling. The doors, which usually looked like a translucent veil, a shimmering waterfall of a force field that kept oxygen and gravity in while allowing the PJs to pass through unscathed, were sputtering, threatening to go completely out.

Well, that hadn't been part of the plan. It was supposed to go out for a few seconds, then come back. Just long enough to create some distraction.

People were definitely distracted. Another group of J'nai and humans poured from the airlock, gasping.

And then she saw them. She grabbed Zoe's arm and pointed.

Struggling toward the airlock were Ty and Sophie.

And in Ty's arms, the limp form of Cat.

"This way!" Zoe said, putting an arm around Sophie. Raina pushed through the crowd ahead of them, screaming at them to make way, they had a medical emergency. The crowd parted reluctantly, but they did part. Raina didn't give them an option. She pushed through like a freight train, Ty and the others close behind her. She was vaguely aware of others behind them as well, holding injured arms, or limping heavily. In all the activity, it would be easy enough to dismiss Cat's comatose state as another victim of the force field accident — or so she hoped.

"Medical emergency! MOVE!" she shouted, using her arms to force her way through. The crowd was loud and packed with people yelling and shouting — but she persisted. She might be shorter than Zoe or Ty, but what she lacked in height, she made up for with attitude — and then some.

"What happened?" she heard Zoe pant behind her, as the crowd finally thinned towards the back of the Rec Dome.

"Long story," Sophie said, also panting, winded. "She passed out on Callisto. Hasn't come to since."

"Also, she kind of blew up Callisto Station," Ty rumbled. Raina's head whipped around, and he shrugged, adjusting his hold on Cat. The girl looked unnaturally pale.

"She … okay," Raina said, taking a deep breath. She pinched the bridge of her nose, breathing in and out again. Shouting at them wouldn't help.

"We can't go to the Medical Bay," Zoe said softly. They had stopped at the edge of the Rec Dome — but Zoe was right. There would be too many questions about how and why Cat had been injured.

"Our room, then," Sophie said, snapping her fingers at her decision. "Raina, run and get Wesley. Zoe, get Aditi. Get them to the room."

"It will be tough to get Aditi away from this," Zoe said, gazing back at the crowded Rec Dome. The claxon had stopped, but red lights still flashed in the hangar bay. Raina thought that meant that the seal had been restored. She hoped.

"It's an emergency!" Sophie screeched. A few neon-haired Einsteins glanced at them, then continued their rapid walk to the mess ahead. Sophie closed her eyes, thinking.

"Get Jaxon, then," Raina said, putting a hand on Zoe's arm. Zoe looked down at her, an unreadable expression in her dark eyes. Raina swallowed hard. After a minute, Zoe nodded, then took off, her long legs soon carrying her out of sight.

"See you soon," Raina said, brushing a frizzy curl out of Cat's eyes. Then, she ran to the medical wing.

Once there, Wesley was easy to find. He was sitting on an empty cot in the main area, legs crossed, looking at something on his tablet.

"Raina," he said, cocking his head. "What are you…"

"Cat's been injured," she snapped, grabbing his arm. "We need you."

He leapt up, tablet abandoned on the cot.

"What kind of injury?" he said, throwing a short white coat over his uniform. He went to the cabinet behind the cot and opened various drawers, grabbing things seemingly at random. Gauze, a thermometer, a blood pressure cuff.

"No idea. They said she passed out," Raina said. She wanted to scream in frustration — they needed to go, *now*. Wesley was hunting for something in the cabinet, slamming drawers shut and rustling through others.

"How long?" he asked.

"I don't *know* — at least a few hours," she said, biting her lip. Finally, he seized a small rectangular device triumphantly, raising the orange case overhead.

"Aha!" he said and stuffed it into his pocket. He dipped his head again to look for something else.

"Oh, come on!" Raina said, stomping her foot. She grabbed his arm and yanked. It threw him off-balance, but he complied and followed her out of the medical wing and down the corridors to Room 10013.

"When did they get back?" Wesley asked. Raina shot him a glance — she supposed Ty had filled him in on their little excursion.

"Just now. We snuck them out of the hangar bay and they're bringing her to our room," Raina explained.

"How did you get them out of the hangar bay?" he asked, hurrying to keep up with her.

"I shut off the force field over the PJ entrance. Set off some alarms," she said shrugging. So, the field had been down longer than she'd expected — no one had gotten seriously injured, right? She was lucky to have gotten Wesley out of the medical wing before any wounded had arrived, she thought.

"And how did…"

"More walking, less talking," Raina said, gripping his arm and propelling him forward, for all that he was over a foot taller than her. He was all gangly limbs, draped in his white coat like a cape fluttering out behind him. He reminded her of a crane or a stork.

She threw open the door to her room and pushed the stork inside.

"Got him," she panted, slamming the door behind her.

Cat was laid out on her bunk, the lower one, nearest the door. Wesley rushed to her side, fumbling in his pockets for that orange device. He stuck her finger with a needle and ushered the drop of blood into a cartridge at the end of the device. The screen started a countdown, promising results.

"What is that?" Sophie asked. Raina looked — Zoe wasn't back yet.

"It'll give me some basic labs on her," he said, checking her pulse, pulling up her eyelids. Checking to make sure she was breathing. He moved with a rapid efficiency even Raina couldn't criticize. This was his element; Cat was his patient. She stepped back, arms crossed.

"What happened?" he asked, removing the stethoscope from his ears. He glanced to the device — still ticking.

"Um," Sophie said, biting her lip. She looked at Ty, who shrugged.

"We don't really know," Ty rumbled. "She pushed a metal strut, then fainted."

"What he means to say is that our tiny little kitten here launched a two-ton — conservatively — metal beam across Callisto like it was nothing, setting off a chain reaction that ultimately detonated the fusion reactor," Sophie said, flipping her long hair back over her shoulder. "And then, she fainted."

Wesley looked at Sophie, as if expecting her to say 'Gotcha!' or some such thing, but she didn't.

"I mean, the gravity is much lower there, right?" he asked quietly, stepping back from Cat's bunk.

"Gravity emitters were still on, a solid 1 G in the station," Sophie said.

"And the beam weighed how much?" Wesley asked, his voice even softer.

"I couldn't move it," Ty offered. "Wouldn't even budge."

"She was like, in a trance," Sophie said, waving her hands. "The beam had fallen and blocked our exit. We had no way out, until she blasted that thing."

"Did she... did she complain of a headache prior to the event?" Wesley asked, not taking his eyes off Cat.

"Yes," Sophie said, nodding emphatically. "Why, does that matter?"

"Maybe," he muttered. The little orange device beeped, and he picked it up.

"Ok — her blood urea nitrogen is elevated; her glucose is low…"

"What does that mean?" Raina asked, tapping her foot.

"She's hungry. And thirsty," Wesley said, straightening. "She needs fluids, and an MRI. We have to take her to the medical wing."

"And tell them what, that she collapsed after throwing a 4,000-pound metal beam like a javelin?" Sophie said, frowning. "No way. Treat her here."

"No," Wesley said, shaking his head. Raina had to hand it to him, she was a little impressed with the way he was standing up to Sophie. "Take her to the medical wing. We'll tell them she collapsed in the Rec Dome after Raina's stunt — I mean, the force field malfunction," he said, glancing at her. Raina nodded.

"He's right, she needs a real doctor," Raina said. "No offense," she added, and Wesley nodded.

"None taken. Besides, my attending knows her. Knows we've been watching her."

Sophie clearly didn't like this, but she was outnumbered, and she knew it.

"Fine!" she said, throwing up her hands. "Let's go."

They finally made it to the medical wing, Ty once more carrying the unconscious Cat. Zoe was there already. There were a few more people in the large bay, at least half a dozen with small injuries — cuts, bruises, maybe one with a broken arm, Raina thought, checking each as they passed. Nothing major. Inwardly, she beamed. She'd created quite the distraction.

Ty lay Cat down gently on an empty cot at the back of the bay, Wesley rushing around her, hooking up monitors around her arm, on her finger. Sophie stood at the head of the bed, fingering strands of silver-streaked brown hair. There were more and more of them, it seemed, like strands of glitter, or stars.

A dark-skinned man in a power wheelchair came over, his fingers grazing a control panel on the armrest.

"Wesley, what is this?" he asked, gesturing to the crowd gathered around Cat's cot. Raina scowled at him.

"Doctor Adebayo, these are Catherine's roommates," Wesley said. "They found her collapsed in the Rec Dome and called me for help."

"Well," the doctor said, eyeing each of them. "I'm going to have to ask you all to leave. We'll update you on her status as soon as we are able."

"No way," Raina said, putting her foot down — literally. "We're not going anywhere."

"Now, miss..."

"No," she said again, crossing her arms. "And it seems to me you're wasting time arguing with me when you should be taking care of my friend."

Doctor Adebayo threw up his hands.

"Would that we all had such loyal friends," he said gallantly, maneuvering his chair to Cat's bedside. "Would you at least step back? You're in the way."

Raina — and the others — acquiesced, giving the doctor and Wesley room to work.

"She'll be fine," Zoe said, putting an arm around her. Raina sniffed.

"You don't know that," she said. Zoe squeezed her shoulders.

"I do," Zoe said firmly. "Because they know you'll unleash hell if anything happens to her."

At this, Raina couldn't help but laugh, a short sound, cut short by another sniffle.

"Damn right," she said. "Did you end up finding Aditi?"

"No," Zoe admitted, "but I did find Jaxon. He said he'd find us when he could."

Sophie pulled her tablet out of her coat pocket and started typing. Wesley and Dr. Adebayo were in quiet conversation at Cat's side, the older man nodding as Wesley outlined a plan. A moment later, and they were wheeling her to a back room for "imaging."

Raina, Zoe, Sophie, and Ty stood there for a moment, not sure what to do next. Sophie continued to type furiously on her tablet, until —

"Aha! We've been summoned to Dean Prasad's office," she said, stashing the tablet back into her coat. "Let's go."

A diti was alone when they arrived, but Jaxon got there at nearly the same time. Aditi waved her hand around her office.

"Don't worry, I had the bugs removed. It's safe to talk here," she said. Sophie let out a long breath and collapsed into a chair opposite Aditi's desk. Ty moved to stand behind her, placing a hand on her shoulder. Sophie beamed up at him, but Raina could see the dark circles under her eyes. Sophie would have been mortified if Raina mentioned them though, so she kept quiet.

"How is Cat?" Aditi asked, as calm as if she were asking about the weather.

"We don't know," Sophie said, biting her lip again. "She's in the medical wing. Dr. Adebayo and Wesley are taking care of her."

Jaxon moved to take the other chair in front of Aditi, so Zoe and Raina stood back, behind Sophie, like sentinels.

The teal-skinned J'nai prince leaned forward, moving his chair so that he faced Sophie instead of Aditi.

"What happened?" he asked, hands clasped in front of him, face grave. Sophie took a deep breath, and filled them in. On the files she'd managed to download from the computers in the Bridge. On the way the station had collapsed around them, trapping them.

And then how Cat had single-handedly launched a steel strut halfway across the moon, collapsing what was left of the station. How they'd been about halfway back to Ganymede, Cat lying unconscious in the Bridge, when the ship's computers had noted the 'spontaneous' emission of radioactive particles from Callisto — the fusion core had failed, and the tritium had leaked, possibly forever contaminating the planet's useable water supply.

Sophie glanced for a moment between Aditi and Jaxon, but they didn't reprimand her, so she continued. She mentioned how the trip back was moderately horrible due to the Xenon drives and subsequent

G-forces but otherwise unremarkable, except that Cat hadn't woken up.

"I mean, I checked her pulse, and that seemed all right. She was breathing. She just wouldn't wake up," Sophie said, tears starting to fall. Ty's hand on her shoulder tightened, and Sophie grabbed at it, seemingly glad of the contact.

"So, it appears that Cat is what, telekinetic?" Aditi asked, leaning back in her chair. Her lips were a thin line.

"Telekinetic? I am not familiar with that word," Jaxon admitted, looking lost.

"It means she can move things with her mind," Raina said sharply, as the implication of Cat's stunt sank in.

"And ... this is something that humans do?" Jaxon asked, incredulous.

"No," Zoe said. "But it is something that *this* human does. Something that Cat does, apparently."

"There has to be a reasonable explanation," Aditi said, sitting up. "A fluctuation in the gravitational field of the station, perhaps. The gravity emitters were old, unstable, it makes sense."

"No. It's happened before, here, on Ganymede," Sophie said. All heads turned to her, and she sighed.

"She gets headaches, and then things happen. Usually it's lights flickering or something, but she broke a part of the big telescope once, and she blew up a light in the medical wing — just ask Wesley," she said. There was a long moment of silence.

"Interesting," Jaxon said. Raina glared at him.

"Interesting? My friend is unconscious, you blue elf! She might not ever wake up! She did this for *you*, made this crazy trip and all for you, and you say she's INTERESTING?"

"Whoa now," Zoe said, reaching for her. Raina ripped her arm away, furious.

"My apologies," Jaxon said, unruffled. "I did not mean to offend. Of course, I wish Cat the best, and I will make sure that all J'nai resources are put at the disposal of your medical teams to help her when she is awake again."

"Some promise," Raina huffed. "We can't even contact Terra Prime. How are you going to get your fancy doctors here, huh?"

"I'm working on it," he said, a small smile on his lips.

"It's all my fault," Sophie said, slouching in her chair. "Cat wouldn't have gone if I hadn't asked her to."

"Sophie, it's not your fault. You three pulled off a remarkable feat," Aditi said soothingly. "I only regret putting you in this position to begin with."

"No," Sophie said, shaking her head. "It needed to be done."

"I just wish we didn't come back empty handed," Ty said, looking at Jaxon. "I'm sorry, there was no salvaging any of the communications equipment, and then we had to leave in a rush. Whatever is left is useless now."

Jaxon waved a hand, dismissing the apology, but then —

"What of the data you pulled off the computers?" he asked.

"Project *Tabula Rasa*?" Sophie said, sniffling.

Aditi and Jaxon exchanged a glance.

"You don't think …" Jaxon started.

"Savaryn never … he would never…" Aditi interrupted.

"What? What is it?" Raina asked, frustrated. Her hands clenched at her sides. Aditi took a deep breath.

"Sophie, may I see the thumb drive?" Aditi asked, holding out her hand. Sophie handed it over, and Aditi plugged it into the laptop on her desk. The rest of them crowded around behind her, peering at the screen, but the words didn't make sense. It seemed to be a series of word documents, some with just long strands of letters for thousands of pages or more. A, C, G, and T, on repeat, in various configurations.

"Aditi, what are we looking at?" Sophie asked as Aditi scrolled through, clicking and moving.

"Project *Tabula Rasa*, or 'blank slate,'" Aditi said, her voice barely a whisper. "I thought this was hypothetical, a rumor, but…"

"When Iyle and Savaryn started working together, they wanted a way to exterminate the Qaig, in retaliation to what had been done to my people," Jaxon said. He stood up, arms crossed. "This is not something I am proud of. But the project was an idea, a kind of biological weapon, that would infect and kill the Qaig. Like a virus, it would replicate, over time destroying all Qaig. It would take time, years even, to be symptomatic, ensuring that it would spread without detection among all of the Qaig colonies."

"That's… definitely illegal," Zoe said, frowning. "Isn't there some sort of law against using biological weapons?"

"Only on Earth," Aditi said. "No such laws govern Terra Prime, or Ganymede. There were supplements added to the Geneva Protocol in the 1970s of course, but the Admiral ignored them. But this idea was shot down, years ago."

"If it was shut down, then what are we looking at here?" Sophie asked, the lines of letters streaming by on the screen.

"I don't think," Aditi said slowly, leaning back, the screen frozen on a journal entry, presumably by some scientist working on the project. Whatever Aditi was reading had her stunned. Her hands drifted from the computer, as if she'd been a puppet whose strings had just been cut. "I don't think there was ever a radiation leak on Callisto. I think Savaryn was trying to cover up *this*," she whispered, and gestured at the computer. "The virus they came up with didn't just kill Qaig.

"It killed all the J'nai on Callisto, too."

CHAPTER 18
NORA, THE RAPSCALLION

"Well ..." Nora said, frowning. That wasn't supposed to happen. Her extrapolation had been accurate — how were the Qaig here so early? Her gaze — and Soren's — were fixed on their consoles, at the glowing icons of the enemy ships.

"What's the status on the subluminal drives?" Soren asked, her voice soft, like she didn't really want Nora to hear her or much less answer. Like she knew what Nora would say.

"Not good," Nora said, pulling her chair back up to Bastian's console. *Her* console. Her heart thudded painfully as she thought of Bastian, unconscious and broken just a few feet away. He'd know what to do in a situation like this, she thought. He always knew what to do.

She pushed those thoughts from her mind. The two large Qaig ships, like skyscrapers laid on their sides, were moving towards them. Even at their sedate pace, they didn't have twenty minutes. Even pushing the *Rap* to full thrust — which wasn't much at this point — they didn't stand a chance.

And then, a swarm of smaller Qaig scouting ships whirled out of each larger ship, heading toward them like a deadly horde of bees.

Well, that settled it. Nora couldn't outrun *that*.

"Thalia, we have company," Nora shouted into her headset, hoping Thalia hadn't removed hers yet.

She hadn't.

"Looks like you were wrong about the timeframe," Thalia gasped, like she was moving something heavy. Nora rolled her eyes.

"Yeah. Anyway. How much time do you need?"

"A few days would be nice, maybe a week?"

Nora groaned. This was not the time for Thalia's sarcasm. Soren strode over, taking the headset from Nora and shouting into it.

"You have five minutes before you need to get us back on the Current. Make it count. It doesn't have to be the final fix, we just need you to buy us some time," Soren said.

"Why don't you buy *me* some time?" Thalia huffed, then the channel went silent. Nora and Soren exchanged a glance, then Nora looked back at her console. At the Qaig swarm approaching them, little green fireflies on her monitor.

At the black hole.

No way. It was a crazy idea.

But she was all out of options. And she could do it. She could give Thalia all the time she needed.

Nora grabbed the controls and maxed out the subluminal engines. The *Rap* groaned, a sound like a metallic whale, and responded to the commands, gradually gaining speed.

"We can't outrun them," Soren reminded her, grasping the back of her chair as she looked over Nora's shoulder.

"No," Nora said, pursing her lips. "But if they want to try to herd us like before, they'll have to outflank us. They can't do that if we have the event horizon at our back. Plus," Nora said, gripping the steering with one hand and letting her other start the calculations of the black hole's gravity on the console screen, "we can buy Thalia some time. They'll be too afraid of the gravity to come after us," she said.

"With good reason," Soren said flatly.

"Their sensors have to be more accurate than ours ... no way I can make them cross the event horizon on accident, so I'll have to cut it close," Nora said, mostly to herself as she calculated the course.

"Can you do that?" Soren asked. Her tone was nearly reverent.

"Probably," Nora said, frowning. "Yes. Yes, I can do it. The P2 should be able to get us out of the black hole's gravitational field before we cross the event horizon. The time dilation ... well, I can't calculate it perfectly. But it will be like having a wall on one side of us — they'll only be able to come at us from the other side."

Soren considered.

"Well, I don't have any better ideas. Let's do it," Soren said, returning to her captain's chair. "Caution, Nora. We don't need a lot of time. Don't take any risks that you don't have to.

"Attention, this is Soren," she broadcast over the ship-wide intercom. "We are being approached by a Qaig fleet. Until we can jump to the Current, we're going to be skirting around a black hole to avoid capture. It could get … messy. Hang on."

On Nora's screen, the black hole was just that — a hole. A black circle no more than a centimeter across. The event horizon — that point of no return, that line which, once crossed, could not be uncrossed, not even with the P2 — was a thin ring of green around it. And the *Rapscallion*'s red arrow was making a beeline for that ring.

On her front view panel, the black hole was much more impressive. She hadn't gotten a good look at it before because it was mostly at their stern and, more importantly, she'd been fighting for her life and hadn't had time for sightseeing.

It wasn't really black, or at least not all of it. It was a massive dark sphere, with a halo of reddish light around it — an accretion disc, from matter it had caught in its gravitational tendrils. Around the equator there was another halo of light, a ring, like those of Saturn. It made the black hole appear to have two halos at perpendicular angles, when Nora knew really there was only one — it was the massive gravity of the black hole itself that bent the light at such an extreme angle that it made the light appear as if it were an equatorial ring. She made sure to snap a few photos with the ship's lead camera as they went. She wanted to be able to look over them later — if there was a later. She wouldn't believe she had the audacity to do such a crazy stunt otherwise.

They were at an incredible distance from it still. In size, she had nothing to compare it to. On her screen, the measurements of the black hole itself were something like a hundred miles across, but the rings spread out significantly farther, as did the event horizon. It was hard to focus on anything — not even the impending capture or death behind her — when confronted with such a view.

"Here's hoping the gravity from the black hole will mess with their traction beams, too," Nora said, mostly to herself again. She took the *Rap* on a course parallel to the event horizon, hopefully close enough that no Qaig ships could flank them, and far enough away not to be pulled into the black hole themselves. The best she could hope for was a stalemate that would be broken when Thalia fixed the P2. Hopefully, it wouldn't take weeks to fix it, as Thalia had initially stated. Nora wondered if she could stray a little closer to the black hole — but she couldn't bear the consequences if she was wrong. If she returned to a Ganymede that was ten, or twenty, or fifty years older than it had been when she left. If her roommates had died of old age, while she had remained young.

She looked up, and the Qaig ships already seemed to be holding back — not as brash as she was about the effects of the black hole.

She ran the calculations again, using her best estimates from the ship's equipment and sensors. The *Rap* ran a steady course as she furiously typed — fingers that had once danced across ivory piano keys now unerringly calculated the ship's trajectory. Numbers and letters fell from her lips as she mumbled, "… where c is the speed of the light, M is the mass of the black hole… *zut*, well, we have the radius and the gravitational constant so…"

Equations tumbled onto her screen. She'd memorized them in her physics class — but never did she think she'd be using them like this. The idea that the event horizon — that limit beyond which the escape velocity would have to be faster than the speed of light — wasn't a sharp, well-defined boundary but possibly something fuzzier was a reality that she didn't want to think about too much. She just wanted to stay close, but not too close. Keep her ship in the Goldilocks zone. If the Qaig ships started to flank her, she moved closer to it. When they backed off, she knew she was straying too far towards the black hole. She only hoped that they wouldn't use that to their advantage and trick her into moving too far back to use the horizon as her safety blanket anymore. So far, so good.

"Just keep at it," Soren said, standing, her back cracking as she stretched. "I'm going to check on the crew, see if I can't persuade Thalia to hurry up," she said. She left the Bridge, then stopped, looking back at her grenade launcher. She met Nora's gaze, grinned, considered, then left without it.

"Sure," Nora said, breathing out. No big deal. She popped in her earbuds, turned up the Rachmaninoff, and flew on.

I t took Thalia about sixteen hours, but she got them back on the Current, and it seemed like this time, it would last. Nora hadn't had too much trouble from the smaller Qaig ships. As she'd thought, they couldn't maneuver her the way they had before, not when she had the gravity well at her side. She'd gotten Thalia the time she needed. Nora felt like she'd gotten away with the heist of the millennium.

Towards the end though, the Qaig had realized what the *Rap* was up to and had switched from their attempts to capture the *Rapscallion* to an active destruction mode again. The *Rap* had taken a number of hits, and she honestly wasn't sure the shields or the subluminal engines could take much more.

Soren had rushed up to the Bridge, strapping herself into her chair in a flurry of movement.

"We're on, get ready," she'd said. Microseconds later, she'd felt the familiar *pop*, like a champagne cork, as they entered the supraluminal superhighway of the Current.

Asher had come back to the Bridge then. There were streaks of blood — Bastian's blood — on his uniform. Nora couldn't look at him. Given how long he'd been absent from the Bridge, she could only imagine Bastian's status was critical.

"How is he?" she asked through gritted teeth. The *Rap* was pulling, like it wanted to jump back off the Current, a maneuver that would splatter them in a trail a million miles long across the universe. Asher worked at his console to her right, plugging in their coordinates and destination. It looked like they'd actually been going the wrong way from Ganymede during their short jumps, but since they were all pretty short, it would take them just slightly longer than the usual 72-hours to get back.

Back home. Nora swore she'd kiss the ground of the hangar bay the moment she got off the *Rap*.

"Stable," Asher said at last. "We couldn't keep his pain controlled with the medications without sedating him. Daven intubated him," Asher said. The last member of Thalia's crew and the only J'nai, Daven, was an enigma. He was gaunt, and gray, and bald. And grumpy. But apparently brilliant, and Nora was grateful for whatever medical training he possessed in addition to his astrophysics background. Still, being intubated didn't sound like a good thing.

"And his ... wounds?" Nora asked. With Asher's coordinates entered, the *Rap* evened out, no longer veering left and right like a shopping cart with a wonky wheel.

Asher glanced back at Soren before speaking.

"Daven and Donovan are working on that now, cleaning them up and putting in some stitches," Asher said, his voice flat and calm. "He'll need a proper doctor once we get back. Then we'll see."

"Then we'll see," Nora said. Asher didn't mention Bastian's eyes. That couldn't be a good sign.

Nora took a deep breath, relaxing slightly. The *Rap* would be somewhat on autopilot for a while, as long as Thalia kept them on the Current. It didn't need her constant supervision for the moment.

She rolled her head on her shoulders, hearing creaks and pops. How long had she been sitting in that chair? Her stomach rumbled, so it must have been a while.

"Why don't you take a break," Soren said. "I'll watch the system for a while. Get some food, take a nap. I'll wake you when we need to switch."

Nora nodded, suddenly exhausted. A nap sounded amazing.

She drifted down the hall, feeling like a ghost, to the kitchen, where she helped herself to a meal bar and some water. She stood in the small galley, leaning back against the sink. From here, she could see the door to the captain's quarters. Which was now the sick bay, where Bastian lay, unconscious, maybe permanently blinded.

The meal bar tasted even more like dirt than usual, but she swallowed it down.

On her way to the cargo bay, to gather her shower things and a clean flight suit, she spotted Harris and Sun outside the crew quarters. The door to the room was cracked a few inches, and they crowded to get a glimpse inside.

"Oh, shove off, mate," Harris said. He had a prominent nose and a mole on his right cheek — a cheek which was now squashed against the wall, as Sun pushed down on his shoulders so she could peek inside, too. Nora drifted silently over to them. Did she want to look inside? Did she want to come face to face with the terror that was the Qaig? Her curiosity bested her, and when Sun and Harris edged back from the door to continue their shoving contest, she jumped in and put her eye to the crack.

Whatever she'd been expecting, the truth was a million times stranger. He — it? — was like a seven-foot human-frog hybrid. Even sitting slouched on the bottom bunk in the crewman's quarters, it was clear that he was too big for the space. His head was shiny and slimy and domed, and his green-brown mottled skin was covered with fine warty growths that appeared to be dry and cracking. His eyes were closed, and he appeared to be resting or maybe sleeping. Breath gurgled out through his wide, lipless mouth in a kind of crackly noise. Thick chains had been wrapped between his wrists and ankles, effectively chaining him to the bed, though it didn't look like he'd made much of an attempt to escape. He wore a green suit that appeared to have been modeled after J'nai EVA suits, adapted for his own unique anatomy. His hands were webbed and clasped together in his lap.

His eyes opened; great yellow orbs scored with vertical pupils caught Nora in a gaze as fierce as a laser. Nora leapt back — toppling Harris and Sun over in the process. The door slammed shut, the sound reverberating down the hall. Sun shoved Harris off her, muttering something in Chinese.

"Sun! Get your ass back down here," Thalia's voice screeched from engineering down the hall. Harris and Sun exchanged a glance, then hurried towards her. Nora looked back at the door — the creature inside wasn't making any noise. Her heart, though, was hammering so hard in her chest that she was sure he could hear it. This was the enemy, who she was sure would destroy them all the second he got loose. She felt fear, true — but also curiosity, and maybe a little pity for the creature they'd brought on board and chained. She tried to sort out her feelings as she made her way to gather her things and then head for a shower, but if anything, she only felt more confused.

Cleaned and fed, she felt nearly human again, and more tired than she'd ever been in her life. She wanted to sleep forever — but first, she had to see Bastian. She'd put it off long enough.

She stood outside his door for what seemed like an eternity, before knocking. No one answered, so she opened the door. It was unlocked, which momentarily made her grin.

The sight before her, however, wiped any trace of amusement from her entire soul.

Bastian was laid out on his bed, a blanket pulled up neatly to his waist. The left side of his chest had been cleaned and dressed with large white bandages. His shoulder was also wrapped. A tube — a breathing tube — was in his mouth, taped in place. A machine on wheels was at the head of the bed, clicking and whirring rhythmically as it breathed for him. In and out. In and out. In his right arm were two IVs, with bags of colored fluids running into them.

And his face. She couldn't see anything of his face, of his sharp profile, of his steel-colored eyes. The left side of his head was wrapped in a lopsided gauze turban that covered his eyes. What she could see of his right cheek was swollen, already purple.

"Sit down," Daven said, when he caught sight of her at the door, unmoving. Nora's feet didn't want to obey her brain's commands.

"Nora, glad you're here," Donovan said. He looked as exhausted as she felt. "We could use a breather. Can you sit with him for a minute?"

She looked at the bed, at Bastian. Her heart seemed to be beating so hard, she couldn't speak past the lump it made in her throat, so she nodded instead.

"Good. Listen, we're just going to get some food, supplies — you don't need to do anything. In fact, *don't* do anything. Don't touch anything," Donovan said. Daven was his silent gray shadow, nodding.

"Can he hear me?" Nora asked, moving to take a chair that

Donovan placed near the head of the bed. She sat, but gingerly, like she wanted to bolt. Donovan shrugged.

"Who knows. Maybe? We've got him pretty drugged up, so he doesn't pull out his breathing tube," he said, then left the room. "Back in five!" he hollered, as the door shut.

And then, they were alone. Just her and Bastian, alone in his room. Again. She thought of the last time they'd been here, what he'd said. What she'd felt. It ached like a physical wound in her chest.

"The door was unlocked," she blurted, as an excuse for her entry, then winced. She wasn't sure he could hear her, but if he could, he would have laughed at that. Or smirked. She looked at the screens behind him — there didn't seem to be any change in his heart rate, if that's what the squiggly line meant.

She looked down at his left hand, gently laid across the top of the blanket. It looked gray, somehow, instead of his usual golden tan, but the fingers still looked strong, full of life. She reached out, running a finger along his. It *felt* warm. She took his hand in hers — a move so bold, she would never have attempted it had he been awake. His hand was warm, but limp. Callused and strong, but unresponsive. She held it anyway.

"You saved me," she whispered, gripping his hand tightly. Tears choked her, clouded her vision. She cleared her throat. "It should have been me."

She sat there with him in silence. Then — just in case he *could* hear her, she started talking to him. She talked more than she had in the entire time she'd known him. About how she'd flown around a black hole. She talked about her parents, about how she would have loved to take him to New Orleans because of the jazz he loved so much. How she promised she'd get the *Rap* back to Ganymede as fast as possible.

She wasn't sure how long Donovan was gone. It must have been more than five minutes. At one point, she lay her head down on her arms, still holding Bastian's hand. She'd fallen instantly asleep. This was how Donovan found her, and he'd gently shaken her awake.

"Hey," he said softly. "Go to your bunk. I got him now."

She moved like a zombie, her feet like lead, but she made it back to her cot in the cargo bay. She laid down, pulling the blanket over her head.

And then the alarms started.

"Nora, Bridge, now!" Asher called down at her. She groaned. She wanted to pull the pillow over her head, but even that wouldn't block out the alarm blaring every other second. She pulled herself off the cot and somehow made it up the stairs and down the hall.

The Bridge was a beehive of activity. Soren was seated at Nora's console and jumped up when she saw her enter.

"Good, hope you grabbed some coffee on the way up — no? Well, I'll get you some. Sit down," she said, ushering Nora back into her seat. Alarms and flashing signals glared at her from the console — the supraluminal drive was overheating, something was wrong with life support, the temperature controls were off again, and the gravity emitters were on their last dregs of battery if something didn't get plugged back in.

"Ok, let's do this," Nora muttered. Thalia and her crew — Sun, Harris, and Daven — huddled in the far corner from her, talking animatedly, Thalia puncturing her speech with various emphatic hand gestures. Soren grabbed Asher by the shoulder, steering him from the Bridge.

"Catch," Soren called over her shoulder, and tossed a headset to Nora. She fumbled, dropped it, recovered, and put it on.

"Testing one, two," Nora said. Soren gave her a thumbs up, pointing to the headsets that she — and everyone else — now wore.

"Don't know when we'll get the intercom back. Asher and I are going to work on the life support system, Thalia and her crew are going back to engineering to cool down the P2. If you see a new signal come up or one goes away, you tell us," she said, leaving the Bridge. Nora nodded. Thalia and her crew left soon after, so it was just Nora all alone in the Bridge. Thankfully she'd been able to mute the alarms, but new icons kept popping up on the console.

"Soren, uh, oxygen level dropped a point. System says maybe there's a … wait, never mind," she said, frowning. "Wait, it's back, definitely dropping."

"Noted," came Soren's terse reply. The headsets were a bit like a walkie talkie — Nora had to push a small button on the mouthpiece to transmit, but anything that anyone else transmitted came through just fine.

An hour passed, then two, then Nora lost count. Every new alarm that came on, the overhead horn sounded again until she muted it. She couldn't put in her earplugs and listen to Bastian's music with the headset, so she just kept muting the alarm, like playing a game of Whack-A-Mole. The *Rapscallion* shuddered around her, creaking and groaning like an old house. Whatever the others were up to, they did seem to be making slow progress on the problems. She wasn't sure the *Rap* would be able to be whole again, repaired back to its former glory, with the way they were patching up every single system.

At some point, Donovan brought her a cup of coffee. He'd been keeping watch at Bastian's bedside, adjusting meds, monitoring his breathing tube, changing bandages.

"How is he?" Nora asked, sipping the blessed beverage. It did lift the fog in her brain a little. How long had she been awake? Days? She'd lost track.

"Honestly, not great," Donovan said. He took off his glasses and passed a hand over his eyes, massaging the space between his brows. "His face is a mess. He's going to be in a hell of a lot of pain when he wakes up. Whatever rust or dirt that was on that panel that hit him, it infected the wound already. He's got a fever, and we don't have any antibiotics on board. I wrapped a few ice packs on his wrists and put some in his armpits. It seems to help," he said, shrugging. Nora's heart clenched. It was remarkable that despite everything going on — the ship literally trying to fall apart in the Current around them — that she still had energy to worry about Bastian. Silently, she willed the *Rap* to go even faster. They were still at least 48 hours out. She wondered if she could boost the P2 somehow, cut that time down.

Once the immediate crises had been averted, the P2 warm but no longer critically hot, they started taking shifts. Nora slept for about five minutes, or so it felt, before Asher woke her up. She could mostly manage the *Rap* in the Current by herself, which left the rest of the crew free to continue work on the ship itself. Soren's engineering background was invaluable, and Thalia and her crewmates were managing to keep the P2 functional. Donovan and Asher took turns caring for Bastian. Afterwards, Nora would say those last two days were a blur. Alarms went off, the siren sounded, she'd alert the crew and mute the alarm. Donovan tried talking to the Qaig, but he was getting nowhere. Even the catastrophic became somehow mundane after two continuous days of stress.

Finally, they approached Ganymede. The *Rap* was held together with duct tape, but she'd held up. Nora called the time to arrival over the headsets, telling Donovan to get Bastian ready to transport. She wanted him to be in the cargo bay, ready to go the instant they touched down.

"Yes, madam bossypants," Donovan had replied. Nora rolled her eyes. Bastian's fever had not broken, but neither had it worsened. She'd managed to spend only a few moments with him during their trip, during which she'd been shocked by the grayness of his skin, the slack body, the swelling of his face and bruising of his chest. She hadn't been there when they'd changed the gauze turban on his face, and from the looks on Donovan's and Asher's faces when they discussed it, she was glad.

Finally, finally, after a million years, they made it to the Ganymede Star Port. The *Rap* crashed through the ring's opening and the P2 cut off. Momentarily, the subluminal drive sputtered, and failed, the *Rap* drifting, before re-engaging and roaring to life.

Then the gravity emitters failed, and if Nora hadn't been strapped to her chair, she would have floated right off. She could feel her greasy hair flying out behind her, a tangled curly cape.

"Ganymede, this is the *Rapscallion*, requesting permission to land," Soren called over the intercom.

"Roger that, *Rap*, glad to have you back. Permission granted," came the reply. A dozen or more PJs were at the Star Port, awaiting a potential Qaig attack. There was no way the Qaig could have — or would have — followed them this far, right? She was too tired to even care.

The *Rap* limped back to Ganymede, a process which was agonizingly slow. The gravity emitters kept re-engaging and then failing, making her stomach feel like she was on a roller coaster. She could hear Donovan and Asher carrying Bastian on a stretcher to the cargo bay, and cursing intermittently as the gravity went on and off again. She couldn't tear her eyes off the front view panel, but her heart stopped with every lurch or bump that she heard.

Ganymede Station came into view, the stark white domes and halls glittering below her, the most precious thing she'd ever seen. Her view blurred for a moment, then cleared as the tears clouding her eyes fell. She sniffled, wiping her face on her sleeve, and brought the *Rap* around for landing. She didn't have energy left to be afraid or even wipe away the tears streaming from her eyes anymore, so she just let her training take over. Bastian's training.

It wasn't the prettiest of landings, but she didn't scrape the sides of the hangar bay on entry and only skidded a few feet as the *Rap* touched down. She let out a shuddering breath and released her grip on the controls. Well, it seemed like her stunt with the black hole hadn't caused any serious time changes, and for that — and a hefty amount of luck — she was immeasurably grateful. Her fingers were cramped, and she rubbed them, trying to straighten them out again. She jumped out of her skin when Soren put a hand on her shoulder, squeezing gently.

"Well done, cadet," Soren said warmly. "You made us all proud."

Nora ducked her head, a flush of heat warming her cheeks.

"Come on. Let's get off this rust bucket," Soren said, and turned Nora's chair. Nora got up and followed the yellow J'nai down the hall to the Cargo Bay, where Daven was lowering the walkway. A crowd appeared at the opening, and a medical team rushed forward to greet Donovan and Asher. They started talking rapidly, getting vital signs, information about Bastian's injuries as they whisked him off the ship and out of sight. Daven carried the compact ventilator and wheeled the IV pole behind them.

Nora craned her neck to see him, but the mob at the end of the ship blocked her view.

"He's strong. He'll be fine," Soren murmured as they descended the stairs together. Nora nodded, Soren's confidence giving her strength.

She'd just made it to the base of the stairs when a cluster of girls tore free of the crowd and swarmed her, wrapping arms tightly around her and shouting her name. She couldn't even speak, just sagged into their welcome and started crying.

"What happened?" Sophie asked, taking Nora's head between her hands. Nora just shook her head — she didn't have the strength for words. They were here — her friends were here. She hugged them back tightly, tears dripping from her nose, her chin as she cried.

"YOU DID WHAT?" Admiral Savaryn's voice thundered from the cargo bay of the ship. He stood there, a massive, intimidating presence, glowering down at them. Soren ignored him.

"Nora needs rest, and food," Soren said, ushering the girls off the ship. "Take her back to her room and keep her there. I'll deal with the Admiral."

"Ugh, and maybe a shower," Zoe said, wrinkling her nose. Nora giggled. She couldn't help it. All of the pent-up fear and anger and who-knew-what was breaking free, like a tidal wave. She giggled hysterically and couldn't stop.

"Soren, you brought a QAIG to GANYMEDE?" came another voice from inside the ship. Nora could hear a rumble and a low roar, along with a clank of chains. Soren crossed her arms and turned to face the Admiral.

"Yes," Soren said crisply. "I had hoped it could give us some insight. And I expect it will be treated with …"

"Come on," Sophie said softly, cutting off the verbal feud between Soren and Savaryn, putting an arm around Nora. Zoe and Raina flanked her other side, half-carrying her down the ramp. "We don't need to be here right now."

"Where's Cat?" Nora asked, looking around. Cat wasn't there. That was strange, right? Shouldn't Cat have been there to meet her? Nora's roommates exchanged worried glances.

"She's fine," Sophie said quickly. "But … we have a lot to catch up on. We'll tell you one you've rested."

They made it through the crowd and back to their room — the walk was the longest she'd ever endured in her entire life; she was sure of it — and Nora collapsed into a chair at the table. She'd never been so glad to see their little room, to be home. She closed her eyes, just wanting to sit and enjoy it for a moment — enjoy not being on a ship that was about to fall apart around her. She was back; she was safe. Her face scrunched as she thought about Bastian — not all of them had made it back safe. She put a hand over her eyes, as if the pressure could push the tears back into their ducts.

"Nuh-uh," Sophie scolded, tapping her shoulder. "Shower, then bed. Get up."

"Soph, give the girl a minute. Can't you see she's toast?" Zoe said, taking a seat as well. Zoe put a warm hand on Nora's shoulder. Nora opened her eyes — her vision clearing after she wiped away some of the moisture — and did her best to smile at her roommates, to prove that she was okay, but the absence of their fifth member made the room feel incomplete somehow.

"Where's Cat?" Nora asked again. Fatigue made her words feel thick on her tongue, and sound slurred in her ears. Again, those silent exchanged glances between her roommates.

"Well..." Sophie started.

"Look, let's just do this," Raina interrupted. She jumped up from her lotus pose on the floor. She looked like she'd been doing her best to repress whatever emotions she was feeling, but they were getting ready to boil over. She was literally trembling with the effort, so her roommates stopped what they were doing, and listened.

Raina held up her hand, and ticked off the following bombs—

"Savaryn and Queen Iyle are brainwashing the J'nai and us against the Qaig, who might not be all that bad after all — we don't really know," she said. Nora blinked, but didn't say anything. Another finger raised.

"And they're trying to commit genocide against the Qaig with this crazy bioweapon called *Tabula Rasa* but keep killing J'nai on accident because, who knew, the species were related like a million years ago and their DNA is too similar. That's what happened at Callisto — there was no radioactive leak. Savaryn killed J'nai and had to cover it up."

Another finger ticked.

"Oh, and Sophie and Cat went to Callisto Station with Ty because Jaxon and Aditi told them to, and Cat blew it up. Oh, and she's psychic. Or telekinetic or whatever you call it. She can move things with her mind. We think. Mostly she breaks things. And now she's in a coma."

Her ring finger raised.

"Ty and Sophie are a thing now, officially. Finally. And," she said, taking a deep breath as she reached her pinkie finger, "I'm in love with Zoe."

CHAPTER 19
NORA, GANYMEDE STATION

"I need espresso," Nora said after a minute. She closed her mouth — somewhere along the way, it had dropped open while Raina was talking. *Tabula Rasa?* Killing J'nai? Cat and Sophie had gone to Callisto? And who the hell was Jaxon? Suddenly, her trip to Terra Prime and back, even with a Qaig on board, sounded bland in comparison to what had transpired on Ganymede in her absence. Raina crushing on Zoe was the least surprising thing out of the whole bunch, though it still made her head reel.

Nora looked at Sophie, begging her for caffeine. Sophie just batted her eyes innocently.

"What makes you think I have access to the top-secret Terra Prime ultra-caffeinated beans?" she asked sweetly. Zoe rolled her eyes, but Nora noted a faint pink stain on her swarthy cheeks, and that she was carefully avoiding Raina's gaze. She hadn't moved a muscle otherwise, hadn't stirred from her seat. She seemed as dumbstruck as the rest of them. Nora suppressed a smile — while Ty and Sophie going 'official' wasn't that much of a surprise, hearing Raina's confession had been. She really hadn't seen that one coming, and apparently neither had Zoe or Sophie, though neither looked displeased.

"Look, we all know you had Cat make you a jerry-rigged espresso machine out of parts from the Chem Lab," Nora said. "Now's the time to get it out and put it to work."

"Yes, ma'am," Sophie said, eyes twinkling. She grabbed the machine from the locker by her bunk, along with a softball-sized bag of amazingly fragrant coffee beans. Sophie took a deep breath as she opened the bag, inhaling the scent with a sigh of pleasure.

"Now," Nora said, standing, suddenly feeling a thousand years old. "I need a shower. I can't even process what you just told me until I get clean." She felt like she'd literally have to peel her flight suit off, it was so grimy. She didn't even want to think about what state her curls were in.

"Ugh, I can smell you from here," Zoe said, grinning as she rocked back in her chair, the front two legs perilously far from the ground.

"You're one to talk," Sophie fired back. "Did you even bother to shower after your last workout?" She'd filled a beaker with water from the bathroom and set to work.

"Uh, didn't exactly have time to, with Nora's return," Zoe said, grinning, but unperturbed. Sophie wrinkled her nose. Raina had taken a seat on the windowsill on the other side of the room and was gazing wistfully out at the surface of Ganymede, rolling out in brown rumpled hills all the way to the black horizon. Zoe kept glancing at her, trying to make eye contact, but Raina seemed drained, and just kept her gaze on the window. Nora rubbed her eyes — they felt gritty, like the rest of her.

Within minutes, espresso as thick as black oil trickled down the tubing of Sophie's machine.

———

It took a few hours, but eventually they were caught up on each-other's adventures.

"I can't believe Ty flew you to Callisto by himself," Nora said, blinking hard. The espresso had given her a burst of energy, though now not even that particular rocket fuel could keep her eyelids open. She yawned, so hard that her ears popped.

"You flew the Current by yourself," Sophie countered, sipping delicately from a small beaker, which she'd refilled several times with espresso already.

"That's different," Nora said, but she couldn't remember the rest of her argument. She yawned, loudly this time, feeling her jaw crack. She ran a hand through her damp — but blissfully clean — hair, massaging her scalp. Even her *scalp* hurt, she was so tired.

She could barely begin to contemplate the implications of her roommates' discoveries while she'd been gone. It was no great surprise that Savaryn was keeping things from them — but it was nice to know that Aditi was still on their side. She wondered aloud about the bioweapon that Savaryn had commissioned. Sophie said she was looking into it, to see if it was real, and if there'd been an antidote made. She'd learned about Jaxon, the J'nai Alpha who was Aditi's partner-in-crime, who wanted to get to the bottom of what was really going on. And she'd told them all about the disastrous trip to Terra Prime, about the Qaig prisoner they'd taken. She told them about Bastian's injury, and her voice had cracked when she mentioned that he might lose his eyes. This last had elicited a collective gasp from her roommates, and then, despite the caffeine and the adrenaline, Nora had yawned so hard that Sophie had finally cut her off.

"That's it, missy," Sophie said, standing. She put her hands under Nora's arms, helping her up "Bed. Now. We can finish our talk later."

"Yes ma'am," Nora said. She groaned as she stood, feeling weak and shaky, grateful for Sophie's help. She wasn't sure how she did it, but somehow, she climbed the ladder to her bunk above Sophie's. Being back in her bunk — being *home* — brought a feeling of euphoria. Seeing her parents' faces smiling out from the photo on the shelf in her bunk — with those silly Christmas sweaters — made it feel like maybe they would have been proud of her. She touched the picture gently. She smiled, feeling a little delirious. She fell asleep within nanoseconds of her head hitting the pillow.

CHAPTER 20
ZOE, GANYMEDE STATION

Z oe prided herself on her instincts. She liked to think they had been honed over the years, after battling punks in the streets back on Earth, and then whipping herself into the best physical shape of her life here on Ganymede. Not much surprised her, and not much got past her.

Raina, though, had torn right through those "instincts" and gone straight for the jugular.

It wasn't that she was unhappy, exactly — more like stunned. And for the rest of the evening, Raina wouldn't even look at her. Zoe didn't think she'd meant let that last part slip out — then again, it could have been the impetus for her entire little tirade, like she'd been holding it back for too long already.

Zoe was exhausted. Not exhausted like Nora probably — the girl looked like the walking dead — but still, tired beyond reason. And still stunned. Raina liked her. Raina. *Raina.* Liked her. Okay, yeah, there were still the Qaig and impending apocalypse and whatnot, but Raina *liked* her!

After Nora went to bed, Sophie mumbled something about going to sleep, too. Raina followed suit, avoiding Zoe's gaze, and climbed into her bunk, drawing the curtain tight. Zoe clambered up the ladder to her top bunk, settling her too-tall frame into the space. It was about as cozy as a coffin. She wasn't sure how someone of Ty's stature could stand it.

She flopped back onto her pillow, her mind spinning like a hamster wheel. She heard Raina shifting below her, like she couldn't get comfortable. Zoe bit her lip — she should say something. She should say something, right? What did one say when someone else — the someone else she'd been dreaming about for weeks now, or maybe longer — blurted out that she felt the same, in front of everyone? Well, not everyone — just Nora and Sophie, but if she knew anything about Sophie then she felt everyone on the station really would know by the end of the night.

Zoe pulled up her tablet and punched in her password.

Hey, she texted. Raina squirmed below her, and she heard the soft tap of fingers against glass.

Hey.

Zoe's fingers hovered over the tablet. Ok, that went well.

Would you like to go get a coffee or something sometime?

God, that was even more lame typed out than it was in her head. She heard Raina snort, and a little jolt of uncertainty shot through her.

We get coffee together every day, Raina typed back. Zoe rolled her eyes. Duh.

Yeah, but we could make it like a date. I'll bring you flowers from the Greenhouse and everything.

A pause.

So — you're not mad at me? Raina typed.

Why would I be mad at you? Zoe asked, her fingers poised for more. Well, now or never, she thought. *I've been trying to ask you out for weeks.*

Another pause. Raina shifted around some more. Sophie abruptly ducked out of the room. The timing was so suspicious that for a moment Zoe wondered if she had hacked their tablets or read their minds — Sophie seemed capable of doing both sometimes.

Then Zoe became acutely aware that she and Raina were now alone in Room 10013 — except for Nora, who didn't really count because she was likely comatose. She grinned, preparing to write something scandalous —

And then Raina's head popped up over the side of her bunk, and

Zoe yelped, fumbling her tablet, startled for the second time today. She'd really have to work on those instincts.

"Hey," Raina said, a small smile on her face.

"Hey," Zoe said, her heart racing for reasons that had nothing to do with surprise. She tried to sit up in the bunk but had to settle for kinda-hunched-over instead. Raina held her eyes for a long time. Zoe could swear that the Sun itself could have gone supernova in that moment, and she never would have noticed.

"Coffee would be great," Raina said at last. Zoe grinned, relieved and a little giddy.

"It's a date," she said.

CHAPTER 21
SOPHIE, GANYMEDE STATION

Sophie spent a few minutes in her bunk, thinking, listening to Nora's steady breathing above her. She'd looked exhausted — something beyond exhausted. She'd pushed herself beyond any conceivable limit and had saved her entire ship. Sophie had only managed to put herself, Cat, and Ty at enormous risk, and who knew what would happen with Cat now. Sophie was checking in with Wesley about every five minutes on their tablet messaging app — Cat still hadn't woken up.

She chewed on her bottom lip as she thought, then checked the time on her tablet — she still had a few minutes before curfew. She got up, told Raina and Zoe that she was off, and left the room. Raina and Zoe had been working in their own respective bunks, not talking, though Sophie suspected they were shyly texting each other on the messaging app on their tablets, judging from the giggles coming from them. She snorted — it was about time.

She headed down the corridors at a breakneck pace, and into the medical wing. The lights were dimmed a little with the oncoming night, and there weren't many people about. There was one other medical trainee there, a handsome one she'd seen before, who stopped to gawk at her for a minute before returning to his task.

She went to Cat's "room" in the main wing, with walls of crinkly green curtains, and peeked in. Cat appeared to be sleeping, her head tilted to the side. Without her glasses and with the little brown coils of her hair falling on her face, she looked even younger than she usually did. She turned to go when she saw Wesley approaching, his nose buried in his tablet. He nearly stumbled into her.

"Ah, Sophie! Sorry. Just, um, coming to check on Cat before I have to leave," he said, craning to look past her. His face softened as he looked at his charge.

"She's sleeping?" Sophie asked softly. He nodded and motioned for her to follow him from the Medical Bay.

"She's still exhausted, but otherwise she seems okay. She woke up for a bit after you left, but she is really wiped out. Judging from her labs, her muscles underwent tremendous stress from her actions. She has rhabdomyo — uh, she has muscle breakdown, and we've got to keep her well hydrated," he whispered. He hung his white coat on a rack by the door, tucking the tablet into his uniform pocket as they left.

"Can she come home ... I mean, back to our room soon?" Sophie asked. Wesley hesitated but then nodded.

"Dr. Adebayo wants to watch her a bit, run a few more tests, make sure her kidney function stays stable and things like that, but I expect so, yes."

"Ok," Sophie said. She paused just outside the door, considering, twirling a strand of hair around one finger.

"Was there something else on your mind tonight?" Wesley asked, cocking his head. She shrugged, letting her hair fall over one shoulder. Then she looked back up at him and decided to just go for it.

"I need you to teach me medicine," she said. He blinked. His mouth opened, then shut again.

"That's a tall order," he said. He shifted his weight from leg to leg, glancing at his watch. It was just a few minutes until curfew now, and she knew she was cutting it close.

"I mean, not all of it, obviously," she said quickly. "But — when we were out there, there was nothing I could do for her. I knew she was breathing, and I could feel a pulse, but that was it. I was entirely help-less the entire trip back and when you — you just ran to her, knew exactly what needed to be done, what testing to do. If something had happened to Cat because of me, I ... I don't know what I'd do," Sophie said. Wesley nodded, considering.

"You need to do our Basic Life Support course, BLS. You'll learn to check vital signs, do CPR, all that stuff."

"Yes, yes! I need to learn that. Can you teach me?"

Wesley shook his head.

"It would take hours, and I, I am just not qualified to..."

"I'll do it," a voice said, as the handsome trainee she'd seen earlier came out of the Medical Bay. He was about Wesley's height, with tousled blond hair and a snubbed nose, wearing a long white coat over scrubs. He gave her a wide smile. "Hi. I'm Liam." He held his hand out to her.

"Sophie," she said, shaking it. "You'll do what, exactly?"

"I'm Wesley's upper-level resident," he said, clapping a hand on Wesley's shoulder. "I used to teach the BLS classes, but we haven't had any since, you know, the Qaig thing."

"And you'll teach me?" Sophie asked. Though Wesley would have been good, she supposed learning from his teacher was even better. She did catch Wesley's eye, but Wesley didn't say anything. In fact, his mouth was pressed tightly shut.

"Are you free for lunch tomorrow?" Liam asked, checking something on his tablet.

"To study," Sophie added.

"Right. To study," he said. "Meet me here. We can probably get you through the course in a few days over lunch breaks, if you want."

"Thank you," Sophie said, and his cheeks went a little pink. She meant it, too, from the bottom of her heart. She couldn't stand the thought of how helpless she'd been, the risk she'd put her friends through.

"Sure. Happy to help," Liam said, clapping Wesley once more on the shoulder before walking off.

"Curfew time, don't get caught out or Adebayo'll have my hide," he called back. Wesley grunted.

"You don't like this plan?" Sophie asked, when Liam was out of earshot. Wesley's face darkened, and he scowled, which was something Sophie had never seen him do before. Usually Wesley was pleasant, professional even — something was definitely rankling him.

"I do not like *him*," Wesley muttered, jerking his head in the direction Liam had gone. Sophie arched an eyebrow, looking down the corridor, and shrugged.

"Believe me, I can handle him," she said, crossing her arms. She meant that, too — she was familiar with the effect she had on men, had recognized it in Liam's glazed look.

"Just be careful with him," Wesley said. Sophie turned back to give him a snarky reply but stopped when she saw the way his eyebrows puckered. He was worried for her.

"Why?" she asked.

"He... gets a little handsy with the female staff," he said. Sophie nodded. She'd been dealing with handsy men for years.

"Do you think he can teach me what I need to know?" she asked. Wesley considered for a moment, then nodded. Okay. That was enough for her. She'd take precautions. She'd make sure they were never alone, never out of earshot of other people. She might not have Raina's fighting spirit, but she had a set of lungs that would make her shriek echo over Ganymede if she needed it. She grinned, satisfied that she had a plan in place, and walked with Wesley back towards their rooms. She would never, *ever* feel that helpless again.

CHAPTER 22
NORA, GANYMEDE STATION

Nearly twenty hours later, after the longest sleep of her life, three espressos, and a 3,000-caloric lunch, Nora stood outside Admiral Savaryn's rooms. The last time she'd spoken to him had been just before the mission, when she'd been floored to learn about the P2 drive and had been thrilled to be chosen to be a part of the team. Despite the fact that only a week or so had passed since then, she felt about a million years older. She'd have to ask Sophie to start doing Botox on all the wrinkles she felt forming on her forehead.

"Gotta go in sooner or later," a voice chirped behind her. "Might as well be sooner."

Donovan came up beside her, looking awkward and stuffy in his pressed uniform instead of his usual rumpled T-shirt. Nora took a deep breath, pushed open the door, and stepped in.

The Admiral's room felt enormous. The inside of the room — or rooms, actually — was spacious and sparse. She had entered into a sort of sitting room, complete with orderly chairs and minimal attempts made at making the space actually comfortable. She made her way down a short hall past two more closed doors, then into a conference room with a long table. At the head sat Admiral Savaryn, his face drawn and red as he talked quietly to Soren. Next to him, Soren gleamed, sitting tall and straight and proud in her Ganymede Station uniform. Beside her sat the XO, MacGregor, his hands clasped in front of him. A few other officers she didn't recognize — both human and J'nai — also sat at the table. They followed Savaryn's words with rapt attention.

"Come on," Donovan said, pushing past her. Nora swallowed the lump in her throat and followed him into the room.

"Sit," Savaryn said, his voice booming. Nora grabbed the closest chair and sank into it. A moment later Asher came into the room, too.

"Where's Thalia and her team?" Nora asked Donovan. He shrugged and pushed his glasses back up his nose.

"Jail, hopefully," he said. Asher leaned over.

"Getting debriefed down in the Hangar Bay, having the engineers look at the P2," he said. Nora nodded, then realized that Savaryn's mercury-colored gaze was locked on her. She squirmed, feeling her face heat.

"Is it all right with you if we get started then, cadet?" he asked. Nora nodded, feeling sweat break out on her neck and trickle down her spine. She wondered if he knew that she knew about Callisto now. How Ganymede Station would react, if that news about Callisto and *Tabula Rasa* became public. She'd heard about his new rules — no gathering in groups, no loitering anywhere that wasn't a task space, to start — and couldn't help but feel he was worried about it, like his tightening of the leash on Ganymede was a reaction to the control he could feel slipping away from him. It gave her courage, in a way, knowing that she held this over him. He didn't know it, of course, but it gave her courage all the same. She sat up a little straighter and stared right back at him.

"So, for the official record," MacGregor said, breaking the tension. "Captain Soren, please start at the beginning. You were supposed to gather intel as to the situation at Terra Prime, and to test out the P2 drive. In your own words please, tell us what happened."

Savaryn's gaze shifted to Soren, who took a deep breath, and began.

A fter what felt like an eternity but was actually maybe two hours, Nora left the Admiral's quarters and let out a shaky breath. Soren had praised her flying skills, which made her prouder than she'd ever felt. Savaryn hadn't said much during the debrief, and neither had his lackeys — they just nodded, taking notes on tablets, whispering a little to each other. MacGregor had asked few questions, mostly about the Qaig that Soren had brought to Ganymede. When the topic had shifted to the Qaig prisoner, Nora had been dismissed. She felt wrung out. She wanted nothing more than to go back to sleep — but her roommates had been messaging her tablet all during the meeting, and so she made her way over to the medical wing to meet them.

Inside, she'd see both Cat and Bastian, both possibly still unconscious or asleep. Though physically she was mostly recovered, she wasn't sure about her emotional side, wasn't sure that she could handle whatever she was about to see and hear.

"You've got this," Raina said, putting her arm through Nora's elbow, dragging her forward. "Come on. You can't come all this way and not go in."

Sophie and Zoe padded quietly behind them. Nora had heard soft whispers from Zoe and Raina earlier when she'd awoken, but the girls had quieted as soon as she got up. She wasn't clear if some sort of agreement or relationship had been discussed. Zoe and Raina weren't avoiding each other, exactly, but neither were they talking much to each other today. They did exchange a lot of glances though, especially when they didn't think anyone was watching.

They entered the long medical wing, with its rows of cots to either side, each pod separated from the other by sage-green curtains.

They went to see Cat first. Nora was surprised to see Wesley sitting on the cot, talking quietly with Cat — who was awake!

"Finally!" Sophie screeched, throwing herself on Cat, covering the smaller girl with hugs. Wesley stood quickly, face coloring, and excused himself. As he walked by, Raina grabbed his arm.

"How is she?" she asked him. He looked at Cat, something unreadable in his bright hazel eyes.

"See for yourself. Physically though, she's fine," he said. "Goodbye, Catherine."

He stuffed his hands into the pockets of his short white coat and left.

Nora looked at Cat, who was flushed pink all the way to the roots of her frizzy hair.

"Hi, Nora," she said shyly. Nora sat on the cot, putting a hand on Cat's leg. It was like they all wanted to touch her, to reassure themselves she was okay. Zoe and Raina stood on Cat's other side, not touching each other. Cat had an IV in her arm, into which clear fluid was dripping.

"Hi yourself," Nora said, grinning. "Sophie told me about your little adventure."

Cat looked around, and spoke quietly, afraid of being overheard.

"We told Doctor Adebayo that I fainted in the Rec Dome. Wesley knows the truth, though," she said. Nora nodded.

"Is it true that you blew up Callisto Station?" Nora asked. Cat winced and pushed her glasses back up her nose.

"Unintentionally," Sophie said, shrugging. "What I'm interested in is whether Cat can control this ability."

"I don't know," Cat said softly. "Wesley hasn't heard of anything like this in the other clones. Headaches, seizures, that kind of thing — we've been discussing possibilities."

"Like you turning into the Hulk?" Zoe asked, smirking. Cat smiled.

"Something like that. He thinks maybe the radiation that Marie Curie was exposed to may have done something to her DNA. The other Curie clones here haven't had any issues or ... episodes, but he's not sure if there were any Curie duds that never made it here. He's going to do some research on it," Cat said, smoothing the blanket over her legs. The motion made the silver strands on her head glimmer — were there more of them today than there was the last time Nora saw her? It looked like it. Cat was positively salt-and-pepper now.

"Well, I don't care why it happened, just don't you dare scare me like that again!" Sophie said, smacking Cat's arm. "If *I* get a gray hair from the stress, I'm blaming you!"

"Bastian's awake now, if you wanted to know," Cat said to Nora, nodding toward the other side of the aisle. "Wesley says he's been asking for you."

Nora cringed, though Sophie let out a soft wolf-whistle.

"I'll just, um," Nora said, backing up. "I'm just going to see what he wants."

"Take your time," Sophie said, waving her fingers and giving Nora a wink. Nora flushed and ducked out of the curtain, relief sweeping through her that Cat was all right and Bastian — well, at least he was awake and talking. Whatever injury had knocked him unconscious must not have caused any major damage. She felt lighter, like a great weight had been lifted from her shoulders, and she fairly bounced over to the other side of the medical wing.

It was easy to tell which cot was Bastian's — there was a crowd outside, J'nai and human. Soren was there already, and Asher and Donovan, too. They must have come over straight from the debrief, too — and they beckoned her over when they saw her. There was an air of forced levity between them, which made her immediately apprehensive.

And then she saw Bastian. He wore a hospital gown now, which covered the worst of the bruising along the side of his chest. His left arm was in a sling. Over his face, a clean gauze bandage was wrapped across his eyes, and over the left cheek, like some kind of crazy turban.

"Nora's here," Soren said, guiding her to the chair by his bed. Bastian smiled — despite it all, he *smiled*. She smiled back, flushing self-consciously, and sat next to him.

"Hi," he said. His voice sounded raspy.

"Hi," she said back. "How… how are you?"

"It looks worse than it is," he said.

"How can you tell? You look like shit," Donovan said, then squawked, as Soren dug her elbow into his ribcage.

Bastian smirked.

"Still better looking than you," he said, and they all laughed, though again the sound was forced. Nora was having a hard time concentrating on anything other than his injuries — she found herself cataloging them, feeling guilty about each scrape, each bruise, each broken bone. She was so grateful to see him awake and talking, she had so many things to say to him — and yet none made it past her lips, not with so many other people around her.

"I hear you did some pretty fancy flying back there," Bastian said, interrupting her internal struggle, turning his sightless eyes towards her. She swallowed hard, wondering about the gauze, wondering what was beneath it. If she'd see his blue-gray eyes again.

If he'd ever see her again.

"I had a good teacher," she said, trying to sound upbeat, but the words came out a little choked. He smiled again despite the sob in her voice, his little half-smile, and her heart skipped a beat.

"I've never flown around a black hole, or outflown a Qaig ship, not to mention several dozen of them," he said, tilting his head. "Those moves were all your own, Eleanora Clark."

She flushed.

"All right, all right," a richly accented voice said. A dark-skinned man in a hoverchair came over and shooed them away. "He's only just woken up. He needs his rest."

"I slept for three days, sir," Bastian said, exasperated. "I'm ready to go."

"You're due for another antibiotic infusion. And the J'nai surgeon is ready for you. We'll take you back soon," he said, then looked up at the crowd around Bastian's bed — not just the crew of the *Rapscallion*, but also some other officers and pilots. "What did I say? Shoo!"

"Yes, sir," they mumbled, and slowly dispersed. Soren took Asher and Donovan by the shoulders and steered them out. Nora watched as he left the Medical Bay, and it felt like the contents of her stomach had lodged somewhere in her chest.

Bastian was wheeled back for surgery — to repair the ripped skin of his face, and to see if his vision could be salvaged — and Nora still couldn't shake the feel of his hand in hers, how limp and lifeless it had been when she held it on the flight back from Terra Prime. The fact that he was awake now, talking and making jokes ... he was stronger than she gave him credit for, which was saying quite a bit. Despite it all, he hadn't been afraid, hadn't been upset about his eyes — or if he was, he hid it well. He didn't seem to be in much pain either, so either the doctor was doing a good job with his pain medication or, more likely, Bastian was hiding that as well. She was both in awe at his strength and somehow irritated by it. She was told the surgery would take several hours, at minimum, and her roommates steered her back to the cafeteria for another meal while they waited.

"You think they'll expel us if they find out what we did?" Zoe asked, around a mouthful of protein bar. The cafeteria was largely deserted — everyone else was at their assigned tasks. Aditi had personally pardoned Room 10013 from their tasks for a few days — to help Nora and Cat recover, she'd said.

"And what, ground us? Keep us locked up in this station with no outside communication and force us into indentured servitude? How is that different from what we're doing now?" Sophie said, flipping her hair over her shoulder. She was typing away on her tablet, messaging either Ty or Jaxon, Nora imagined.

"... good point," Zoe said.

"Besides, he's a genocidal power-hungry maniac," Raina said. "I say we tell everyone."

"Not yet," Sophie said, tapping her tablet. "Jaxon has a plan. But don't worry," she said, a fearsome glint in her green eyes. "He'll get what's coming to him."

A few hours later, Wesley sent them all a text, notifying them that Bastian was out of surgery. Nora flew to the medical wing, waving to Cat (who was still under observation for the moment), and made a beeline for Bastian's cot.

"He's still pretty groggy from the anesthesia," Wesley warned. He was making notes on his tablet, checking the vital signs on the monitor. A nurse in green scrubs pushed something into the IV.

"And there's something else," Wesley said. Nora made to go sit by Bastian, but Wesley put a gentle hand on her arm, stopping her. She turned, looking up at him, her eyebrows knitting together. More bad news? She wasn't sure she could handle it. Wesley took a deep breath and took a quick glance at Bastian. He lowered his voice, pulling something up on his tablet.

"We did some more imaging, to check for other injuries. It's not uncommon for someone to not feel a relatively minor injury when they're distracted by the pain …" he drifted off. Nora swallowed hard and nodded. Wesley continued.

"So anyway. The broken ribs, clavicle, we knew about. But … what do you know about Bastian's past?" he asked. Nora shrugged, confused.

"As much as anyone else, I suppose. He grew up in France, then was recruited here."

"Did he ever talk about his past injuries?" Wesley asked. Nora shook her head. It wasn't too surprising that he'd had injuries before, after all, he was well-versed in martial arts and ran their cadet "Fight Club" training program. He was bound to have some old breaks. The first time Nora had hit a punching bag, her hand had been sore for days.

"It's just — I don't know," Wesley said. He shifted his weight from foot to foot, uneasy.

"What is it?" Nora asked. Wesley licked his lips, pulling up x-rays on his tablet.

"These," he said, pointing to thin white lines through various bones in Bastian's hand, his arm, his legs, and ribs.

"What am I looking at?" Nora asked.

"These are healed breaks. Old wounds," Wesley said. Nora wasn't sure what to say — there seemed to be a lot of them.

"He leads 'Fight Club,' you know," Nora said, reaching for the only plausible explanation she could think of. "I'm sure he's taken his share of hits."

"Nora, he got these as a child," Wesley said gently. "These are old, from before his time here on Ganymede. He never said anything to you about his past?"

Nora's gaze drifted to Bastian, who looked asleep. She shook her head.

"I think … I think Bastian may have been beaten. Repeatedly, over years. These kinds of breaks," he said, pointing to the x-ray of Bastian's chest, at the thin white lines tracing through his ribs, like spiderwebs. "These breaks take a lot of force."

Nora let out a breath, and it shuddered through her chest. Ok, so Bastian had been injured in his past. He never talked about his time on

Earth, before Ganymede. She thought back to that night in the Green-house, a million years ago, when she'd asked him about his home. He'd immediately shut down, refusing to talk about it. She hadn't thought much about it until now.

"Ok, thanks, I'll let you know if I find out anything," Nora said. The words felt stiff on her tongue, automated. She couldn't take her eyes off Bastian, asleep before her. She gave Wesley's arm a squeeze, then made her way to Bastian's side.

CHAPTER 23
SOPHIE, GANYMEDE STATION

After she'd seen Cat, Sophie went about her usual assignments, which today consisted of staring blankly at her computer screen in her little cubicle until the lunch break bell rang. Honestly, she could run these programs in her sleep. Aditi had given her the day off, but she'd gotten a message that any hours missed would have to be made up later, so she'd come in anyway. With Cat on the way to recovery, Nora either in the Medical Bay or the hangar, and Zoe and Raina trying to be inconspicuous about their mutual attraction in their own room, Sophie felt the need to make herself scarce and get out of the way for a bit.

Today, though, she had something to look forward to. As soon as the break bell sounded, she leapt up and headed to the medical wing, downing a protein bar as she went. She was just wiping the last crumbs from her mouth when she spied Liam waiting for her by the door. His gaze went to where her fingers lingered on her lips, before returning to her eyes. She put her arm down and put on a bright smile.

"Hello, Liam! Thank you for meeting me," she said. He nodded and held the door open for her as they walked into the medical wing, down the long center aisle and to another hall at the back. This hall was narrow and lined with small rooms to either side. Some of the doors were open, revealing rooms with a few people reading some x-rays, or looking into microscopes, or simple storage areas. At last, they came to a room with half a dozen desks and a white board. On a table at the front lay a mannequin — a man's head and torso made of tan plastic — with some other equipment nearby to treat their "patient."

Again, Liam held the door for Sophie, which was rather gentlemanly of him, but when he shut the door to the room behind them, Sophie turned and opened it wide.

"Sorry. Claustrophobic," she said, and gave him a smile that was apologetic and not at all flirtatious. He shrugged.

"Okay, I might get paged during this, so if I do, I'll just step out for a few minutes," he said. "Perks of being in charge."

She nodded and selected a desk at the front of the little classroom.

"Well, I don't want to waste your time," she said, getting out her tablet and preparing to take notes. "Let's get started."

She had to admit, Liam was a pretty good teacher. He clearly liked it, or at least liked being the center of attention, *her* attention. He talked about the different modules he'd be walking her through, including assessing vital signs, CPR, and how to check a heart rhythm and use a defibrillator. She was practically wiggling with anticipation. She should have done this long ago, before she'd ever risked her friends in that crazy Callisto stunt.

After about forty minutes, he did get paged on his tablet, and said he had to go. Sophie thanked him and gathered her things.

"See you tomorrow?" he asked, still looking at his tablet. Whatever he saw there he didn't like, as he was practically glowering.

"Tomorrow," Sophie said, and showed herself out. She could feel him walking behind her as she went down the corridor, but he didn't say anything. Wesley's warning rang out loud and clear in her mind, and she walked a little faster. She took a deep breath once she reached the central Medical Bay, and hustled over to see Cat before the afternoon session of her task began. From the corner of her eye, she spied Nora at Bastian's side across the aisle and grinned to herself. Bastian must have finally gotten out of surgery — as curious as she was, she decided to let Nora have her moment alone with him, and she slipped quietly out of the front door of the Medical Bay.

CHAPTER 24
NORA, GANYMEDE STATION

Bastian lay on his cot, appearing relaxed. A hard shell of an eye patch covered his right eye; the left side of his face was still swathed in gauze. He couldn't see her, but at the sound of her footsteps, he stirred.

"Hey," Nora said softly, sitting by his bedside. Bastian's hand moved towards her, and after a second of hesitation, she took it. He squeezed her hand gently before letting her go, his head turning towards her slowly, like he had to focus to move a single muscle fiber.

"Hey," he said thickly, like his tongue was swollen. "The surgery went well."

"It did?" Nora asked, her heartbeat accelerating. "Does this mean ... your vision..."

"They were able to save the right eye," he said, leaning back into his pillow with a sigh. "The left, not so much."

"Oh," Nora said, feeling like a deflated balloon. "Oh Bastian, I'm so sorry."

"No," he said firmly, then again, gentler, "No. You don't feel sorry. It is what it is. I still have one eye, and they tell me the vision will be fine. That's a lot to be grateful for."

"But... you can't fly," Nora blurted out, then covered her mouth with her other hand. Great. Way to kick a man when he was down.

"No," he said slowly, and let out a sigh. "So, I'll do something else. Guess they'll just have to make me a captain for real, then."

She chuckled, but it sounded sort of like a sob. He wouldn't need his depth perception as much to captain a ship. She imagined if flying was taken from her, she'd feel like a falcon with clipped wings. Bastian, though, he just ... transformed. Took on another form altogether, never even missing a step.

"Are you... does it hurt much?" Nora asked. The swelling over his jaw and collarbone didn't seem as bad, though they were still violet. His usually-razor-sharp cheekbones were barely discernable between the gauze and the near-black bruising.

"Pain is inevitable," Bastian said with a small sigh, adjusting his back on the cot. "Suffering is optional."

"You give the man a little morphine, and suddenly he's a philosopher," a voice said. Nora turned, to see a handsome teal J'nai man with gold and white tattoos come to stand at the foot of the bed. He was accompanied by Soren, who stood silent, her hands clasped behind her back.

"That sounds like Jaxon," Bastian said, turning his head towards the sound.

"Good ear," the J'nai said, grinning. He stood casually, his hands in the pockets of his uniform. Royalty, Nora remembered from the tattoos. That's what had Soren so stiff and formal. Should she stand? Bow? She wasn't sure, so she just sat still.

"And you must be Nora," he said, extending a hand to her. He had a firm handshake.

"I am," she said, puzzled. What was a J'nai royal doing here?

"How are you feeling, Benoit?" Jaxon asked, moving to stand on the side of the cot opposite Nora.

"I've had better days, honestly," he said. "They told me to expect a few more days here, I need some strong antibiotics, and another tetanus shot."

"When will you be ready to fly?" Jaxon asked. Nora whipped her head around.

"FLY?" she screeched. "He just had surgery! He's not ..." she trailed off. Probably not a great way to talk to royalty. She pinched her lips together, trying to suppress the flush she could feel rising to her face.

"What she means," Bastian said, "is that I can't fly. You cannot have a one-eyed pilot with no depth perception."

"How about a one-eyed captain?" Soren asked. It was the first time she'd spoken, and for a moment Nora had forgotten she was even there. Soren looked to Jaxon, as if expecting a rebuke for speaking out of turn.

"Well, how's tomorrow then?" Bastian asked. Nora shook her head, not believing any of this.

"Look, subtlety isn't my strong point, so I'll just say it," Jaxon said, leaning against the medical cabinet. "You're up to date on what Sophie and her team found on Callisto?"

"*Tabula Rasa*? Yes, I heard," Bastian said. Nora's palms were sweating.

"It gets worse. The virus had gotten out of containment, killed dozens of J'nai. The reason the Qaig haven't come to Ganymede? They're afraid Savaryn will unleash it. We've also discovered that your admiral has been keeping this virus here, somewhere, as well. And in the event that the J'nai ever turn against him, well... he has options."

Nora's blood ran cold. The Admiral wouldn't dare — would he? The virus, here? Her skin crawled at the idea.

"And Cat ... I mean, were Cat and Sophie and Ty exposed to it, on Callisto? Did they bring it back here?" she asked. Jaxon shook his head, and she felt relief rush through her like a wave.

"No. As far as we can tell, the virus is killed by the vacuum of space. It didn't survive on their suits or in the cargo bay of the ship. I've had Soren run some tests," Jaxon said. Soren pursed her lips.

"But..." Nora started. Her mouth went dry. "Sophie said ... they took their helmets off, when they were on the Bridge. And the Bridge had been sealed. You don't think..."

Jaxon and Soren exchanged a glance. Nora counted her heartbeats, which were racing, the fastest metronome she'd ever heard. *One-two-three-four...*

"No," Jaxon said, drawing out the word slowly. "If they had come into contact with it, we would have detected it on their suits." Nora felt reassured by his conviction — at least there wasn't the J'nai equivalent of Ebola getting ready to decimate Ganymede.

"A virus couldn't live for so many years without a host, anyway," Soren said, shaking her head. "Any free virus on that station died out, long ago. And now," she said, taking a deep breath. "Now we know Savaryn has it. And could release it at any time, if he thought the J'nai were a threat to him or his station."

"He wouldn't," Nora whispered. "Queen Iyle, the J'nai, they wouldn't turn against us, would they?"

"We are adaptable," Jaxon said simply. "It's one of the great advantages of our race. But we are not always, historically, the most peaceful of races. I believe we threw the first punch in the war with the Qaig, so to speak."

"So where would you like me to fly you, Jaxon?" Bastian asked, interrupting.

"Terra Prime," he said. At this, Bastian laughed and shook his head.

"We just got back from there. It's swarming with Qaig; you'll never get past them to the planet."

"I don't plan to," Jaxon said. "I want to talk to them. Make a deal."

"What kind of deal?" Nora asked, incredulous.

"Peace between our races," he said, and he said it with such earnestness that Nora nearly believed him. But was such a thing possible?

"How?" she asked. At this, he grinned.

"By overthrowing Queen Iyle, and taking her place on the J'nai throne," he said. "If I do that, I'll have the power to make a treaty with them, and with the humans. No more peace by holding a virus over our heads."

"Savaryn won't agree to it," Soren said. "He won't let you take a ship to Terra Prime." At this, Jaxon snorted.

"He will. I'm an Alpha. He cannot refuse my request to return to my home, especially if I have a crew willing to take me."

"The *Rap* will take a while to repair," Nora said, looking at Soren. Soren winced.

"What did you do to my ship?" Bastian asked, startled.

"Look, we got back in one piece, mostly," Soren said, grinning a little. "It's just that life support, the carbon dioxide scrubbers, the subluminal engines, the P2..."

"Don't forget the gravity emitters," Nora threw in.

"Right, and the gravity emitters. None of those work. Well, they do, but they're patched together with duct tape and glue, and I think what you call paper clips. But the rest of the ship is more or less intact."

"Oh, and the ..." Nora started. Bastian put up a hand to stop her.

"Okay, I get it. Can we get another ship?" he asked.

"How about the *Desiderata*?" Nora asked, grinning. Bastian cocked his head to one side, but Soren nodded.

"Good ship. I'll look into it," she said.

"But the P2 barely worked last time," Nora said, frowning.

"But it did work," Jaxon said, irrepressible. "Soren and Thalia have assured me, this time, we will succeed."

"Thalia?" Nora said, blinking in surprise. "She's in on this scheme?"

Jaxon shrugged.

"Not really. She thinks she's fixing it for Savaryn."

Nora considered. So, Thalia wasn't on their side, but the Admiral's.

"Okay. Let's say this works. You go to Terra Prime, and do what? Overthrow Iyle, get yourself coronated or whatever? You still have Savaryn and his bioweapon to worry about," Nora said.

"Yes, well," Jaxon said with a tight grin. "We're working on a way to get Savaryn to ... step down."

"Your Mutineers?" Nora asked, thinking back to Sophie's description. He nodded. So, like Sophie said, the Admiral *would* be punished.

"The Qaig have the upper hand now. They have superior firepower, superior numbers, and have your home world hostage. Why would they agree to peace with the J'nai? Or humans?" Bastian asked. Nora frowned, but he was right. Jaxon straightened, a steely glint in his eyes.

"Because if they don't, I'll release *Tabula Rasa* on the Qaig home world."

"You wouldn't," Nora said, the phrase escaping her louder than she intended. She caught Soren's eye. She didn't know how many Qaig lived on that planet — or even where it was — but she imagined it was a lot. If the *Tabula Rasa* was a deadly as she'd heard, they were talking about the annihilation of millions — or potentially billions — of lives. *One-two-three-four-five-six...* her heartbeats pounded, filling the pause between the question and answer.

"I would," Jaxon said. Though his pose remained casual, his mouth was a hard line, his jaw tight. The words barely made it past his clenched teeth.

"They agree to peace, we destroy the *Tabula Rasa*," Soren said. She fidgeted, uncomfortable with the plan but either not seeing an alternative or refusing to speak further in front of an Alpha.

"Do you have the *Tabula Rasa*?" Bastian asked. Jaxon and Soren exchanged a glance.

"Not yet," Jaxon said slowly. "We're not sure where Savaryn's keeping it."

"So, you're just going to what, ask him to hand it over?" Nora asked. She pinched the bridge of her nose as she thought.

"That is unlikely to work," Bastian said. Nora snorted.

"So, we'll steal it," Jaxon said. Nora didn't like how his eyes glittered.

"Once you find it," Nora said. She let out a long sigh and closed her eyes, recounting the ludicrous plan out loud.

"So, we find the virus, steal the virus, then convince Savaryn to let us take a ship. Then we replace Savaryn, you replace Iyle, and we get the Qaig to agree to keep the peace. Simple enough," Nora said.

"Of course, we need a pilot," Jaxon said, looking at Nora. His gaze was piercing, and it made her squirm. No way. No way in Hell was she going through that again. And Bastian was in no shape to go!

"I'm in," Bastian said. She rolled her eyes and looked at Bastian — was he seriously considering this? Going *back* to Terra Prime, after what they'd just been through to get home?

"Me too, and the rest of the crew," Soren said. "Bastian can captain, and I'll run engineering and keep Thalia and her crew in line. Nora?"

Nora swallowed hard.

"No."

The voice wasn't Nora's. She raised her eyes from the floor scuff she'd been examining to look at Bastian. His jaw was set in a tight line.

"She is not going," he said, his voice firm. It was suddenly so quiet, Nora wondered if he could hear her heartbeat hammering in her chest.

"Excuse me?" she squeaked.

"You're not going."

"What gives you the right..."

"I am the captain!" he said, then lay back on his cot, as if the vehemence of his words took the last bit of strength from him.

"The last thing we need," he said, slowly, carefully, each word measured, pitched so that Soren and Jaxon could hear him just as clearly. "Is an untested, untrained Fax cadet on board. I cannot be there to pick up your slack this time. We need an experienced pilot."

She could not have been more surprised than if he'd physically struck her. She blinked, disbelieving. Cold dread pooled in her stomach.

"You don't mean that," she whispered. The words barely made it past her lips. She looked to Soren — her mentor — for help. This wasn't like him — Bastian wasn't the kind to tease. Soren wouldn't meet her gaze, keeping her laser green eyes instead fixated on Bastian.

"I do," Bastian said, blind eyes still turned towards Soren.

"I am the only one besides you who's flown the P2! No one else could evade the Qaig like I did!" she said, stammering, the words coming out in a gush. Tears sprang unbidden to her eyes, and her hands and teeth clenched. The *Rap* and its crew were her crew! Her family! He would deny her this? A rush of pride welled up in her chest, squashing the cold. Though she'd said the words unthinking, they were true. No one could do what she could do. No one had the experience with Qaig-controlled space, with the P2, with this crew like she did. No one. Not even high and mighty Bastian Benoit.

"Exactly," Bastian said, sounding bored. "If *you* could do it, I am sure someone with actual flight experience would have no trouble learning the new system. Chen, maybe. Or The Abbott. And they could have kept my ship from being shredded in the process."

Whatever she'd discovered about herself in that moment, whatever had swelled inside her, burst, like taking a pin to a balloon. Tears ran down her cheeks. She stood, stiff-backed, not making eye contact with either Soren or Jaxon, and fled the Medical Bay.

CHAPTER 25
SOPHIE, GANYMEDE STATION

The next day, Sophie again went to her task, and then to the medical wing over lunch. She wasn't overly fond of the antiseptic smell, but a girl had to do what a girl had to do. She didn't see Liam outside today, but she already knew where to go, and went ahead inside. She had planned to see Cat, but she saw Wesley sitting on her cot, talking quietly with her. Cat had drawn her knees up to her chest and was nodding her head animatedly at something he saw saying. Sophie liked Wesley — he was a bit of a nerd, but he seemed like a good guy, and he was very cute. Cat could do worse. She passed by the cot with just a wave to Cat and a wink and made her way back to the classroom.

"Sophie, hey," she heard, and turned to see Liam hurrying out of one of the other rooms, which looked to be some sort of study lounge.

"Hi," she said brightly. "Ready to go?"

"Yeah," he said, and followed her into the classroom, closing the door behind them. She took her seat, ready to get started.

"Ok," he said. He looked a little agitated, a little flushed. Perspiration beaded his forehead, but he cleared his throat and continued.

"Ok, today we're going to work on some CPR," he said, and gestured for her to come up to the dummy on the table. She did, hands on hips as she waited for instructions.

"You're going to want to give good, hard compressions," he said.

He demonstrated how to position her hands, locking his elbows, and delivering a few rib-crunching reps. She winced — it was brutal.

"Yeah, if you do it right, you're going to crack some bones," he said, nonchalant. "But you'll restart a heart, so it's a good tradeoff. Now you try. Don't forget — keeping the proper pace is essential."

She licked her lips and stepped up to the dummy. She could do this — it felt totally awkward, looking at this rubber torso, but when she thought about Cat and how she'd been unresponsive for hours after their little escapade, her own heart clenched tight, like she'd never be able to get a deep breath again. So, Sophie put her hands together like he'd shown her and pushed down.

Nothing happened.

"Harder," he said. She tried again. The plastic chest creaked, but barely budged. He'd made it look so easy — but then again, that's why he was teaching the course, right?

She gave it a few more tries, leaning her entire body weight down on the dummy, with minimal improvement. This dummy, unfortunately, was a goner.

"Here, let's try this," he said, grabbing a small step stool. He came around behind her and put it at her feet. She stepped up on it and tried again — the increase in her leverage made a big difference, and the chest compressed nearly as much as it had when Liam did it.

"Better," he said, and she startled a bit when she realized the sound was coming from very close to her right ear. He was still standing behind her. "Like this," he said. His arms came around her, his hands over her hands, a hot pressure keeping them in place. An old, familiar feeling like bile rose in the back of her throat.

"You need to lean into it," he said. She could feel his chest pressing against her spine, and the hairs on the back of her neck prickled. His voice was low now, and a little raspy. She swallowed hard, her gaze flickering to the door — to find it closed. When had it closed? How had she let him close her in here? She was smarter than that! Her gaze flicked back to the dummy, her mind running a million thoughts per second.

"I think that's enough for today," she said in as breezy a voice as she could muster, and went to step off the stool, but his arms were still around her, and instead she only spun in his embrace, backed up against the table. She brought her hands up and shoved against his chest, but he didn't budge. He was stronger than he looked, hard muscle covered with his layers of scrubs and white coat.

"Thanks, I got it now," she said, keeping her tone light, but he didn't release her. Instead, he leaned towards her, and her pulse skyrocketed.

"You are such a little flirt, aren't you?" he said, grinning down at her, his teeth too white in the unflattering overhead lights. One big hand drifted downwards, grabbing her hip, pulling her into him.

"Let. Me. Go," she said, glaring. Her heart was hammering. This classroom was at the end of the corridor — with the door closed, would anyone even hear her if she screamed? It might be enough to startle him, anyway, buy her time to escape —

"Tell me, are you really claustrophobic?" he growled, his arms tightening around her. His intentions were clear — he was not letting her go. He bent his head, as if to kiss her —

And she kneed him in the groin. His face contorted as he dropped.

"Bitch," he whimpered, but she whirled away from him, her chest heaving, gasping for breath. She grabbed her tablet and ran, flinging the door open and taking off down the hall. She slowed her pace only when she got to the main aisle of the Medical Bay, smoothing her hair back and putting her movie-star smile back on. She waved to Cat as she passed, not stopping, not turning to see if Liam was still behind her. Head held high, Sophie exited the medical wing, Stage Left.

S ophie's mood became progressively more taciturn as she ignored Liam's repeated messages on her tablet — *Missed you today, make sure you study up on the AED section for tomorrow*, just like nothing had happened. Well, there was a snowball's chance in Hell that she'd ever go back to his little 'study sessions.' She should have been more careful — if something had happened between them, she'd have no one but herself to blame. Wesley had warned her, after all, and she'd still willingly gone with Liam, let him take her to some quiet little corner, let him box her in. Sophie hadn't told her roommates about what had happened yet — and she wasn't really sure why. Was it pride? It was a little embarrassing, though the feeling of her knee driving into Liam's sensitive parts kept her from feeling *too* ashamed about it. What she needed was a distraction, and for once, the gods or fate or whomever smiled down on her. She looked back down at her tablet. A message was being blasted across all of the tablets and computers on Ganymede Station. As she read it, a smile returned to her face. This message added a sparkle to her day that not even Liam could diminish.

That Friday, no one was allowed to work past three o'clock.

Because Admiral Savaryn was throwing a giant party.

Well, not exactly a "party," Sophie thought with a grin, twirling a loop of hair around one perfectly manicured nail, but it was close enough. He'd said that there would be snacks, and music, and *time off*, and extended curfew, and ...

"It's party time, girls!" Sophie shouted, throwing her hands in the air and nearly launching her tablet into orbit in the process.

"Got it!" Zoe shouted, her cat-like reflexes snagging the tablet millimeters from the window. She tossed it back to Sophie like a Frisbee.

"Thanks," Sophie said, grinning. "Did you read it?"

"Yeah," Raina said, yawning. "What's this, he wants to thank us all for our hard work by arranging some little treats? Does he really think that will work?"

"That depends. Will there be pizza?" Zoe asked, scanning the message on her own tablet.

"I mean, more likely that it's a smokescreen or something, right? A way to placate us all, keep us blind to whatever shady affair he's planning, keep us from suspecting him of doing anything illegal," Cat said. But Sophie was at her locker already, a black dress and stilettos in her hands.

"So... we're not going to go?" Nora asked, covering her mouth as she yawned. She looked awful — well, more awful than she usually did lately. Her pale complexion only made those horrible dark circles under her eyes more pronounced. Nora could use some fun, she thought. And some concealer.

"Oh no, we're all totally going," Sophie said, depositing her party attire back into the locker. "But let's not let our guard down, either. I bet that party will be a perfect time to sneak around, maybe even get into the Bridge and snoop around the mainframe. I bet Aditi would let me in."

"Spoken like a true super spy," Zoe said, rolling her eyes.

"Well, I'm in," Nora said. "It might be a good time for us to start looking for where Savaryn's storing the *Tabula Rasa*."

Sophie tossed her long hair back over her shoulder.

"Way ahead of you, darling," she said. She picked up her tablet and opened a program. A head popped up on the screen — a frowning, disembodied head.

"Ladies, meet Adam. Adam, ladies," Sophie said.

"This is Callisto's AI?" Nora said. They crowded Sophie's tablet. The face continued to frown, eyes flicking eerily to each of their faces, using the tablet's camera to scan them.

"Well, I'm working on plugging him into Ganymede," Sophie said. "I figure if anyone knows where the virus could be stored, he would."

"I am being blocked by a firewall, Agent Hedy," he said through the tablet's speakers.

"Agent Hedy?" Nora mouthed, giggling. Sophie grinned.

"Yeah, sorry, working on that, Adam. I'll check in with you later," she said, and closed out his program.

"So ... he's kind of like a virus himself," Sophie said. "If I can get him into Ganymede's system, he should be able to find the *Tabula Rasa*. Then during Savaryn's party, we steal it!"

"Well, I like this plan," Raina said. Zoe snorted, crossing her arms.

"Anything to piss off the Admiral."

"We'll need a portable containment system," Cat called from her bunk. "Something that can keep a steady temperature of at least minus-70 degrees. I can probably have something done by the party."

Everyone was quiet for a long time.

"What?" Cat said, not emerging from her hideout.

"I think we've corrupted you," Zoe said, cackling. Cat grumbled in response.

"I don't suppose there's any chance of an antidote to this virus? Or like, a vaccine?" Raina asked. They all looked at Cat, whose eyes went wide.

"What? I'm a computational physicist, not a genetic engineer," she said.

"Just check, okay? I bet Wesley can help," Sophie said. Cat turned pink.

"But we're still going to the party," Sophie insisted. "We must make an appearance. After all, it would be suspicious if none of us went."

"Let's see what Adam can come up with," Nora said, thinking. If there was anything that was going to show Bastian how capable she was, it was finding the virus. She'd only agree to hand it over once he reinstated her on the crew. The idea kind of made her nauseated, but since he was being an unreasonable jerk, she was left with few alternatives. "We can maybe take turns leaving the party, or something."

"Okay!" Sophie said. "A party AND a heist! And I'll get to wear my heels!"

"Most fabulous super spy ever," Zoe said, grinning.

"And we'll all dress up! And I can do your hair, and your makeup, and..." Sophie continued, rummaging in her locker.

"Well, the rest of us have nothing to wear that's not station-issued," Nora said, frowning. Zoe and Raina shrugged, too. Sophie put her hands on her hips. "Unless you're thinking of bedsheet togas again?"

"Well then it's lucky we have friends in the 3D-printing department, isn't it," Sophie said, grinning.

"Who?" Cat said, emerging at last from her bunk, like a wide-eyed chipmunk emerging from hibernation. Her hair was a bushy halo around her pale face, the silver strands reflecting the light.

"Me!" Sophie said, beaming. "I've been designing a few things this year — nothing fancy, but well, a girl can't wear uniforms all the time now, can she?" She pulled up a dozen designs on her tablet and passed it around. Her roommates made the appropriate *oohs* and *aahs*, which made her beam, her previously foul mood all but forgotten. They were pretty neat designs, if she did say so herself, full of swooping swirls and futuristic shapes and cut-outs. One never knew when the opportunity to dress to impress might come along, and it was best to be ready when it did.

"Making clothes from recycled plastics, worn-out uniforms, and metal fibers? This sounds neat," Zoe said, craning her neck to look over Raina's shoulder at the tablet. "I've been wanting to give that a try." She stretched, cracking her spine as she reached for the ceiling.

"Well, now we've got a little time to try it out," Sophie said. Her fingers twitched — this was exactly the sort of excitement she needed to banish the yuck of yesterday's interactions. "Let's go! I want to be first in line when the printers open today."

As it turned out, there was a mad rush for the 3D printers. They weren't even close to being first in line, but since Sophie offered to design outfits for other students and even some of the graduates, she was assured that her own requests would be done in time for the party.

"And… what's that?" Nora asked, when they all returned to the room later. There was a black box with a red satin ribbon on Sophie's bed. She gave Nora a wink. She hadn't told Ty about Liam yet — not that there was a reason to. Nothing had happened. Still, she may have blown him off last night when he'd wanted to meet up. She felt the teensiest bit guilty about that — but seeing the gift he'd left made her feel warm and giddy, so much so that the guilt barely tinted her mood.

"Ty said he was dropping off a little birthday gift for me," Sophie said, running a finger over the smooth ribbon. Nora smacked her forehead, and the other girls gasped in unison.

"Your birthday! Sophie, I completely forgot! And I didn't get you anything! Ohmygosh, I am so, so sorry!" Nora said. She looked positively panicked; her face drained of all color. Sophie rolled her eyes — it was no big deal.

"Darling, you returned from your crazy little escapade in one piece. That's gift enough for me," Sophie said, giving her a bear hug. Nora yelped but returned the hug.

And then they were tackled by Zoe, Raina, and even Cat. A jumble of limbs and shrieking laughter, they held on to each other for a long time. Sophie's heart glowed — who needed presents when she had her crazy roommates?

"Well, let's plan our own party!" Nora said as they disentangled themselves. Sophie's green eyes twinkled, and she clapped her hands together. It was all the encouragement Nora needed.

"Raina, Zoe — ice cream and espresso beans," Nora said, pointing to the door. Sophie giggled with delight, Liam all but banished from her mind.

"Yes ma'am!" Zoe said, throwing her a salute. Raina rolled her eyes but nodded with a smile.

"Cat, let's get those Christmas lights from last year back up, and let's make a playlist," Nora said. Cat gave her a grin and a thumb's up.

"All right, roomies. Back here, after dinner, don't be late!"

CHAPTER 26
NORA, GANYMEDE STATION

Nora made a quick trip over to the medical wing, wanting to talk to Bastian again, alone. Despite Thalia's comments about her being 'just a bus driver,' she knew that no one could have handled the *Rap* like she did. She just wished none of it had been necessary. She was only fortunate that her training had made the maneuvers largely second nature. Except for that bit with the black hole. She grinned — she still wasn't sure how she'd actually managed to pull that one off. She resolved to spend some more time in the Sim Gym so that she wouldn't get rusty.

Despite whatever Bastian had said — and in front of Soren and Jaxon, no less — she was determined to prove herself and get back with her crew. She *would* be going to Terra Prime with them. She wondered if she could somehow rig up a P2 simulation — she bet Cat could help, or maybe Sophie with her programming skills. She rubbed the back of her neck absently — she really didn't want to tell either of them that Bastian had kicked her off the mission.

What a jerk. Here she'd thought she'd finally made an impression — no, more than that, that he actually cared about her, and he'd dismissed her completely. It made her feel about two inches tall, like a green cadet all over again. She'd never even heard of the other two pilots he'd mentioned as her replacements. At least she had Sophie's birthday bash to look forward to, after this unpleasant encounter.

She made her way back to see Bastian, to give him a piece of her mind, first swinging by the cafeteria to pick up two cups of black coffee as a peace offering. After all, if he hadn't been injured trying to protect her, it would have been him piloting the *Rap*. Instead, he'd never pilot any ship ever again. The recycled plastic mugs she was holding threatened to crumple under her grip.

She made her way down the long center aisle of the Medical Bay, lost in her thoughts. She didn't even notice the tall blond woman at Bastian's side until she nearly stumbled on her, the coffee sloshing precariously in her hands.

"So, I hear this is all *your* fault," Olivia said softly, looking pointedly at Nora.

"Hi, Olivia, it's nice to see you too," Nora said, setting down the drinks and crossing her arms. Olivia was holding Bastian's hand, sitting calmly at his side. He seemed to be sleeping or perhaps faking it to avoid Olivia. It didn't seem like something he'd do, but she'd realized lately she didn't really understand him as well as she'd thought.

"I'm glad you find this funny," Olivia said, pushing a strand of hair back from her face with a manicured talon. "He was the best pilot this station had."

"No," Nora said, defensive. "I am. But he's a close second."

She'd hoped that the comment would rile him, that she'd get some flicker of reaction from him if he was only pretending, but no emotion registered, no twitch of his lips.

"Oh, come on," Olivia said. Bastian stirred, and it was then that Nora's attention was directed at him for a moment — she noted the pallor of his face, the sweat beading on the blond hairs above his lips. Olivia stood, looking every inch the protective girlfriend. She stalked out of the room and drew the curtain, blocking Nora's view, the curtain rings clanging against their metal support rods.

"Bastian was a hero," Olivia said, pointing at Nora. "And thanks to you, he will never fly again."

"Is he okay?" Nora asked, trying to dodge past her to look at Bastian, but the woman was fast, and blocked her way.

"Of course he's not okay! He's blind, you idiot!" she shrieked. Nora's face flushed. She hadn't asked him to save her.

"Hey," Nora said. Bastian hadn't looked good at all. She could hear a small moan coming from behind Olivia, and the sound nearly broke her heart in two.

"Look," Nora said, squaring off. "Why do you care so much all of a sudden? Last I saw of you, he was very clear about *not* wanting to be involved with you," Nora said, recalling that heated conversation before the Qaig attack. Olivia turned red; her eyes, feral. Then, of all things, she smiled. She smoothed her jacket and turned a too-sweet look to Nora.

"Maybe," she said. "Why, are you jealous, little Hypatia? Oh, isn't that sweet, you've got a crush! Can you imagine, an officer like Bastian, with a cadet like you? And a Fax, no less? And what would the Admiral say, I wonder."

Nora felt heat rush to her face. As if she wasn't reminded constantly of their age difference, the fact that he was technically her superior officer, that he was the Ace himself, and she was a nobody.

"And what makes you think that Bastian would ever want to be with the person who made him lose his sight? He blames you, you know," Olivia continued.

Nora gaped at her. She was as stunned as if Olivia had actually slapped her. The worst part was, Olivia was right. How could Bastian ever actually want to be with her? No wonder he couldn't even stand to look at her, didn't even want her on his ship. And who cared anyway, she didn't want to be with *him*, either, not after he'd embarrassed her, not after he'd kicked her off the mission. Olivia preened, looking like a Nordic goddess with her long blond hair and statuesque height. Nora felt child-like next to her, suddenly very aware of how disheveled she must appear compared with Olivia's flawless makeup.

"Whatever," Nora grumbled, and shouldered past Olivia.

Bastian looked awful. She pulled his blanket down to find his hospital gown dark with sweat, clinging to his chest as if it were adhered. The bandages on his head were thick with caked brown blood, where they weren't matted to damp skin. He moaned again, his hand finding hers, seeking comfort. It was clammy, and she held onto it tightly.

"Bastian?" she asked. He didn't respond. "Bastian!"

"What's going on?" Wesley said, pulling the curtain back. He took one look at Bastian and sent a quick page on his tablet. Nora could hear tablets *ping* all over the Medical Bay, and a host of nurses and students came rushing over, accompanied by Dr. Adebayo.

"Move, please," the man said, in his lilting voice, unhurried. "Vitals — ah. Wesley, is he responsive?"

Wesley stood at the head of the bed, talking into Bastian's good ear. Bastian shivered, as if he was freezing, despite the sweat pouring off him.

"Septic," Dr. Adebayo muttered. "You," he said, pointing to a nurse. "Get the fluids running. Jennifer," he said, gesturing to another student. "Prep the OR. We'll need to remove that dressing." People rushed to do as he asked.

"What's going on?" Nora asked, horrified. Olivia had fled.

"The cuts on his face might be infected again, or he could be developing tetanus," Dr. Adebayo said, looking briefly at her. "We'll have to take the dressings down, and I need to be in the operating room in case we need to sedate him and clean out the wounds. Let's go!" he said. As he and Nora had talked, everyone else had been moving in a flurry of activity. Bastian had been hooked up to monitors on his arm and fingers, checking his pulse and blood pressure.

"Let's go!" Dr. Adebayo barked again, and as one, the group of people grabbed the side of Bastian's cot and wheeled him off. Wesley looked back over his shoulder once, shooting an apologetic glance to Nora — and then the doors closed behind them, leaving Nora alone.

How on Earth was she supposed to plan Sophie's party when she couldn't stop thinking about Bastian? About the horrible things he'd said to her, and about her — and what was worse, what Olivia had said? Had he told her about getting Nora off his ship? He blamed her. Something inside of her felt tight, like a vice around her chest. She wouldn't put it past Olivia to make things up to taunt her, especially if she saw Nora as a threat. But he'd broken up with her. Told her that there was nothing between them. She'd heard it with her own ears.

Besides, she'd thought that, maybe, he'd felt something for her. Something deep inside her felt squirmy, uncertain. After that time together on the *Rapscallion*, that night in the captain's room, when he'd said he wished *she* was the one sneaking in to be with him, when he'd touched her face… she shook her head. No, it was just her overactive imagination, which apparently was desperate for attention.

But then he'd held her to him after the Qaig had arrived — had held her, comforted her, when they thought they were all going to be blown to bits. Was that just the action of a friend? She didn't have much experience with such things. But now? Now that he'd sacrificed his sight, his dreams, to save her? He'd kick her off his ship because he couldn't stand her that badly? And now, what if his wounds had gotten infected? What did that mean for his recovery? Would he ever be the same again?

Sophie would know what to do, she thought. She should definitely talk to Sophie. Her pace picked up, and she ran through her list of errands with robotic efficiency. Sophie would know, she kept thinking. But the squirmy feeling twisted in the pit of her stomach.

"Hey," Raina said, catching up to her in the cafeteria. Nora was startled and actually jumped at the sound. She had wandered there after picking a few things up from the 3D printing lab for Sophie's party, although celebrating was the last thing on her mind at the moment. She didn't even really remember walking there. She couldn't help replaying the last moments she'd seen Bastian over and over in her head.

"Geez, you look like someone just told you we're out of coffee or something," Raina said, peering up at her, dark eyebrows furrowed in concern.

"WE'RE OUT OF COFFEE?" Zoe yelped, grabbing Nora's shoulder, coming up out of nowhere. Raina rolled her eyes. People filed past them into the cafeteria dome.

"Not yet," she said. "It's just an expression. Anyway, Nor, what's bothering you?" They moved towards their usual table.

"Bastian," Nora mumbled. "He's sick, I think. His wounds are infected. They took him back to surgery." She couldn't stand telling them the rest of it. The worst part was that she didn't blame him, not at all. She could barely stand herself.

"Oh man," Zoe said, sitting down hard. "Is he going to be okay?"

Raina elbowed Zoe hard in the ribs.

"Of course he is!" Raina hissed. "Nora, he'll be fine. Don't worry."

"Who's fine?" Cat said, coming over with her dinner tray.

"Everyone, we're all fine," Zoe said, giving her a thumb's up. Cat looked at them suspiciously, but said nothing else, and took her usual seat.

"We're all fine," Nora mumbled, and dragged a fish stick idly through the ketchup. The thought of eating made her stomach clench, like she might throw up, so instead she made ketchup designs on her plate while her roommates finished eating.

I t was hard to get into the celebration later, but Nora tried, for Sophie's sake. She'd ordered rolls of red ribbons from the 3D printing lab, and between the curling strands of ribbon and Cat's lights, Room 10013 had never looked more festive. Raina and Zoe had procured some ice cream and those illicit Terra Prime espresso beans, and soon the smell of coffee filled the air. Sophie had set up her tablet to play music and was already dancing. Real coffee was starting to run low — thanks to the blockade at Terra Prime, and the two-month-long lag from getting anything from Earth — and people were starting to get cranky. The chemists had started plying people with caffeine tablets, but without real coffee, Nora suspected there would be a mutiny. At least for now, though, those thoughts were pushed to the back of her mind. She'd enjoy each sip of her espresso while she could.

"Best roommates ever!" Sophie beamed, grabbing Nora's hands and yanking her up from her perch on the window ledge. "Come on! Dance with me!"

"Happy birthday, Sophie," Nora said instead, and hugged her friend tightly. Sophie stiffened.

"Ugh, *cher*, what's going on?" Sophie asked, pulling back, peering up into Nora's eyes with her own emerald-green ones, lids dusted with glittery gold powder in celebration. "Is the party too much? With all you've been through, maybe we should just forget it."

"Oh no," Nora said, wiping her eyes at the tears which had suddenly gathered there. She gave Sophie a smile, but it was clear that Sophie wasn't buying it. "It's fine. I'm just tired."

"We're all fine," Raina echoed, rolling her eyes and turning down the music. "But Bastian's sick. Nora didn't say two words at dinner. She's worried."

"Oh," Sophie said, putting a hand on Nora's arm. "What happened?"

"Infection," Nora mumbled. She checked her tablet for the ten-millionth time. He should have been out of surgery by now. She should have heard *something*. Unless — and her chest ached with the thought — unless Wesley was updating Olivia, instead of her. Unless something had gone terribly, horribly wrong.

"Cat, send Wesley a message. See if you can get some updates," Sophie commanded. Cat flushed.

"Um, why would he tell me?" she muttered.

"The two of you are friends, aren't you?" Sophie asked, arching an eyebrow. Cat wouldn't meet her gaze.

"Something else is eating at you," Sophie said, studying Nora's face. "Out with it."

Nora shrugged and sat at the table. The air of cheeriness that they'd achieved seemed to have gone out of the room, like a deflated balloon. Sophie stopped the music on her tablet.

"Did something else happen?" Sophie asked softly, then straightened. "Was it Thalia?"

"Oh, if it was, I will kick her…" Zoe started, then trailed off when she noticed everyone staring at her. She frowned, stuffing her hands into her pockets. "I just don't like her. No offense, Nora."

"It's okay," Nora said, with a tired grin. "I don't think I like her most of the time, either."

"So…?" Sophie prompted. Nora sighed, and put her head down on her folded arms, so she wouldn't have to look at anyone.

"Olivia was there today," she mumbled. She heard Sophie drawn in a sharp breath, and Raina hush someone, followed by a "Just let her talk!"

"She said Bastian ... he told her that he blames me for the loss of his sight," she muttered. No one spoke, and when she raised her head, her roommates were exchanging incredulous glances. Nora felt ridiculous. Of all the things she should be worried about right now — the Qaig imprisoned on Ganymede, the uber-virus Savaryn had stashed away somewhere, the suicidal peace-mission Jaxon wanted to go on — and she was moaning about a *boy*. How cliché. Though she really couldn't blame him if he did hate her. She might feel the same, in his position.

"Nora, I know for a fact that Bastian is *crazy* about you," Sophie said emphatically. "Everyone can see it. He's sick, probably on all kinds of drugs, and he could be hallucinating for all we know," she said, and raised a finger. "Also, Olivia is a snake."

"Oh, that's not even the bad part," Nora said, grimacing. "Bastian kicked me off the *Rapscallion* crew."

"He did WHAT?" Sophie shrieked.

"Yep," Nora said, and leaned back in her chair, staring at the twinkling lights strung from the ceiling. "Said he needed someone with more experience next time. That he couldn't keep picking up my slack. And no wonder, he probably can't even stand to be around me right now anyway."

"Well — I mean, that's just ..." Sophie sputtered, her hands fluttering. "Ugh!"

"So — I take it this means that there's another secret mission lined up?" Raina asked, picking at her nails. The other girls swiveled, looking at Nora.

"Jaxon wants to go back to Terra Prime," Nora said. Screw secrecy, she thought. "Use the *Tabula Rasa* as a negotiating tactic to get the Qaig to leave. He asked my crew to take him." *My crew.* The words echoed inside her. Mine. Soren and Asher and Donovan and even Bastian. Hell, she'd even take Thalia and her ilk if it meant she was flying again.

"Sounds dangerous," Zoe said. Sophie nodded, her lips pressed tight. Nora frowned, trying to work through the mess of emotions in her head. Besides, it wasn't like anything had happened between her and Bastian. He owed her nothing. Olivia was right, she was just a girl with a crush. But that didn't mean she couldn't still train, couldn't prove that she was ready beyond a shadow of a doubt to go with her crew. She deserved to go to Terra Prime — she *would* go. Who else knew the *Rapscallion* like she did? Who else had flown with the P2?

When she thought this, a plan began to form in her mind– well, more like a crude sketch than an outline. She ran it past them, and her roommates cheered, and then Nora felt a little better. She'd show Bastian what Eleanora Clementine Clark was truly capable of. She couldn't restore his sight, but she could go and protect her friends, her second family. She would go to help Soren and Asher and Donovan. She would show them all that Nora was a force to be reckoned with, and that she would not back down from a challenge.

"I got Adam uploaded," Sophie said softly. Nora jerked her head up.

"What?"

"Into Ganymede," Sophie said, pulling up the program on her tablet. "He's integrating himself into every wire, screen, and camera in the station. Like how he could manage everything on Callisto, he's doing it here, too. I mean, I don't think he'll actually be able to control much, but he can monitor things, maybe manipulate camera feeds, and run thermal scans. He's already found a few places where Savaryn could be hiding the virus."

"What are we waiting for? Let's go!" Zoe said, heading for the door.

"Maybe let's make a plan first?" Raina said, gesturing towards the table. Zoe shrugged.

"Okay, yeah, good idea," she acquiesced, flipping a chair around and sitting backwards in it.

"All right, now who brought me ice cream?" Sophie asked, clapping her hands. "Ice cream and plotting! This is the best birthday ever!"

Raina rushed to get the containers. They shared spoons and plans, dividing up and marking locations on their tablets. And for the rest of the night, Nora forgot about Olivia and Bastian. Mostly.

The next morning, there was a message from Wesley on her tablet.

He's fine. Wounds okay. Getting antibiotics.

She sighed, and some of the pressure inside her eased up.

That morning, her roommates were going back to their usual assigned tasks. Or so she thought — until Sophie let out a prolonged *siiigggggghhhhh* as they left the room.

"Yes?" Nora asked. Sophie rolled her eyes.

"Looks like I got reassigned. Someone must've snitched and told Savaryn I'd automated my searches so I could ... do other things instead of work. I swear, that man has it out for me," she said.

"Where are you headed then?" Zoe asked over her shoulder.

"Compost duty."

CHAPTER 27
SOPHIE, GANYMEDE STATION

Adam had pinpointed a dozen locations with temperatures that Cat said were sufficiently cold to store the *Tabula Rasa* virus. The problem was, most of them were heavily patrolled — a few areas in the medical wing, the deep freezers in the kitchen, and a few small areas on the periphery of the station that were kept at Ganymede's ambient temperature of around -200 degrees. They'd have to wait for the party, when most of the station would be in the Rec Dome and investigate then.

So, since Nora wasn't otherwise occupied, Sophie begged her with her biggest, flutteriest smile ever to accompany her down to the greenhouse.

"Look, I'll keep you company, but I will not be messing with the compost," Nora said.

"And you expect *me* to? I could break a nail!" Sophie said, flashing her manicured talons, then smirked. "Betcha I could reprogram the cleaning bots to shuttle the compost for us," she said.

"I will not be taking that bet," Nora said, grinning.

They made it to the greenhouse, and through the airlock. Sophie hadn't spent much time here — the humidity absolutely did horrors for her hair — but she had to admit, it was a nice change of scenery from the usual stark white and blue of Ganymede Station.

There were only a few others at work in the Greenhouse this early in the day. Nora sat by the fishpond, dragging her fingers in the water as the tilapia — aka tonight's dinner — nibbled at them. The Greenhouse was a huge, humid dome, made of hundreds of clear, triangular panels that gave a great view of Ganymede's surface and of Jupiter above.

"Okay," Sophie said, sitting by Nora. "Looks like they actually want me picking fruits and veggies instead of working with the compost today."

Nora didn't have Sophie's talent of arching a single eyebrow, but she gave it her best shot. Sophie looked at her with an expression of complete innocence.

"What?"

"Who'd you con into switching with you?" Nora asked. Sophie huffed.

"That nice Tesla over there," she said, giving the boy a little wave. He flushed and went back to his task.

"Well, let's get to it," Nora said, standing and brushing her hands off on her pants. "You don't want him to get in trouble for not finishing his task now, do you?"

"Whatever do you mean?" Sophie asked, fluttering her eyelashes. Nora groaned, grabbed her, and headed towards the tomatoes.

That morning, they picked tomatoes, cucumbers, berries — the Greenhouse flourished year-round. Despite their best efforts, they both ended up with dirt under their nails and streaked across their faces before noon.

"So, do you want to talk about it?" Nora asked, wiping a hand across her sweaty forehead.

"About what?" Sophie asked, giving a tomato a yank and adding it to the basket at her feet, which was already close to overflowing.

"About whatever's eating away at you," Nora said. "Whatever's got you ripping into those veggies like you'd rather they were someone's face."

Sophie sighed.

"I definitely do *not* want to talk about it. There's nothing to talk about," she said, taking down another tomato — gently.

"Did you break up with Ty?" Nora asked. Sophie sighed.

"No," she said. She hadn't spoken to him since the incident with Liam, true. But she wasn't avoiding him. She just wanted to make sure that when she told him what happened, he didn't blame her. She could be a flirt, she knew, but that didn't give anyone the right to touch her like that without her permission.

"Uh, Soph?" Nora said and tossed her a towel. Sophie looked down at her hands — red tomato guts were leaking from her hand, where she'd clenched so tightly, she'd ruptured the little veggie. Or fruit, technically.

"Ok, yeah, there's something. I … well, I went to see Wesley the other night," she said, wiping her hand. Nora paused and looked at her.

"Sophie, you didn't…"

"What? With Wesley? Please," she said, laughing. "I mean, he's a nice boy and all, but he's not Ty," she said. Nora looked relieved, but didn't say anything else, waiting for Sophie to proceed.

"I wanted him to teach me CPR and things, you know, because of what happened with Cat," she said, carefully wiping her fingers, not looking at Nora. She did want to get this off her chest, but she didn't know if she could while looking her best friend in the eyes.

"And he was busy, so this other medical trainee offered to help. Liam. And I met with him over a lunch a few times. He was a good teacher," Sophie said. She knew she was rambling. Why did she feel she had to justify this? Explain everything?

"And then he just … caught me. Held me, wouldn't let me go. There's a bruise on my arm, here. He called me a flirt and tried to kiss me and… No one was around and the door was closed, so I panicked and, well," she said, eyeing a cucumber on the next row with a wry grin. "Let's just say he'll be walking funny for a few days."

"Sophie," Nora said, her voice a whisper. Sophie looked up and found that Nora looked blurry — no, it was her eyes that were blurry, with tears that threatened to spill down her cheeks in a very undignified sort of way. She sniffed, looking up at the lights. That was supposed to stop tears from falling, wasn't it? Cat had told her something about that once.

And then Nora's arms were around her and damn it all if the tears

didn't start falling anyway. She buried her face in Nora's mass of curls
— really, she should offer to cut it or something for her — and
scrunched her eyes tight.

"I'm so sorry," she said, which only made Sophie sniffle harder. She
was shaking, actually trembling, with the emotion.

"It's not like anything actually happened," Sophie mumbled, eating
a mouthful of hair as she spoke.

"No," Nora said, taking Sophie by the shoulders. "No. If he
touched you at all without your consent, I don't care if you *were* flirting
with him, then it is not okay!"

Sophie sniffled.

"He bruised you!" Nora said, horrified. Sophie covered the spot on
her arm, but it's not like Nora could see it through her uniform
anyway. The movement just confirmed the injury though, and she
could see the incredulity in Nora's eyes.

"Well, it doesn't matter. It's not like I ever need to see him again,"
she said. Nora took her shoulders and steered her to a little bench and
sat her down.

"It does matter. He made you feel bad. That matters," Nora said.
Sophie shivered, and leaned on Nora, glad of her friend's company.

"Does Ty know?" Nora asked. Sophie sat up straight, biting her lip
as she considered.

"No," she said. "And he doesn't need to. It's fine."

"You haven't talked to him since it happened, have you?" Nora
asked.

"Damn you and your intuition," Sophie said, but giggled. Another
tear dripped from her traitorous eyes. "No, I haven't told him. No one
else knows. And no one else needs to."

"He needs to be punished," Nora said, eyes wide. "You should tell
someone. Aditi, maybe."

"Oh no," Sophie said. "I do *not* want my personal business
splashed all over this station, thank you."

Nora sat with her quietly for a few minutes. If there were other
people in the Greenhouse now, they thankfully left them alone. Sophie
took a few deep, slow breaths, like Raina had shown her. It helped a
little.

"What if the next girl he traps isn't as strong as you?" Nora asked. "What if it was me?"

"It's not going to be you. You're too smart for that," Sophie said, but she felt the fight leaving her. She was exhausted — emotionally wrung out. Telling Nora helped, and that would be the end of it. She didn't need snide comments from other cadets every time she passed, about how Sophie was such a flirt, it was all her fault, it was bound to happen to her sooner or later, how she'd deserved it.

"Come on," Sophie said. "I don't want that poor Tesla boy to suffer if we don't get all the tomatoes picked."

Nora stood with her, but didn't say anything. She didn't have to. Her hazel eyes were pleading — Sophie grabbed the basket and turned away.

CHAPTER 28
NORA, GANYMEDE STATION

Nora went with Zoe and Raina to the hangar bay after breakfast and checked in with Soren. The yellow J'nai woman was hard at work already, her flight suit splotched with grease. She was perched on top of the *Rapscallion*, working on the P2.

"Hi," Nora called, waving. Soren waved a hammer at her, pleased to see her. Nora's heart soared — Bastian or no Bastian, this was *her* crew.

"Morning, cadet," she called. "Hey, can you grab Asher for me?"

Nora nodded and ducked into the cargo bay. She breathed in deeply of the smells of the engines, the metallic tang in the air. Somehow, despite everything, the *Rap* felt like home.

She climbed the stairs at the back and made her way down the hall to the Bridge, where she found Asher working at his console.

"Soren wants you," she said. She tried not to stare at the dark stain beside her console. Hers, not Bastian's. The pieces of wire and metal fragments had been cleared away, but the stain of Bastian's blood remained. She could almost hear her own screams echoing down the hall. She shuddered, looking away.

"On it," Asher said, not taking his eyes off the screen. "Hey, did you see Bastian this morning? Soren said he looked better."

Nora mumbled something. She was glad, but that didn't mean she wanted to run back to the Medical Bay to see him. Again.

"Where's Donovan?" she asked. His bobbleheads had been neatly re-arranged, but the anxious man who owned them was nowhere in sight.

"Interrogating the Qaig with Savaryn," Asher said, and briefly glanced up at her.

"Are they getting anything useful?" Nora asked. She scratched the back of her neck.

"I don't know," Asher said. "But Soren wanted Donovan to be there. Something about keeping the Admiral honest," he said.

Nora wasn't surprised — animosity toward the Qaig was at an all-time high, despite what Sophie had learned. Aditi and the rest of the mutineers hadn't made their knowledge public. She figured that people would be calling for Savaryn to execute the Qaig soon, if they weren't already. She left and went back to help Soren with the repairs.

The work kept Nora's mind from straying too much. The more she worked, the more surprised she was that the *Rap* had held together at all. It was an absolute mess. She'd heard nothing further from Soren or Jaxon about returning to Terra Prime, so she just kept working on the repairs. Her mind did drift back from time to time, to that night in the captain's quarters on the *Rapscallion*, when Bastian had brushed the hair back from her face, when he'd told her he wanted more, wanted *her*. Her cheek still tingled when she thought about it, like the touch had somehow permanently singed the nerves there. But what had he actually said? Had she been reading into whatever he was going to say, just hearing what she wanted to hear?

And what was she going to do about what happened to Sophie? She had to respect Sophie's wishes, didn't she? She swung her hammer a little harder at the thought. If Soren suspected a reason behind Nora's industriousness, she didn't say anything. Another reason Nora liked the J'nai woman.

"Hey Soren," she asked, when she caught her staring. "Will you teach me to curse in J'nai?"

The woman grinned.

"The English language isn't enough for you to express your frustrations?" Soren asked, but she was sitting back, watching Nora, a teasing smile on her face.

"Nope. I picked up a little French..." from Bastian, she thought, but shook her head to clear it. "Sometimes things get bad enough that cursing in one or two languages isn't enough. Unless you know some Qaig swears?"

"Unfortunately, I do not have the talent that Donovan has when it comes to deciphering the Qaig speech," Soren said, expelling the word of the enemy race like it tasted bad. "It all sounds like the croaking of one of your frogs to me."

"Has he sorted out that audio file yet?" Nora asked, wrapping a bunch of wires together. Soren blinked, her green eyes going unfocused for a moment.

"The audio file. The one the Qaig transmitted after they intercepted us at Terra Prime," she said, then spat out a string of unintelligible sounds, though it sounded like a lot of j's and vowels.

"That," Soren said, raising her hammer. "That is how you swear in J'nai. I had forgotten about the file. We may have deleted it when we purged and encrypted the *Rap* when we had moved on to, as you say, Plan C, but I will have Donovan take a look."

The next few days passed in a busy blur. Nora kept occupied with work in the Hangar Bay, which was both mentally and physically exhausting. Soren taught her how to weld, patch, and repair just about every segment on the ship. How to reapply the Vantablack coating to parts of the supercomputer system that had cracked. And to curse in J'nai, her attempts at which caused Asher to practically roll across the Bridge with laughter.

But at least, in case of another emergency, she wouldn't feel so helpless. She was grateful for the mentorship. And Cat had helped her with the P2 simulation, so whatever spare minute she wasn't in the Hangar Bay, she was in the Sim Gym, running task after task until her body was sticky with sweat and her back ached and her vision went cross-eyed from the strain. And then she'd run one more. Though the simulation modules were blocky and claustrophobic compared to the real ships, the controls and alarms and view screens were close enough to give her a real challenge. And this area wasn't in use much, anymore. Any cadets who'd had hopes of flying had been grounded by the Qaig attack, and she'd had to actually brush some dust off the "mockpit" she'd used. She tried not to think about the long nights she and Bastian had spent here together, a lifetime ago, when he was first training her, but it was like the memory still haunted the place. She could almost hear his footsteps outside the simulator sometimes, like he was there, still watching, still judging. Still apparently finding her lacking.

So, she did another simulation, this time one where the P2 caught fire mid-jump. And another, where Qaig ships were waiting for them on the other end. And another. And another. She didn't hear from Jaxon much, other than to let her know that he and Aditi were working on a message for the Qaig, and that he planned to ask Savaryn for a ship soon.

She also didn't go back to see Bastian again. Her roommates asked her a few times if she had gone, or had planned on going, and she'd shrugged. Wesley had sent her another message, that Bastian was doing well, but that was it. Well, she was glad he was doing better. If he wanted to see her, he'd let her know. She had more important things to deal with, like repairing the *Rapscallion*, and proving to them all that she was the best choice for the mission. That she belonged with the crew, as much as any of them.

After a long afternoon spent in the "mockpits," Nora's back was killing her, and she had to blink several times before her eyes would focus on the hallway before her. Blinking alarm messages still swam in her vision, claxons still echoing in her eardrums. She had about ten minutes before curfew to make it back to her room, which should be plenty of time. She pulled up her tablet to check for messages — none from Bastian, which she pretended didn't sting — and turned a corner

—

Knocking right into the station's XO, Arthur MacGregor. He was so tall that when he turned in surprise, his elbow nearly clocked her in the side of the head, and she had to duck.

"Oh! Um, sorry," she said, rubbing a hand across her aching eyes. "I didn't see you there."

"Obviously," MacGregor said, and though his voice was grating, there was a slight lift to his mouth.

"I didn't realize being a bus driver required so much practice," a mocking voice said. Nora looked around MacGregor — and found herself looking into a pair of hazel eyes, identical to hers, but narrowed in fury. "Do you have clearance to be in here? Let me guess, Aditi gave it to you?"

"Thalia," Nora said, stunned, then blinked. "I heard you were on house arrest. Indefinitely."

Thalia shrugged, her electric-colored hair moving in effortless waves.

"Whether you like it or not, the station needs me," Thalia said. "And if you want to thank me for saving your life, now's a good time."

"Likewise," Nora spat.

"Ladies," MacGregor interrupted, raising a hand. Nora could practically hear Thalia's teeth grating as she clenched her jaw.

"I was just taking Ms. Jones to review the P2 upgrades," he said. "And then she'll be going right back to her room." Thalia rolled her eyes.

"Upgrades?" Nora asked, surprised. She wondered what kind of upgrades he was talking about, if that meant he and Savaryn were planning another run to Terra Prime, just like Jaxon was. Was there more than one P2 drive now?

"Nothing for you to worry about," Thalia said, flipping her hair back over her shoulder. "The way I hear it, you won't be leaving this station anytime soon, either. Didn't Bastian kick you out?"

And Thalia walked off. MacGregor ran a hand through his white mane, but turned, and caught up to her quickly. He was saying something to Thalia, but Nora couldn't make out the words.

She thought about their interaction as she headed back to Room 10013. Thalia's words stung, but it was the fact that she'd been talking with MacGregor that really had Nora intrigued. She still wasn't sure whose side Thalia was on — other than her own — and MacGregor was also an unknown. Aditi had said as much. He was a Fax, but one in danger of being demoted for his 'sympathies' towards the Qaig. She wondered if maybe he would align himself with Savaryn, and look out for his own interests the way Thalia did, or if he'd align with Jaxon?

Ugh, her brain hurt. She didn't want to think about Thalia, or Bastian, or the Qaig, or the stupid virus.

She only wanted to think about how to get her crew and her ship back. And maybe another cup of coffee.

CHAPTER 29
NORA, GANYMEDE
STATION

"You did WHAT?!" Sophie shrieked. It was curfew, Cat was already in bed (reading on her tablet, of course) and Zoe and Raina were brushing their teeth in the bathroom. Nora looked up from her own tablet — she'd been reading over her simulation results at the table — and caught Sophie's shocked expression. Sophie had her tablet in hand and must have just read some kind of message. Nora's stomach plummeted when she realized what the likely message was.

"Yes, I did it. I told Aditi," Nora said, crossing her arms. There was no point in denying it. And she did *not* like the way Sophie was fuming at her, like she was the one who was in the wrong here.

"You had no right!" Sophie yelled. Her face was red with fury, her eyes glittering.

"Um, what's going on?" Zoe asked, toothbrush still in her mouth — one glare from Sophie, though, and Zoe put up her hands in surrender.

"I had every right! You are my friend, and you were hurt!" Nora yelled right back. Her hands clenched at her sides, and hot tears threatened to spill down her own cheeks.

"Wait, who hurt Sophie?" Raina asked, coming out the bathroom, looking as ominous as a tornado. Nora leaned back, waiting for Sophie to speak. Sophie was shaking, and pacing, and stomping her feet, looking like some sort of caged wildcat.

"It doesn't matter! I asked Nora not to do something, because it was none of her damn business, and she did it anyway! Some best friend you are," Sophie said, still pacing. Nora couldn't help it then; the tears really did start falling.

"And if the next girl he assaults doesn't get away? This isn't the first time he's done this! If someone didn't speak up, it will happen again, or worse!" Nora shouted. She was glad there was a table in between them. Cat shrank back into her bunk, making herself as small and invisible as possible.

"Sophie," Raina asked, her voice calm, belying the murderous gleam in her eyes. "Did someone hurt you?"

"No," Sophie said, sticking her chin into the air.

"And those bruises on your arm just showed up out of nowhere then?" Nora said. Sophie glared at her, crossing her arms to cover the spots, now faded to a sickly greenish hue.

"Okay girls, you're going to have to catch us all up here," Zoe said, turning a chair around backwards and straddling it. Sophie turned her glare on Zoe now.

"It's not your business, either," she said, through clenched teeth.

"We're your friends, chica. Don't act like we're the bad guys here. Tell us what happened," Zoe said. Raina also took a seat, crossing her arms, her fists clenched. She looked like a teakettle on the verge of boiling — Nora half-expected steam to be coming from her ears in a minute.

"Nora's a traitor, that's what happened," Sophie said, and walked to the bathroom, slamming the door behind her. Nora wiped tears from her cheeks and rolled her eyes.

"Sorry," she said to her roommates after a moment, after she'd gotten her breathing under control. "Sophie was in trouble, I didn't know how to resolve the problem, so I went to Aditi. I don't know what happened after that," Nora said.

"What happened," Sophie said, flinging the bathroom door back open, "Is that Liam's been kicked out of the medical program. He's on nighttime janitorial duty now, until further notice."

"Then he got off lightly," Nora said. "Shouldn't you be happy? He's being punished."

"Wait, wait," Zoe said, hands up. "So, someone came after you?

You told Nora, Nora told Aditi, and now the guy's cleaning toilets forever? So, what's the problem?"

"The problem is that Sophie was assaulted by some jerk and didn't tell us! What did he do to you?" Raina asked, fuming.

"I didn't tell you because I didn't want this," she said, pointing at Nora, "to happen. It's no one else's business."

"Whatever this guy did to you, if he touched you…"

"I'm not a whore!" Sophie yelled, chest heaving.

Silence fell over Room 10013. Cat shifted in her bunk. It was a small movement, but the rustle of her blankets seemed as loud as a grenade exploding. For a long minute, no one spoke. Then, at last, Zoe's cool head prevailed.

"No one said you were, hon," Zoe said, her voice calm. "Now if you want to tell us the whole story someday, that's fine, but don't go biting off Nora's head. She was trying to help."

Sophie seemed to deflate and sat down hard on her bunk. She put her head in her hands, her long dark hair falling like a veil, hiding her face, hiding her.

"I'm going to castrate the bastard," Raina muttered. Zoe shot her a look, and Raina shrugged. "Fine, I won't. But I can't promise he won't accidentally fall down some stairs or something."

"He's going to tell everyone," Sophie said, her voice a whisper. Cat finally came out of her bunk — like a rabbit checking to make sure there weren't any predators around — and padded to Sophie's side. She put a hand on Sophie's knee, and Sophie looked up. Her green eyes were rimmed with red.

"So what," Cat said firmly. Sophie giggled, as surprised as the rest of them at Cat's comment. "No one who knows you will believe him, and that's all that matters. You are a good person, Sophie."

Sophie let out a choked sob and threw her arms around Cat. She was shaking, and soon great heaving sobs were wracking her. Zoe, Raina, and Nora joined them, cramming into the little bunk together, holding Sophie — and handing her tissues and glasses of cold water — until the storm abated.

S ophie had outdone herself.

Nora spun in front of the bathroom mirror, admiring the way the navy-blue dress swished. It was hard to believe this whole ensemble had been printed. There were even metallic threads woven through it, glimmering like starlight. Though it had taken Sophie a few days to settle down, Nora guessed they were best friends again. If the dress was an apology, then it was an apology definitely accepted.

"My turn!" Zoe said, joining her. She was grinning widely, her teeth brilliant white against her olive complexion. She'd combed back her hair with some kind of gel, and wore a short, one-shoulder dress in white and gold. She looked like a classical goddess, and Nora told her so.

"True," Zoe agreed, admiring the way her muscles were shown off by the cut of the fabric.

"Don't hog the mirror," Raina said, crowding in with them. Zoe made way for her, whistling appreciatively. Raina glared at her, but she was smiling, too. Raina looked like a sci-fi princess; Sophie had designed her cut-out purple dress in a sequence of three-dimensional hexagons and diamonds, and Raina's long hair had been braided into a dark coronet.

"Yes, you all look lovely, feel free to smother me with your thanks and compliments," Sophie called. Her insistence that they all take this opportunity to dress up had been infectious, a welcome distraction from the doom-and-gloom of the station lately.

They piled out of the bathroom. Cat was dressed in a simple — but lovely; sophisticated even — gray dress. She was seated at the table, poring over something on her tablet as Sophie worked on her hair.

Sophie was wearing the short, fitted black dress and towering heels she'd been saving for just such an occasion.

"Soph, what is *that?*" Zoe gawked, pointing.

"Oh, this little old thing?" Sophie said, tossing her long hair over her shoulder so they could get a better view of her necklace. The massive red jewel at her neck twinkled with the motion. "My birthday gift, from Tylajah. Oh, that boy makes my heart race," she crooned.

"We call that an arrhythmia, Soph. You might need to be shocked by those paddle things," Nora said.

"Must have missed that section during my basic life support training," Sophie said. Nora flushed — she hadn't meant to bring up that bad memory of whats-his-face, the jerk. It was just a joke. She rubbed the back of her neck and shot Sophie an apologetic glance. Sophie glared at her, but only for a moment, before returning to Cat's hair.

"Man," Zoe said, whistling, admiring the necklace, deflecting the palpable tension once again. "Well done, Ty."

"Where did he get it?" Nora asked, taking a seat across from Cat so she could appreciate Sophie's necklace. It was as big as a quarter, a flawless crimson, and hung on a simple chain.

"You know how those boys down in engineering make lab diamonds for the drill bits and such?" Sophie said, placing pins in Cat's tamed mane. "Turns out, it wasn't that hard for them to switch things up and make a ruby. He printed the chain from some leftover asteroid alloy."

"Dang, girl," Zoe said. "I might have to go have a talk with those guys. Raina, we could have you dripping with diamonds, a true Rani."

"Ugh, no," Raina said, but her cheeks turned pink.

"Suit yourself," Zoe said, grinning.

"So, Nora," Sophie said, nonchalant. "Any word on whether Bastian will be making an appearance at the party?"

Nora frowned.

"I don't know; I haven't heard from him."

Sophie arched an eyebrow.

"Oh? And you haven't talked to him, either?"

"Not a word," Nora said through tight lips.

"And …"

"Come on, Soph, give it a rest," Zoe said quickly. "Besides, we're going to be late!"

"Fashionably late," Sophie mumbled, putting the finishing touches on Cat's hair. "Done! Let's go!"

W hen they arrived at the Rec Dome, it seemed like most of Ganymede Station was already there. The lighting in the dome had been dimmed to approximate twilight levels, and the wide paved area near the Hangar Bay had been cleared of benches. People had gathered there, talking and drinking — some sort of punch being handed out from a table at the far end. A platform was set up on one of the small astro-turfed hills, and on it was a microphone and —

"A piano!" Nora shrieked, clapping her hands despite herself. Her roommates turned to look at her, amused.

"How on Earth did they get a piano here?" she said. One of the graduates, she couldn't remember his name, was seated at the wondrous object, his hands picking out a lively melody. Her fingers twitched, aching to try it out. They hadn't carried it all the way here from Earth, had they?

"3D printed," Raina said. "They've been out here installing it all day, tuning the darn thing."

"I mean, they can 3D print a telescope, why not a piano?" Cat said. Nora grinned. She had to try it. She'd bide her time, maybe when so many people weren't around … oh, she couldn't wait. Her mood soared, despite the adrenaline also flooding her system — tonight, Room 10013 was on the prowl for *Tabula Rasa*, with the party providing the perfect cover.

They made their way further into the dome, greeting friends and classmates. Jane, the blue-skinned J'nai exchange student Nora'd met on their first day of classes — what seemed like an eon ago — was there, still wearing her pigtails, talking with Asher and another J'nai in animated tones. Nora hadn't seen her in forever and waved when she caught Jane's eye. The girl waved back with a grin. She didn't see Soren, but that didn't surprise her much — if she had to bet, she'd say that Soren was still working on the *Rapscallion*. She'd even taken to sleeping there, most nights.

They drifted towards the table with the punch. On the way, Sophie let out a squeal and pounced on Ty, who was making his way through the crowd followed by his roommates. She gave him a swift kiss on the cheek and looped her arm through his.

"Ladies," he said, acknowledging the rest of them with a nod, but he only had eyes for Sophie. Sophie bit her lower lip and dragged him over to the dance floor. They were lost in a sea of people in just moments. The piano music had stopped, and a DJ with bright pink hair — an Einstein clone — was setting up speakers on the platform. Shouts were coming from the crowd on the dance floor as the excitement built.

"Hello," Greg said, coming towards the group. Nora was startled to see him and felt a pang of guilt in her gut. She hadn't thought about Greg in ages. Once, not that long ago, seeing him approach would have made her feel warm inside, even giddy. Since Bastian though, everyone else seemed dimmed by comparison, like dwarf stars next to supernovas. Not that Bastian was in her life, at this point. The realization made her stomach clench to the point of nausea.

"Hello," she said, suddenly finding the DJ very interesting to watch.

"Ah, Catherine, I've been looking for you," Wesley said, following Greg over to their group. "I was about to get some punch — I think it's peach-flavored, if no one's spiked it yet," he said, his gaze drifting to Nora. Nora put her hands up and laughed.

"We just got here! No illicit booze, I promise. And seriously, after last time? Spiking the punch is the last thing on our minds," Nora said. Wesley grinned and offered his hand out to Cat.

"Let's get some," he said. For once he wasn't wearing scrubs or his white coat and looked rather dashing in jeans and a dark sweater. Cat flushed to the roots of her hair and shyly took his hand. He smiled down at her, and led her off, leaning down to talk to her. To her amazement, Nora saw that Cat was chatting just as animatedly right back. Cat, her shy little roommate!

"If he breaks her heart, I'll snap him in two," Raina murmured, following Nora's gaze. Greg laughed nervously.

"Seriously?" he asked.

"Oh, she's serious," Nora said with a wicked smirk. "Cat's a little… naïve. We just want to look out for her."

"I don't think you have to worry," Greg said, stuffing his hands in his pockets. "Wesley is intrigued by her. His words. And it takes a lot to get his nose out of his work."

"Speaking of noses ..." Zoe said, glancing at Raina, who shrugged.

"After Raphael, I hope people think twice about taking advantage of her. And I guess she's not as defenseless as she looks," Raina said. Nora paused — Greg was aware of what Cat had done on Callisto, but she didn't feel comfortable broaching the subject further in public like this. Too many people knew about Callisto now, as far as she was concerned. Jaxon's mutineers, all of Ty's roommates, the crew of the *Rapscallion*. She trusted most of them, but how much longer could they all keep such a secret?

"Rumor has it Raphael didn't get the break re-set. Thinks it makes him look distinguished," Greg said instead, and Nora couldn't help but chuckle.

Then the music started, with a rapid bass beat that soon had half the population of Ganymede Station jumping in and dancing. The sound was so loud, Nora could literally feel her eardrums pulsing.

"We're going to check out the greenhouse!" Zoe called. Nora cupped her ear.

"What?"

"Greenhouse! Virus storage!" Zoe yelled into her ear. Nora nodded. Raina and Zoe left, hand-in-hand, looking for all the world like they were off to find some dark corner together — and in a sense, they were. But the corner they were looking for was a frigid -70 degrees and may or may not contain a virus capable of annihilating every J'nai in the station if it ever got out. They were going to check the greenhouse's cold storage (for storing seeds from Earth and Terra Prime, indefinitely), and then come right back. If they found *Tabula Rasa*, they would return to Room 10013 and put it in the storage device that Cat had designed. If they didn't have any luck, they'd come tap Nora for her turn.

Greg had been saying something, but Nora missed it as she watched Raina and Zoe walk off. Instead, she waved a polite goodbye and headed for the punch tables.

"Hasta la vista," he said.

Nora made it about halfway — pushing slowly through the throng of bodies, thankfully away from the blasting speakers — when she looked back over her shoulder. Where she'd been standing just a minute earlier, Greg now stood talking to —

Olivia?

Nora stumbled, turned to look where she was actually walking, apologized to the person she'd bumped into, and looked back again. Greg and Olivia *were* talking, having to stand close to speak over the sound of the music. He looked … taller, somehow. Older while he was talking to her. Like he was standing up straighter. She wondered what they were talking about. Not that it was any of her business.

"Well, fancy running into you here," a voice mocked. Nora turned and found herself face to face with her mirror-image.

"Thalia. I thought you were on house arrest," Nora said for the second time in as many days, crossing her arms. Thalia wore her flight suit, halfway unzipped as usual, with the arms knotted around her waist, showing off her extensive tattoos. She hadn't bothered to dress up for the occasion, and eyed Nora's outfit with disdain.

"Oh, I am," she said airily. "But I got special permission to leave my cell tonight for my good behavior. Plus, I'm bored. I've got the top ten high scores on 'Qaig Attack' now and it's getting tedious."

"Well, then, enjoy the party," Nora said, and pushed past her. She was *not* in the mood to talk to Thalia. She wasn't even sure how she felt about her — thankful, for kind-of saving her life a few times? Angry, for fooling Bastian into thinking she was Nora? Annoyed, for Thalia being a generally obnoxious human being?

But as Nora pushed past Thalia, she realized she didn't see Zoe and Raina in the chaos. She turned, trying to find them. Zoe was tall, she shouldn't be that hard to see. It had been nearly fifteen minutes, she'd had two glasses of punch and was starting to get nervous that either they'd been caught, or worse — that they'd actually found the virus after all.

She finally spotted them though, behind the punch table. Zoe was gazing down at Raina, and both of them had goofy smiles on their faces. Zoe handed Raina something — a bright orange hibiscus flower, which she must have swiped from the greenhouse — and Raina gazed up at Zoe like she was the most precious thing in the entire universe, like no one else existed except them. Zoe looked up and made brief eye-contact with Nora, nodding to go ahead with her own mission. Nora nodded back, and left, a funny feeling in her stomach — was it jealousy, over the intimacy that Zoe and Raina had? Fear, from what she was about to do?

For the first time in a long time, she felt truly alone. Sophie had Ty, she could see them even now, lost in their own little world on the dance floor. Zoe and Raina were inseparable. And Cat had Wesley now. She briefly thought about Bastian, but squashed the feeling, and straightened her spine. She had a job to do.

She made her way back through the crowd. No one stopped her or talked to her — everyone was too caught up in their own conversations. She slipped back out the way she'd come. She felt a twinge of disappointment in her chest that no one at all appeared to be missing her.

She crept down the hall towards the graduates' dorm rooms. For now, she and her roommates shared their living space. After graduation, they'd be given their own rooms. Though smaller, they were more private. Nora hoped that that day would take a long, long time to come — without her roommates, she got the feeling the space would feel pretty lonely. The dorms branched off down a hall that curled outwards, the rooms extending like leaves on a fern.

And interspersed with the graduates' rooms were the officers' quarters. They branched off periodically, and through the windows they each looked like large, white blocks. Some of the windows were open to the vista of Ganymede, and some had drawn shades.

It was down one of these halls that the Admiral's room lay.

Nora continued, rehearsing an excuse in her head — that she had remembered something vital about her last mission on the *Rap*, and needed to tell Aditi right away. Conveniently or not, Aditi's room was two doors down from the Admiral's.

She heard a trill of laughter and paused. Two voices giggled from behind a closed door — but the door remained closed, and she continued on. Her shoes clacked against the bare white floor, and since she was alone, the sound felt amplified.

She passed Aditi's door. *One, two*, she counted.

"Ready or not, Adam," she said, slipping her tablet from a concealed pocket in her dress. She booted Sophie's program, and the grumpy AI sprang into view.

"Can I help you?" he asked.

"I need this door open," she said. "Please."

"Your wish is my command," Adam said. A pause, then from inside the metal door she heard a soft *click*.

"Hey Adam, did Sophie mess with your programming to make you more polite?" Nora said. Adrenaline was making her tremble, making her words tumble out in a rush. She liked that she at least had Adam for company.

"I'm sure I have no idea what you mean," he said tersely. "The cold storage in the Admiral's room is located underneath the desk. And do be quick. The penalty for being caught here would likely be a court martial."

"Thanks," Nora breathed, and slipped inside. She remembered the layout from her debrief visit, and it didn't take long for her to locate his office. She moved as quickly as she could, but each footstep felt as loud as a gunshot in her ears. Her heart was hammering such a rapid staccato that she felt nauseated, and a little light-headed. But she was Eleanora Clementine Clark, and she would not fail.

The office had a metal table that had been fashioned to look like an old wooden desk. Medals and pictures of Savaryn with heads-of-state dotted the walls, some from Earth and some from Terra Prime. There was even a photo of the first J'nai envoy to Earth, taken all those years ago — the Admiral with a tall, white-haired J'nai who must have been Queen Iyle. Even in the picture, they both appeared stiff, cold.

"Might I suggest haste?" Adam chirped. "The motion sensors are detecting the presence of at least two people in the outside hall, and the Ganymede Station software is attempting to bypass the sensors that I have jammed. I estimate no longer than three minutes before you are discovered."

Nora fumbled, pushing the padded chair back from the desk and reaching underneath. She reached around, looking for a latch or button or something. She tried all the drawers, which were locked. Finally, her finger snagged on a seam on the side, and she felt along it until it gave way.

The drawer popped out, and she peered inside. Her breath caught in her throat —

Espresso beans. Savaryn was using the secret cold-storage compartment under his desk for Terra Prime *espresso beans*. She opened each one, to see if maybe something was hidden inside. Their sweet scent perfumed the air — but all she saw were more beans.

"Well, darn," she grumbled, and let out a few curses in J'nai, which made her feel a bit better. She carefully replaced the beans, shut the cooler, and got out of the room as fast as she could.

"Look, I'm blocking the cameras and sensors in here, but you really need to hurry up," Adam said. "I can't keep masking you forever."

"All done," Nora said, closing the door behind her. Her back was slick with nervous sweat, her hands freezing and clammy as the adrenaline continued to prepare her body for a fight-or-flight scenario.

For show, in case anyone was actually monitoring the sensors, she knocked on Aditi's door — as expected, there was no answer, and she turned to go back to the party. The two people Adam had said were coming her way were nowhere to be seen. She headed back to the Rec Dome, her pulse gradually returning to normal as the music and noise reached her ears.

Back at the party, she found Sophie wrapped around Ty on the dance floor. Sophie met her gaze, and Nora shook her head, indicating that she had not found *Tabula Rasa*. Sophie nodded — it was her turn next. Sophie fanned herself, told Ty she'd be right back, and headed off. Sophie would be headed to the Medical Bay, to the cryo storage there. Though Wesley had assured them that there was nothing more than medication and old pathology slides there, they'd still thought it was the most likely place the virus would be.

Nora turned, uncertain of where she should go as Sophie quietly left the room. Without a task in front of her now, she felt a little lost. Adrift. Zoe and Raina were nowhere to be found — the realization of which made her face heat up. Cat and Wesley were in animated conversation over on the quieter side of the dome. He'd helped her search the science labs in the academic wing earlier in the week, but they hadn't turned up anything on the *Tabula Rasa*, either.

Suddenly, the party wasn't all that much fun. She was surrounded by people, with no one to talk to. She wished she was back on the *Rap*. She started making her way back to the other side of the dome. She'd make her way back to the room; maybe tell her roommates she had a headache or something. She looked around — but no one was watching her. She didn't even have anyone to tell her fake excuse to.

The music was just noise, loud and obnoxious. She walked through the crowd and was nearly at the hallway entrance when she spotted Donovan. He looked exhausted, paler than usual, with dark half-moons under his eyes. He wore a T-shirt with dancing avocados on it, topped with an open plaid button-up.

"Hey there," he said. It seemed like he was just on his way in. "Leaving so soon?"

"Uh, headache," Nora said, glancing back over her shoulder. Her eyes again snagged on Olivia — it was hard *not* to see her, with her long blond hair and clinging red dress. She was still talking to Greg, and they'd been joined by a tall blond boy (another Original, she thought, since she didn't recognize him) and — Admiral Savaryn? God, she was glad she hadn't been caught in his rooms. Even now, at the "casual" party, he was in full uniform. As if anyone could forget who he was.

"What on Earth?" she muttered, looking at the three of them. Donovan followed her gaze.

"Ah, Olivia. She and the Admiral have been like BFFs this week," he said. Nora looked back at him, confused.

"Why?"

"Dunno. She's taken an interest in our Qaig friend, though. She likes to watch the interrogations."

"How's he doing?" Nora asked, thinking of the strange creature they'd captured.

"I mean, physically he's — it's? — fine, I think," Donovan said, and took off his glasses to polish them with a corner of his flannel shirt. "We've offered him whatever he wants to eat or drink, and he's comfortable. He'll let me or one of the other translators know if he needs something and Aditi makes sure we treat him with respect."

"So, it's talking now?" Nora asked. He shook his head, looking longingly out at the crowd.

"Nothing beyond its basic needs, but I'm hopeful," Donovan said, then, in a whisper, "We'll get some answers before we leave this station again. We'll get to the truth."

Nora looked back to Savaryn — he'd crooked his finger at Thalia, who was slowly making her way over to the little group of students around him, like she was being pulled with a tractor beam.

"Any luck with that audio file?" Nora asked, tearing her eyes off her clone-twin. She hoped that the file — one that the Qaig had transmitted when they'd first emerged from the Current on the P2 — might shed some light on the situation on Terra Prime. Donovan slowly shook his head.

"I guess it's not really classified, but … they don't want us talking about it. The sounds got really scrambled by the equipment and the encryption and everything, and it's a strange dialect, like listening to someone speak Shakespeare instead of modern English, you know?" he said, his eyes drifting over the crowd beyond her.

"So, you haven't been able to translate it?" Nora asked. Donovan looked down at her, frowning.

"My dear madam bossypants, you *do* know you are talking to the best linguist in the Ganymedean fleet?" he said, pushing his glasses back up his nose. Nora grinned.

"But actually… no. No, we haven't translated it. There's bits and pieces, something about an exchange of information, but that's all we've gotten. Our captive Qaig friend hasn't been much help, either. Either he — it — doesn't understand the message or is choosing not to help."

Nora nodded. He looked back out to the dance floor, and she saw his toe was tapping.

"Go on," she said, pushing him playfully. She wished he'd been able to find out more from the Qaig, from the audio file, but there was time — wasn't there? Before Jaxon revealed his plan, before they needed to find *Tabula Rasa* and make sure it stayed out of Savaryn's hands? She gave Donovan a smile, one that she knew didn't make it to her eyes.

"We can talk shop some other time. Go have fun."

"You sure you're okay?" he asked, but he was already walking off. Nora nodded, a bright smile plastered on her face.

"I'm fine," she said, to no one but herself.

CHAPTER 30
SOPHIE, GANYMEDE STATION

S ophie saw Nora come back to the Rec Dome.
She was on the dance floor with Ty. After all of the headaches and scheming and drama of the past week even she, the Drama Queen herself, was tired of it. She wanted to dance and dance until she was completely out of breath. She wanted to kiss Ty in front of everyone, so everyone could see how she felt about him — but Liam's voice still echoed in the back of her mind. She was a flirt. Everyone knew it. Kissing Ty wouldn't prove a damn thing, it would just inflame the rumors. And she didn't want to use him like that, to prove that she wasn't involved with Liam. She caught someone behind her sniggering — it may or may not have been at her expense, but she shot them a glare anyway.

"Are you all right?" Ty asked. He was close to her, so close, one giant hand resting on her waist, his head bent down to hear her amongst the pounding music. She couldn't help it, though — when he touched her, she flinched.

"Fine," she said brightly, giving him a smile. That's when she'd seen Nora entering the dome, her shoulders slumped. Nora shook her head slowly as she caught Sophie looking at her — rats. No luck in the Admiral's room — well, that meant it was all up to Super Spy Sophie now.

"I just — I have to do something, I'll be right back, I promise," she said, fanning her face as if she were overheated. Ty nodded. He didn't understand, but he gave her space, and she was grateful for that. Ty never pushed. He was as quiet and solid as a rock, unperturbed by the rumors, if he'd heard them.

"I'll be here," he said, looking down at her, something unreadable in his expression. "I'll always be here."

The dance floor was too damn hot anyway, she told herself, as she hustled over to the hallway where she'd seen Nora exit. She waved and smiled at the few others who greeted her — trying to ignore any comments she heard or imagined as she passed. *Flirt. Flirt. Slut. You deserved it.*

She didn't see Nora. She hurried down the hall, her heels clicking loudly. She stopped at one of the junctions, looking down towards the hall with the dorm rooms in it, where Nora'd probably gone, back to Room 10013 — and Sophie went the other way.

She briefly regretted her shoe choice when she entered the Medical Bay, her stilettos a sharp *click click click* on the clean floor. Most of the bay was unoccupied, and the few current patients had their curtains drawn for privacy. No one seemed to notice her loud footwear. She headed straight to the long hall at the back, swallowing the bile that was rising in the back of her throat. She didn't have to go all the way to the end, where she'd been "taught" by Liam. She just had to get to the second door — which Adam had politely left unlocked for her.

It was essentially a giant walk-in freezer. There were dozens of drawers for the pathology slides, each like opening a tiny self-contained refrigerator. There were some larger coolers at the back with medications. She pored over each, until her fingers were turning blue, and she couldn't feel her toes (which was a mixed blessing, because she was starting to get blisters anyway). Nothing looked suspicious or out of place. In fact, most of the place was empty. She hadn't really expected to just find an open vial labeled *Tabula Rasa* — though, that would have been nice. Well, back to the old drawing board. Maybe Savaryn had stored the virus *outside* the station somehow, where the ambient temperature could keep it in stasis. In that case, it might be anywhere on this damned moon. It might be a hundred feet below the ice caps for all she knew, in some top-secret lair.

She contemplated this last thought as she made her way back to the medical bay. Halfway down, she turned back and opened the curtain to one of the partitioned rooms.

Bastian had the decency to look startled, glancing up briefly from reading something on his tablet, before arching an eyebrow at her and returning to his studies. He was sitting up in his cot, legs drawn up, an IV of something clear dripping into the crook of his elbow.

Despite everything he'd been through, he still managed to look insanely hot. His bronzed hair was a little longer these days, brushed to the side and helping cover the injuries to his face, the eye-patch barely visible. He looked tan again — the sickly greenish cast she'd first seen on him after his return was gone. An avid reader of romance novels like Sophie couldn't help but notice that his skin tone only enhanced the glimmer of his blue-gray gaze. Sophie herself spent a great deal of time and energy to look as good as she did; Bastian made it look effortless. Game recognized game.

"Visiting hours are over," Bastian said, not looking up again. She stalked over to him and grabbed the tablet from his hands. He looked up at her slowly, his good eye blazing.

"Can I help you, cadet?"

"Sophie," she said, chest heaving. "My name is Sophie, you bastard."

"I know your name," he said, crossing his arms. If her words bothered him, it didn't show on his face. Though it might be hard to discern any emotion with the amount of bruising and swelling there anyway.

"Then you know that Nora is my roommate. My best friend."

"She's mentioned you," he said, sounding bored. "May I have my tablet back?"

"Not until I'm finished," she said, pulling up a chair to his cot and taking a seat. "Do you have any idea what you've done to her?"

He blinked, but did not answer. A flicker of muscle tightened along his jaw.

"Look, I don't know what game you're playing. She wants to go on that mission. She *deserves* to go."

"I do not play games," Bastian said. "I know she wants to go. But we cannot always have what we want."

Sophie sat for a moment, then handed him back his tablet.

"No," she said quietly. "We can't. But don't pretend this is about Nora being green, or a cadet. You know she's the best damn pilot this station has ever seen, and the hardest working person I've ever met. She's beating herself into the ground because of you! Did you know she designed a P2 simulation for the Sim Gym? That she's been working on it, every second, for days now? That she's running simulation after simulation until she's so tired that she falls asleep at our table at curfew?"

"I am aware," he said. His tone gave away nothing. She'd seen more emotion in a rock.

"Then why are you doing this?" Sophie asked.

"It is none of your concern," Bastian said, and nodded towards the door. "You can leave, *tout de suite.*"

She sat back, crossing her legs, and gave him her best glare, her most pointed arched eyebrow.

"I'm not going anywhere until you explain yourself."

"Then you will be waiting a long time," he said, and returned his gaze to his tablet.

"I'm not in a rush," she said, examining her nails. He looked back up at her, and smirked.

"I hear there is a party tonight," he said, looking her over, taking in her high heels and makeup. "And you have no interest in attending?"

"What's it to you?" she asked.

"Look, if you are planning to spend the evening in here avoiding something, go somewhere else. I'm reading."

"I'm not avoiding anyone," she said, frowning. He glanced at her.

"So, it is an anyone, then," he said. "Nora said you were fearless. This person must be truly terrible."

"The thing is, he's not," she said, and sighed. "He's absolutely wonderful."

"Then what's the problem?"

"We can't always have what we want," she said, leaning back, examining the ceiling. She liked Ty. She adored Ty. She wanted to be with Ty. But something about Liam — God, was he *here*? She hadn't even considered that he might be 'on call' or whatever when she came in — then remembered, he was probably off on his janitorial duties. She shuddered, hating that Bastian saw it.

"Take your melodramatic brooding somewhere else," he said, swiping at something on his screen. "I am busy."

"Like hell you are," she said, then sat up. "Wait, why aren't you at the party?"

"Antibiotics," he said, without looking up. She looked at the IV. The bag of fluids had just a small amount left in the bottom.

"Looks like it's done. Let's go."

"No," he said.

"Why, afraid you'll run into Olivia?" she asked. He snorted, and that's when something occurred to Sophie. He wasn't afraid of running into Olivia. Olivia was there, having a fine time without him. He was afraid of seeing Nora. Which meant…

"Oh. My. God," she said, and put a hand to her mouth. He looked up, annoyed, but when he saw her face, something in his gaze softened — no longer steel-gray, but the soft blue gray of a tumultuous sky.

"You're protecting her," she said. "This has nothing to do with the fact that she's incompetent, or inexperienced, or that you blame her for anything. You don't want to put her at risk. You don't want her on that mission because you don't want Nora to get hurt."

He didn't say anything. He held her gaze, unflinching.

He cared about Nora. He was pushing her away, because he cared for her. He knew the mission was risky. He was willing to take that risk, himself. But he would not risk Nora. Sophie's heart swelled — she knew it. She was right. She'd known all along that Bastian felt something for Nora, though he had a strange way of showing it.

"Well," she said, standing and brushing imaginary dirt from her black dress. "You should tell her the truth and trust her to make her own decision. Otherwise, you're just being a coward. And you've hurt her. Good night."

She left the medical wing, not looking back at Bastian, not wanting to see whatever smug smirk was on his face. She might have heard him laugh, a low, short sound, before she left the room.

What kind of hypocrite was she, she thought, making her way back to the Rec Dome. She could blame Bastian for pushing Nora away, for making her feel inadequate as a ploy to protect her. But wasn't Sophie doing the same thing to Ty? Was she a coward, too? Did she care so much what other people thought about her that she would sabotage the one good, steady thing she had?

Sophie made her way back to the Rec Dome, and to the edge of the dance floor, where she found Tylajah waiting for her, talking with some of his friends.

She grabbed the front of his shirt and pulled him down to her for a kiss.

CHAPTER 31

NORA, GANYMEDE STATION

It was a few hours after curfew by the time Nora snuck back out of Room 10013 — with Sophie's help — and back to the Rec Dome. The rest of her roommates had returned just seconds prior to the extended curfew time, chatting tiredly, their faces bright. Sophie had immediately shed her stilettos and plopped eagerly into a chair, rubbing her feet, lamenting their failed expeditions. Zoe and Raina, Nora noted, had been holding hands when they came in, though they let go on entering, like they weren't sure how to act together while back in the room. Still, they'd gone on and on about the music, and the outfits, and noting who had hooked up with whom. Even Cat had been chatty, discussing the theories that she and Wesley had come up with about her new abilities — something complicated to do with biomagnetism. Nora greeted them all, said she was just feeling tired and so she'd come back a little early, when in reality she'd been back for hours. She'd tried reading, then napping. Nothing worked. She thought about taking a shower and going to bed, but she *really* wanted to try that piano, so she'd stuck in her earbuds and listened to some *Moonlight Sonata* to pass the time, her fingers marching out the notes on her blanket as if she were the one playing.

The station was darkened for the night, and she was nearly caught by a pair of Night Guard patrols that she hadn't heard coming. By the time she made it back to the dome, it was deserted except for the small cleaning bots, scurrying over the grassy knolls and walkways and picking up bits of confetti and other debris from the party. She looked around the dome from her walkway, and when she was confident that no one was around, she made her way back to the piano. In the darkness, the white keys gleamed. Jupiter loomed overhead, casting its reflected grandeur through the massive windowpanes, sparkling against dust motes that drifted through the dome like small stars.

She sat at the bench, gazing at the keys in front of her with a sort of reverence. She couldn't think of the last time she'd played. Maybe it had been a few weeks before she'd left Earth, however long ago that was now. Would she remember how? Her fingers twitched in her lap, and, with a deep breath, she lowered her hands to the keys.

For all that it was 3D printed in space out of who-knows-what, it certainly *felt* like a baby grand. She touched a note, a simple middle C, and let it ring out in the dome. It echoed and rose up and up, into the air above, perfectly in tune. And no one came. No one stopped her. Alone in the entire dome, she felt happier now than she had been during her brief time at the actual party.

Of their own accord, her fingers meandered into one of her old favorites, Chopin's *Nocturne in E flat major, Op.9 No.2*. She started slowly, afraid to make a mistake, to ruin the beautiful notes taking shape, but as she gained confidence, as her brain and fingers remembered this song — she relaxed. The song took on a life of its own. Muscle memory was a crazy thing — even though it had been over a year since she'd last played this song, her cerebellum remembered the notes perfectly. She'd never be able to forget it. She'd played this song a million times on the old upright in her parents' home, then again on a stage at her old high school — music held memory like nothing else, and it flooded her with emotion now.

On she played, and the song filled the empty dome, the notes whirling like smoke. It was as if she was the only person on the whole moon — just her, Jupiter, and Chopin. As the last notes left her, her hands lingered on the keys, reluctant to let go. She let out a long, shaky breath.

It was a miracle she hadn't been caught yet. She suspected Sophie had Adam blocking the sensors again. Either that, or everyone was too tired, or too preoccupied with higher matters to care that she'd broken curfew. She pushed back from the piano reluctantly, afraid to keep pushing her luck. She'd had this time, and it was enough. She should go, now, before she got caught.

"Don't stop," a voice said through the ringing silence. She turned, her heart in her throat.

There, leaning against the doorway, was Bastian. With his hands in the pockets of his impeccable flight suit, he looked as cocky as ever. But the scars — the bandages had been removed, showing three angry red lines slashing diagonally across his forehead nearly to his chin, sharply visible even at this distance. His right eye gazed at her, clear and intense, while his left was covered with a dark patch. A thin strap held it in place, hooking back over his injured ear, which was now camouflaged by his hair. He looked, she thought, like a rakish space pirate.

"Shouldn't you be in the Medical Wing?" she asked. Her heart was pounding — though no longer from fear.

"I was getting, how do you say, stir-crazy," he said. "Besides, I heard they printed a piano for this party. I knew you would not be able to stay away," he continued, making his way to her across the shadowy paths. The bots, she'd noticed, had finished their chores. There was no sound at all except the pounding of her blood in her ears. He motioned to the bench, and she scooted aside, making room for him to sit. With a grin, he put his long fingers to the keys and started to play.

"You just wanted to play it too," she said, her voice a whisper. He chuckled, and she could feel the rumbling vibration of his laugh in her chest.

"Can't both things be true?"

She grinned. She felt at ease again, with him here beside her, like they were back on the *Rapscallion*, working together again, a team again. His hair was still damp, his blond stubble now cleanly shaven, which only made the bruising on his jaw more prominent. She caught herself staring and hastily looked back at the keys.

"Besides," he said, with mischievous look. "Sophie sent me a message and told me you would be here."

Nora rolled her eyes. Of course she had. She'd have to have a few words with her roommate later — though whether she was irritated or thankful, she wasn't sure yet.

"I should get going," she said, and moved to slide off her edge of the bench. Whatever peace she'd felt while playing was evaporating — she couldn't be this close to Bastian. She wasn't sure if she wanted to scream at him or kiss him or smack him, or all three.

"Don't go," he said, and the words stopped her as surely as if they'd been iron bonds. "You promised me we could talk, when we got back to Ganymede, remember?"

She thought back to that night on the *Rapscallion*, when he'd touched her face, when they were alone, when she'd become acutely aware of the chemistry between them, of the electrical charge, of the heat and giddiness that had left her unable to sleep. She'd run that moment over and over in her mind, a thousand times, until she worried she might have imagined or dreamed the whole thing.

"I remember," she said, but the words barely made it past her mouth. She cleared her throat. "But I don't have anything to say to you anymore."

His fingers paused, for just a nanosecond, before continuing the melody. She waited for him to say something, anything — but what was she hoping for? What was he going to tell her? He was acting like he had more bad news to tell her, rather than what she dreamed of him saying.

"Playing is a little different with one eye," he said instead, turning his head to look at his left hand, watching it dance among the keys.

"I … sorry," she said, and meant it with her whole heart. She swallowed, but the movement didn't make it past a lump in her throat, somewhere about halfway down. It should have been her.

"No," he said sharply, his gaze intense, then softer, again, "No. Nora, I do not blame you, I could never blame you, do you understand?"

She nodded, but the lump in her throat didn't budge. To hell with Olivia. Her eyes burned, and she focused on his fingers playing over the keys in front of them, refusing to look up at him.

"If I could go back in time, I would do the same thing again. It is what it is. It is just … different. Now I have to trust that my left hand knows what it is doing on those keys, and feel it, more than see it."

"Trust," Nora echoed, considering. He nodded.

"Trust in your training. Trust in yourself," he said. "Trust the people around you," he said, and put his hands back on the keys. She waited for him to continue. "Learn to see the positive, in any situation. I can still play, after all."

"When it's dark, look for the stars," she said, and smiled, thinking of when he'd said those words to her back in the greenhouse, a few months and a lifetime ago. He whispered it back to her in French now, as he had the first time. The language itself was musical, and a pleasant prickle ran down her arms. The soft tunes wove around them like mist, and she inhaled deeply, wanting to savor every possible sensation about this stolen moment. To revel in the calmness of it, before the universe exploded around them.

"I have not seen you in a few days," he said. She shook her head. She twisted her hands in her lap. She was still wearing her blue dress, and in the dim light the metallic threads glittered like the stars overhead.

"I've … been busy. Wesley said you were doing okay," she said. When said out loud, it sounded lame, even to her ears, and she winced. He noticed the motion.

"Soren came to see me," he said.

"She's been teaching me a lot," Nora said. "We're working on the *Rapscallion*." She looked around for a way to change the subject, and knew she was starting to ramble.

"She says you are a fast learner," Bastian said, glancing at her briefly.

"She's a good teacher," Nora countered.

"She had a lot to say about your flying," he said, still playing. "Cadet or not, Soren thinks you are a real part of her crew now. And her crew is her family."

"I know," Nora said quietly, thinking back to how Soren had once defended her from Thalia. "I feel the same way."

And she did. That lonely spot in her chest felt a bit lighter with saying it out loud. She imagined the crew was his family, too — and wondered whether he was having second thoughts about her banishment. He held her gaze, a small smirk lifting the corner of his mouth. A thrill ran down her, a rush of dopamine making the hairs on her arms stand up. The smirk drew her eye, which then flickered to the green bruising on his jaw. He noted the glance, and turned back to the piano, clearing his throat. Nora was grateful for the reprieve — when he looked at her like that, a strange tickling sensation started in her stomach, and she felt warm down to the tips of her toes.

"I didn't know you could play," she said, changing the subject, anything to calm down the fluttering sensation she was feeling. She wasn't sure if he was playing a specific piece, or if he was making the song up as he went, but it was beautiful, slow, haunting.

"I cannot play much," he said, giving her his half-smile again as his fingers moved, seemingly of their own accord. She watched his face as he played. Sitting next to him, on his right, his face seemed whole. "Jazz, though, comes from in here," he said, pausing briefly to tap one finger against his breastbone, before continuing. "You do not need music in front of you to feel it."

"Do you know any duets?" she asked, and he chuckled.

"I am not sure many classical-jazz duets exist," he said. She swallowed hard, then raised her chin, feeling brave. As if she were someone else here in the darkness, the braver, better version of herself.

"Then we'll just have to make one," she said.

He stopped, and turned to her, his fingers still on the keys as if he couldn't bear to let it go.

"I guess we will," he said. Eye patch or no, his look was piercing, like his gray-blue gaze could see right into her.

"I know about your training in the simulation center," he said, and her pulse quickened. It was not an accusatory statement — in fact, there was something almost reverent in his tone.

"I stopped by to see you there, several times, actually, but I wondered if perhaps you did not want to see me after the things I had said. I — I do not want you to risk yourself by going to Terra Prime with Jaxon," he said. "You are the best pilot — the best person — that I know."

She suddenly realized her mouth had gone dry. He raised his hand, slowly, as if he was afraid she might startle. His lips were turned down at the edges.

"I could not bear it if something happened to you."

He touched her face lightly — at her temple, where the scar from her old wound still showed, then tucked a stray curl back behind her ear. His fingers lingered on the line of her jaw, his thumb trailing near her lips. She swallowed again, finding herself frozen to the piano bench in a kind of delirious, apprehensive haze. Seated this close, she could feel the heat of him, radiating, like a sun.

"I'm going with you," she said. It was almost a whisper, but there was no doubt in her tone that it was a statement, and not a question.

"I know," he said, just as softly.

And then he kissed her. Gently, just a brush of his lips against hers — and then, as he realized she was not going to pull away, the kiss deepened, and he put his arms around her, pulling her to him on the bench, holding on to her as tightly as she held on to him.

And Nora was sure then, beyond any doubt, that there was no force in the universe that could stand against them.

EPILOGUE

"Oh my *god*, I'm going to have so many blisters tomorrow," Sophie moaned. Though more comfortable now that she was out of that tight dress and into pajamas, her toes still stung, and there were spots on both heels that had been rubbed completely raw from the stiletto straps.

"I can ask Wesley if he can get you some antibiotic ointment," Cat offered, pink blossoming on her cheeks. Sophie looked up from where she'd been stretching her aching calves by the window, arching an eyebrow at her roommate.

"Oh? I'm sure you two have much more interesting things to talk about than my poor injured toes," she said. Cat blushed a deeper shade of red and ducked back into her bunk.

"So, no luck searching Adam's cold spots," Raina said. She was setting a slightly rumpled hibiscus blossom into a rinsed-out coffee mug and placed it in the middle of the table. She admired it for a moment, before joining Zoe in her upper bunk. Zoe slung an arm around her, pulling her close.

"Nora didn't find anything either," Sophie murmured, looking out over Ganymede's landscape. Where was Savaryn hiding that damn virus? Adam hadn't been able to pick up any other likely spots on his thermal scans. She sighed. She was glad she'd saved Adam from being

Chernobyl'd. By his very design, he was able to infiltrate and integrate with every piece of the station — well, nearly every piece.

"Speaking of, shouldn't Nora be back by now?" Zoe said, checking the time on her tablet.

"I should hope not," Sophie said, flipping her hair behind her shoulder. "I told Bastian to meet her in the Rec Dome and apologize to her for being such an ass. He might be at it all night … you know, 'apologizing,'" Sophie said, smirking. Zoe grinned and thumped her hand on her bunk.

"It's about time!" she said. Raina rolled her eyes, but she was smiling, too.

The latch on the door clicked off.

Sophie's eyes narrowed, daring Nora to walk through the door and ruin Sophie's perfectly-set-up romantic daydream.

For a moment, the door didn't open. Cat peeked her head out from her bunk, curls gone wild now that she'd untangled them from the chignon. She pushed her glasses up on her nose.

"That door is locked. That door's supposed to be locked," Cat said. The girls exchanged glances.

"Poor girl's too scared to come back in and tell me that my plotting backfired," Sophie snorted, and headed towards the door. It *was* supposed to be locked. Nora should have had to knock to come in, and have Sophie hot-wire the mechanism again — with the curfew in place, that door should have remained locked until morning.

Sophie was about ten feet away when the door finally opened, and she came to an abrupt halt.

Standing in the doorway, framed by Liam, Olivia, and Greg, stood Admiral Savaryn, his face as furious as the Great Red Spot of Jupiter.

ACKNOWLEDGMENTS

None of this would have been possible without the love and support of my family, especially my husband, who will probably be mortified to find himself listed here. I love you to the moon and back. For my kids, who remind me that life is magical; and for my parents, who fostered my love of reading from the very beginning.

For my editor, Ben, whose guidance has been invaluable in this journey. For the BookBaby team, for bringing my stories to life.

And for all those whose steadfast encouragement allowed me to publish the Ganymede series in the first place, especially the Badass Book Club, whose members continue to inspire me — and remind me to slow down and have a girl's night out once in a while.

ABOUT THE AUTHOR

E. M. Leander lives in the American South with her husband, two children, and two cats. A life-long lover of all things literary, when she's not spending free time with family, she can be found devouring books and coffee in equal measure.

ALSO BY E. M. LEANDER

Space Camp:

The View From Ganymede

Daughters of Jupiter

Game of Gods:

Wren and the Tarnished Tiger

Aris and the Obsidian Door

The Immortal Scales

and

Heirs of Flame and Frost

To learn more, visit: http://www.emleander.com